"I cannot believe," he went on, "that Lady Bradbury has the effrontery to think she can forbid me from marrying you when nothing could have ever been further from my mind."

He suddenly stopped, an arrested expression on his face. "In point of fact, you are as well born as many of the debutantes my other female relatives keep thrusting under my nose when I'm in Town, aren't you? The only thing you lack is money. And land."

"That's two things," she couldn't help pointing out.

Which made him chuckle. "There you are, you see, at least you amuse me. At least I can talk to you over the dinner table, or at least I could if Lady Bradbury were not always telling you to hold your tongue."

He placed both hands on his hips and looked her up and down. And slowly began to smile.

"Yes, why not?"

"Why not what?" A feeling of apprehension gathered her stomach into the beginnings of a knot at the devilish expression on his face. Because it looked as though whatever it was he was thinking spelled *trouble*.

"Why not make Lady Bradbury's worst fears come to pass?"

"In, er, what way?"

"Marrying me, of course

Author Note

I love writing Cinderella stories. But in this case, the fairy godmother isn't as benevolent as she ought to be. And neither is the handsome prince particularly charming to start off with!

But this is still a Cinderella story, as my heroine goes from a position of helplessness to taking charge of her own life and enriching it.

ANNIE BURROWS

From Cinderella to Countess

HARLEQUIN®
HISTORICAL™

Recycling programs for this product may not exist in your area.

ISBN-13: 978-1-335-50551-4

From Cinderella to Countess

This edition published by arrangement with Harlequin Books S.A.

For questions and comments about the quality of this book, please contact us at CustomerService@Harlequin.com.

Harlequin Enterprises ULC
22 Adelaide St. West, 40th Floor
Toronto, Ontario M5H 4E3, Canada
www.Harlequin.com

Printed in U.S.A.

Annie Burrows has been writing Regency romances for Harlequin since 2007. Her books have charmed readers worldwide, having been translated into nineteen different languages, and some have gone on to win the coveted Reviewers' Choice Award from CataRomance. For more information, or to contact her, please visit annie-burrows.co.uk, or find her on Facebook at Facebook.com/annieburrowsuk.

Books by Annie Burrows

Harlequin Historical

The Captain's Christmas Bride
In Bed with the Duke
Once Upon a Regency Christmas
"Cinderella's Perfect Christmas"
A Duke in Need of a Wife
A Marquess, a Miss and a Mystery
The Scandal of the Season
From Cinderella to Countess

Brides for Bachelors

The Major Meets His Match
The Marquess Tames His Bride
The Captain Claims His Lady

Regency Bachelors

Gift-Wrapped Governess
"Governess to Christmas Bride"
Lord Havelock's List
The Debutante's Daring Proposal

Brides of Waterloo

A Mistress for Major Bartlett

Visit the Author Profile page
at Harlequin.com for more titles.

Patricia Edith Noone
1924–2019

You always loved books.

Chapter One

'You really are a very silly girl,' said Lady Bradbury, as Eleanor looked out of the window for about the fourteenth time that morning. 'In spite of all your Latin and Greek.'

Yes, she probably was. There was no good reason for getting so excited, just because Lord Lavenham was due to arrive some time today. But she just couldn't help it. From the moment the housekeeper, Mrs Timms had opened up his room to air it, and put in fresh bedding, her spirits had lifted.

'Men like him,' went on Lady Bradbury, 'never marry girls like you.'

'Of course not. I never expected…' She was far too plain, for one thing, while he was the most attractive person, male or female, she'd ever seen. The first time he'd paid one of his visits to his mother's aunt, Lady Bradbury, since Eleanor had been working for her, Eleanor had been capable of doing nothing more than just sitting there, drinking in the sight of him. If she'd been any good at painting, she would have spent hours since then attempting to capture his chiselled features and the lustrous black curls that crowned his head, although not even one of the Dutch masters would be able to recreate that glint of wickedness she'd since come to learn always gleamed from his ebony-dark eyes.

A glint that never failed to make her knees go rather soft and her heart to beat a little erratically, and her thoughts to stray into entirely inappropriate avenues—but never into daydreams of marriage. No matter what Lady Bradbury said, Eleanor was no fool. Not only was Lord Lavenham so incredibly handsome, he was—well, he was a lord. A wealthy lord, with properties all over England, besides this little house in the Cotswolds, while she was merely a paid companion.

'The most you could expect from a man of his stamp,' Lady Bradbury continued, as though Eleanor hadn't spoken, 'is for him to spend an hour or two amusing himself with you while he is in the country and has nothing better to do. Or anyone to do it with. But then he would return to London, leaving you behind, and then where would you be?'

Eleanor had to bite her tongue on the retort that sprang to mind—that it was very unfair of Lady Bradbury to accuse Lord Lavenham of that kind of behaviour. He had never, not once, done any of the things that Lady Bradbury was implying he did. He had never, for example, ogled Eleanor through his quizzing glass, or made inappropriate comments, or tried to grab her, or kiss her on the back stairs. Or anywhere else. Nor did he prey on any of the other female staff, which, so she believed, was the case with men who really were rakes.

But then, after working for Lady Bradbury for only a

few weeks, Eleanor had learned to take everything she said with a pinch of salt. The poor old lady was often in great pain from the arthritis which also prevented her from doing many of the activities she had enjoyed. Consequently, on some days, she didn't have a good word to say about anyone or anything. Besides which, Lady Bradbury had let it slip that she resented the fact that her late husband had left her so poorly provided for that she was obliged to accept the charity of a great-nephew by marriage. That nobody more closely related had been willing to do anything for her.

'I will tell you where you would be,' said Lady Bradbury, answering a question Eleanor had assumed was rhetorical. 'Ruined, that's where. And then I'd be obliged to turn you off without a character.'

'I am sure it won't come to that,' said Eleanor, since she couldn't see Lord Lavenham doing anything so dastardly.

'It will if you continue setting your cap at him, the way you did last time he was here.'

She hadn't set her cap at him. Had she? It was just, well, he was so easy to talk to. Though anyone would be easy to talk to after Lady Bradbury. And she'd grown rather lonely, since working here in a house so far from the nearest village and any sort of social life. Of course she looked forward to his visits and the chance to talk to someone who'd been in the thick of London society, and who had also gone to all sorts of interesting lectures.

But it was more than that. During that very first visit, he'd taken pains to put her at ease after she'd been struck dumb by the physical effect he'd had on her. He'd patiently drawn her out of her shell, until she became comfortable discussing a variety of topics with him. She soon discovered he was extremely intelligent and well read, which had been like finding an oasis in a desert. She'd been so starved of intelligent company since her parents had died. Witty company, at that. His dry comments often made her chuckle. Mealtimes became the main time when they conversed about all sorts of things that didn't interest Lady Bradbury. And afterwards, in the drawing room, they would occasionally carry on those conversations, particularly if he'd brought her a book or a pamphlet he thought might interest her. They talked, that was all. She had never, ever, done anything that could warrant this accusation of 'setting her cap' at him.

She wouldn't know how! She had never been the kind of female who dressed to attract a man's eye and fluttered her eyelashes. She had never simpered or cast out any lures. Plain, practical Eleanor, that was her.

Which was one of the reasons she'd ended up a spinster, working for her living, out in the middle of nowhere.

'That boy,' said Lady Bradbury with feeling, 'is just like his father, you mark my words. *He* had no conscience whatsoever. Lethal to virtue, he was, no matter how carefully a chaperon attempted to guard it.'

Ah. So that explained some of Lady Bradbury's animosity to Lord Lavenham. The way his father had behaved. She had heard rumours, since working here, and, to her shame, was always ready to listen to any gossip that had anything to do with Lord Lavenham, or his family. But this was new. And it helped her to understand why Lady Bradbury was so prejudiced against a man who never seemed to have done her any harm. She'd known she'd find out, if she waited long enough. There was always a logical reason, her father used to say, why people behaved in ways that appeared irrational.

'And as for you,' Lady Bradbury said, 'I would have sent you packing straight after his last visit here, after the shockingly unbecoming way you behaved, if it wasn't for the inconvenience of securing another companion, since so few are willing to work in such a secluded spot. Not that I can blame them. If there was only something to see out of the windows apart from… hills and trees, and sheep. People, that's what I want to see when I look outside, doing things. Not all this barren wilderness.'

Eleanor felt very sorry for Lady Bradbury. Of course she did. Since she was no longer able to do the things she'd once enjoyed, such as playing the piano, or embroidery, it *would* have helped to fill her days if she had a bustling scene upon which to look from her window. She'd probably be far less bad-tempered if she could live somewhere like Bath, for instance, where there would be plenty of other invalidish ladies with whom she could gossip. But when it came to the accusation of behaving in a shockingly unbecoming way, surely, that was going too far.

'And then again, I didn't think he'd be back so soon. Only ever used to visit me, or rather his property,' she said with a screwed-up face 'to go over the account books, once a year, before I hired you on.'

Really? Golly. He must like her, a bit, then…

'And never at this time of year. House parties where

he can carouse with loose women—that's where he generally goes for Christmas.'

Eleanor's spirits plunged as she experienced a vivid image of him carousing with loose women, who would, naturally, also be extremely beautiful. Of course he wouldn't give up that sort of pastime merely to spend time with a plain, impoverished spinster. What on earth had Lady Bradbury been thinking?

'I am sure there must be some perfectly good reason for him coming to Chervil House just before Christmas,' Eleanor began to reason out loud, 'rather than—'

Lady Bradbury banged on the floor with her ebony cane. 'Well, I am not going to permit him to debauch my companion, no matter how much encouragement you've given him, do you hear me?'

Encourage him?

Debauch her?

'I beg your pardon, Lady Bradbury, but I…surely I have never encouraged him to think that…'

'Don't give me that butter-wouldn't-melt look. I may be old, but I'm not blind. Nor deaf. Look at you, all a-flutter because he's coming today. Hoping to take up where you left off last time he was here, no doubt. With all that flirting and giggling…'

This time, Eleanor's face burned with shame. She had done a lot of giggling last time he'd been here. At one mealtime, she'd actually had to stuff her handkerchief in her mouth to stifle her giggles, though for the life of her she couldn't recall now what he'd said that had been so funny. Though with Lord Lavenham, it was often more the way he said things than what he actually said. Or the fact that Lady Bradbury had no idea why Eleanor found what he'd said so amusing.

'I won't have it, do you hear? If you want to keep your position with me, then you will not speak to him while he is here this time.'

'Not speak to him? But I...won't that be rather rude? What if he speaks to me first?'

'That's an example of what you call sophistry, is it? Well, it won't wash with me. I may not have much book learning, but I know what's what. From the moment he sets foot in this house, you will not seek occasion to be alone with him.'

'I have never—' Eleanor said, indignantly.

'You will not enter any room which he is already in and, if he comes into any room that you are in, you will leave it. And you will take all your meals in your room.'

Lady Bradbury might as well lock her in her room and have done with it. Not see him? Not speak with him? Not even with a chaperon present?

No! How could she bear it, knowing he was in the house, but totally beyond her reach?

Oh. She gasped, her hand flying to her stomach, which was clenching in revolt. Lady Bradbury had seen something that Eleanor had only just this moment realised. She *had* formed a *tendre* for him. That was why being forbidden to see him, even though he would be in the same house, hurt so much.

Which meant that Lady Bradbury was probably right to punish her. She ought not to be having feelings for a man so far above her station. A man who could, according to Lady Bradbury, have his pick of the most accomplished, most beautiful, most wealthy society ladies.

'Thank you, my lady,' said Eleanor meekly, because if she really was developing a *tendre* for a man so far above her station, a man who was probably only being kind to her because he felt sorry for her, then it was as well to take steps to prevent her falling any further. Before she made a fool of herself over him.

Chapter Two

Lord Lavenham had been about to stretch his legs out to the fire and rest his booted feet on the fender, after a day spent out on the freezing hills with his gun and game bag, when he heard the sound of footsteps approaching the library door. Footsteps he recognised as belonging to the clusive Miss Mitcham.

Peter didn't know what he'd done to warrant the way she'd been avoiding him ever since he'd come to Chervil House this time, but he was done with letting her treat him like a leper. It was time to confront her.

He kept very still when she opened the door and, to judge from the moment of silence, briefly looked round to make sure he was not there, the way that had been setting his teeth on edge. Because if she saw him, she'd immediately blush, mutter something and dart away before he could so much as get to his feet and say good morning. Fortunately, the height of the wing-backed chair in which he was sitting, and the fact that he'd kept his feet tucked neatly away, meant that she wouldn't be able to see him from the doorway. He wasn't going to make the mistake of behaving as a gentleman should when a lady came into a room and rising to his feet, alerting her to the fact that he was there, or she'd dart off again and he'd be none the wiser.

He held his breath, freezing in place the way he always did when elusive quarry came within range, while she went stomping across the room, muttering something about missing her tea and there wouldn't even be a biscuit like as not. Which almost, almost, brought a smile to his lips. It was so typical of her. The other staff here said she had the patience of a saint to put up with Lady Bradbury's quirks, but every now and then he'd seen the mask slip. Like now, when his mother's aunt had obviously sent her on an errand just as she had hoped to be drinking a no-doubt well-deserved cup of tea.

Only once she'd reached the writing desk by the window, and had pulled open a drawer, did he rise to his feet and take a couple of steps that placed him firmly between her and the door through which she'd just come. The door that was her only means of escape.

She whirled round, a look of horror on her face. A look that curdled his stomach, since he was more used to her gazing at him as though he was some kind of demi-god for a moment or two, before managing to school her features into the prim, polite bearing that she seemed to think befitted the role of paid companion.

She schooled her features now into a deferential mien that perfectly matched the depth of the curtsy she made him.

'I beg your pardon,' she said, keeping her eyes on a point about two inches in front of his boots. Before this visit she had always gazed directly into his eyes with an openness he'd never met with from anyone else. As though she was looking beyond the features that so many others professed to admire, to the man he was inside. 'I was not aware anyone was in here. I do beg your pardon for disturbing you,' she added, before starting to attempt to edge round him.

'If I said you were not disturbing me and asked you to carry out whatever errand brought you here,' he challenged her, 'would you?'

She bit her lip rather than replying. But, tellingly, she continued to try to edge round him without raising her head to look at him properly, as though he were some kind of dangerous beast with whom she dared not make eye contact.

'I knew it,' he said, turning and stalking across the room to slam the door shut. 'I knew I was not imagining the way you have been scampering out of any room I enter and taking ridiculous pains to avoid being alone with me.' He took a stance in front of it, his arms folded across his chest.

She raised her head then and looked frowningly at his position guarding the door, then at the chair in which he'd been sitting. 'So you deliberately lay in wait for me then, did you?'

He hadn't. Not intentionally. Because he would never allow himself to become so intrigued by a woman's behaviour that he...pursued her. He'd just made the most of the circumstances in which he'd found himself. That was all.

'I made sure that I could find out what I've done

to make you treat me this way,' he admitted. 'You are behaving as though I've done something offensive.'

She blushed and hung her head.

'Have I? I cannot think what it could be. And I have been racking my brains to come up with some logical reason for the change in the way you are with me. Last time I was here, I thought…'. He'd thought she'd been enjoying his company as much as he'd been enjoying hers. Unless…

'I don't recall drinking heavily, so I cannot believe I could have behaved badly while in my cups.' All he could remember was laughter and a sense of companionship he'd never felt with anyone else, male or female. A feeling of…connection.

Which just went to show how deceitful feelings could be.

'So,' he said, planting his hands on his hips, 'since you have not had the courtesy to tell me to my face what I have done that makes you feel you have the right to treat me like a leper, this was the only solution.'

'A leper? Oh, no, no,' she said, reaching out one hand to him briefly, before withdrawing it, a look of guilt on her face. 'This,' she said, waving her hand wildly between herself and the door through which she'd been trying to escape, 'is not your fault. It is mine. All mine.'

Which made no sense whatsoever.

'Explain.'

'Oh, dear,' she said, wringing her hands. 'This is all so…' Her face went pink. 'But I do owe you the truth, I suppose,' she said, looking up at him, and going an even deeper shade of pink, 'since I cannot let you go on thinking you have done anything to offend, or frighten me…'

That was one of the things he'd always liked about Miss Mitcham. Her sincerity. She never argued for the sake of scoring points, or said things for effect. She had a quicksilver mind that was always seeking enlightenment, or so he'd thought. He'd also believed she was open and honest. And kind, too. The kindness she showed to Lady Bradbury was the same character trait that was making her swallow what looked suspiciously like acute embarrassment now, so that she could put his mind at rest. Because she was the kind of person who would rather suffer that embarrassment than cause another person pain.

'Lady Bradbury says,' she continued, her cheeks now the shade of beetroot, 'that I have been…er…putting myself forward. Where you are concerned. Of, in short…er…setting my cap at you.'

Setting her cap at him? She'd never done anything remotely like it. She had no idea how to flirt or entice a man. She even dressed so as to disguise her assets, as though she wanted to be all but invisible.

'So,' Miss Mitcham was continuing, as he reeled in disbelief, 'she has forbidden me from being alone with you ever again.'

'She did what?' What did the old woman think he would do if her paid companion *had* been trying to flirt? Reciprocate? Take her up on the offer? A female who was virtually in his employ? Who was, at the very least, living under one of his roofs, under his protection.

'Of course it is not true,' she denied hotly. 'I would never dream of…and neither would you.'

'Of course I wouldn't,' he bit out. At least Miss Mitcham trusted him, even if his mother's aunt didn't. But then wasn't that always the way with the females in his family? Because he looked so very like his father, they kept on saying that the apple never fell very far from the tree. Ever since he'd been of an age to show an interest in the fairer sex, they'd put the worst interpretation on all his amorous adventures so that, in the end, he'd stopped denying that he was a rake in the worst sense of the word. Had, in fact, used the reputation he was gaining to his own advantage.

Being known as a rake meant that women with daughters of marriageable age tended to protect them from him. It meant that he could have encounters with women who made no demands on his emotions, since they all assumed he was only capable of providing brief, physical pleasure.

All of which suited him perfectly. Had suited him perfectly. Until now.

'Especially not with you.' He liked her far too much to use her for a few brief moments of pleasure before discarding her. Besides, she was in a vulnerable position with no male family members to protect her. Dammit, as her employer once removed, it was *his* job to protect her from that sort of attention.

'No,' she said, wilting. 'I am not that sort of female, am I?' she said sadly.

No, and he liked her the better for it. But hold on, it wasn't just the threat of physical intimacy Lady Bradbury had taken steps to prevent, was it? 'But, devil take it, she's forbidden you even to converse with me, hasn't she? It isn't just situations like this you have been avoiding,' he said, gesturing to the closed door. 'You don't even make appearances at the dinner table any more, when your conversation is the one thing that makes my visits here bearable.' And her withdrawal had made him feel the isolation that he normally wore like a suit of armour as a heavy cumbersome thing. A burden, rather than a shield behind which he could stay safe.

Her head flew up. A sparkle appeared in her coffee-brown eyes. 'What a bouncer,' she said, in a way that reminded him of the informality that had started to become such a feature of their interaction. 'You come here,' she said, pointing to his loose jacket and well-worn boots, 'for the shooting.'

'Yes, I do come here for the shooting,' he said, since that was the reason he gave anyone who cared to question his decision to turn down an invitation elsewhere when he took a hankering to spend time at Chervil House. And the shooting was good, especially at this time of year. 'I do enjoy being outside with nothing but a game bag slung over my shoulder, and nobody dogging my footsteps. Nobody whispering gossip into my ear or thinking they can spread tales about me to others about what I may or may not have been up to of late. No image to maintain,' he added, running his hand down the front of a jacket that his valet had attempted to dispose of more times than he could count. 'Just the freedom to tramp across my own land, all day, doing exactly as I please. And,' he added, taking a step closer to her, 'until this time, your presence at dinner to ensure I have intelligent conversation at the end of the day.' She was a very soothing person to return to at the end of a day's shooting. Yes, she was intelligent, but not in that rather sharp, antagonistic manner of some of the society females known as bluestockings. She had a playful intelligence that, coupled with her innate kindness, meant that any disagreement they might have about, say, a book they'd both read never descended to the point of acrimony.

'Well, I'm very sorry,' she said, hanging her head and looking despondent again. Which was all the more disheartening to see, after that flash of humour which had briefly dispelled it. 'But while you are here, I must take my meals in my room. Nor be alone with you, like this, if I wish to retain my post. So...' She began another attempt to sidle past him.

'Just a minute,' he said, taking her by the arm as she drew level with him. 'Am I to understand that Lady Bradbury has threatened to dismiss you if you so much as speak to me?'

'Without a character,' she replied ruefully. 'So if you don't mind, since I really don't want to lose my post and my reputation in one fell swoop...'

He could scarcely believe that the old woman would take out her dislike of him on this poor, defenceless girl. It was the kind of abuse of privilege that had always sickened him.

'How dare she,' he growled, keeping a tight hold of Miss Mitcham's arm to prevent her from leaving. 'She has no right to prevent me from speaking to anyone who lives in this house, since it belongs to me. Or to prevent you from conversing with me, if it comes to that. Especially since neither of us have done anything improper. Good God, it implies that she believes me capable of...of ravishing a woman of gentle birth. A woman who lives under my roof. Does she really think that I have so little self-control that I would forget what I owe my name?'

Miss Mitcham took a breath to make a point. But she didn't need to. He could see what she was thinking. It was written all over her open, honest countenance.

'Yes, yes, they all say I am a rake. And it is true that I spread my favours a touch indiscriminately. But I have never once preyed on the defenceless, or the innocent. I would not.'

'I never thought you would. It isn't that. It's, it's…' Once more, her face turned red. 'It is far worse, at least from my point of view,' she went on, in a rush. 'I mean, she doesn't think you would be doing the preying. She thinks that I am attempting to…er…trap you into marriage.' And then she laughed, a little nervously, with an imploring look in her eyes as though begging him to understand that she was as innocent of that crime as the one of which he'd been accused.

He flinched and let go of her arm which he suddenly became aware he'd been holding on to rather too tightly. 'I don't need protecting from you, any more than you need protecting from me,' he said. 'But this is just typical of the females in my family. They all believe they have the right to interfere with my marital status. As one, they condemn me for loose behaviour while urging me to make what they call a suitable match. And by a suitable match, I mean to the daughter of an earl, if not a duke. A female with an income to match my own, at the very least. And one of a status which will secure my family a place as one of the most powerful in the land.'

She looked confused. 'Isn't that the way things work in your circles?'

'That isn't the point,' he said, whirling away from her and taking a pace across the room. He'd thought she would understand that he could not tolerate the way people, especially his female relatives, behaved as though he owed them something, while at the same time criticising every single blessed thing he did. 'I thought that out here, in the smallest and most remote of my properties, I would be able to escape the…the hypocrisy and the pressures that come with my rank. That I could enjoy the company of a person who just happens to be female, without all the issues of marriage and dynasty, and ambition, blighting it all. And it's all very well you saying that this is the way things work, but…' He paused, turning to her with his hands spread wide in appeal. 'Why should it? Why shouldn't a man choose a wife, a woman he will of necessity be shackled to for the rest of his days, with regard to factors such as compatibility? Or what kind of mother she might turn out to be? Are those things not as important as what she can bring to the family coffers?'

'Well, isn't that what the London Season is all about? All those balls and things? Letting people of your rank mingle, with a view to seeing if they might suit?'

'Hah! A man cannot discover any more about a woman under those circumstances than he could from asking his man of business about her income and background. Women in society dissemble, Miss Mitcham. They pretend to be whatever it is they think a man is looking for, until they get him well and truly hooked. By which time it is too late.'

'I never,' she said thoughtfully, 'took you for a romantic.'

'A what? A romantic?' He all but shuddered with revulsion. 'Whatever gave you that notion?'

'Well, you said you wanted more from marriage than just...'

'I am the very opposite of romantic,' he declared with every fibre of his being. 'Men who fall in love invariably make total asses of themselves.' Even his own brother Sebastian had fallen prey to a pretty face and a coaxing manner, in spite of having a mother like theirs as a warning. 'No rational man should allow emotion to influence his choice of bride.'

She frowned. 'There is a serious flaw in your logic. If a man should not marry for practical reasons, nor for love, then...'

'There is no flaw in my logic,' he retorted. 'I am saying that men should not marry at all.' He began to pace restlessly back and forth as he defended his argument. 'And yet, Season after Season, I watch the latest batch of fools going through what is popularly called courtship. If the man falls for a woman's pretty face and coaxing manner, it is usually only a few weeks after the marriage ceremony before the scales fall from the poor sap's eyes. And then, when he realises how badly he's been duped, comes disillusion and, if the woman in question is particularly cruel—' as Sebastian's wife was '—utter misery. At least, I grant you, if a man marries a woman primarily for financial gain—" as his brother Gerald had done, having witnessed Sebastian's misery, and being of a more practical nature '—he will still have the money in the bank to fund his career, even when he cannot bear to spend more than five minutes in the same room as the woman with whom he struck his deal.'

But it wasn't just his brothers who'd made poor choices. 'Look, Miss Mitcham, I haven't witnessed any man who, having yielded to the pressure put on him by his family to marry, for one reason or another, ended up satisfied with his choice. And the ones who professed to be in love with their brides generally end up the worst off. They face such disillusion that they feel foolish, and resentful, as well as miserable. That can lead to the couple descending into open warfare.' Which was what had happened in the case of his parents. 'And any children unfortunate enough to have been conceived within such a marriage end up as casualties.'

'I am so sorry,' she said, 'that what you have described has been your experience...'

That gave him pause. He might have known that she would know he wasn't merely describing marriages he'd witnessed as an adult.

'You have heard gossip about my own parents, then?'

She nodded.

'I might have known,' he said, shaking his head. 'Their hatred of each other was so notorious that even you, who have never attended a *ton* function in your life, have heard of it.'

'It sounded horrid,' she said, sympathetically, 'but—'

'But this is exactly the type of marriage women like Lady Bradbury expect me to make,' he pointed out indignantly. 'The kind that will be a source of satisfaction to everyone but myself.'

'Which is what made me think you should marry for love, instead, then.'

'No. I've already told you, only a total idiot would marry for love.'

'So that is why you have decided it is better not to marry at all,' she said with a nod, as though reaching a firm conclusion about him. Or seeing the logic in his argument, which somehow dispelled much of the disquiet which had been raging through him since hearing of Lady Bradbury's suspicions. She, at least, understood him.

'I find it hard to believe,' he said, still feeling rather disgruntled, 'that after housing her in this property, when nobody else would do anything for her, Lady Bradbury has the effrontery to think she can forbid me from having any sort of intercourse with you. Or even taking steps to prevent me from marrying you when nothing could ever have been further from my mind.'

'No,' she said, tartly. 'Well, you have made your opinions upon that subject very clear.'

'I meant no offence. Not to you personally. You understand that, don't you? That I never intend to marry anyone, for any reason. Though if I did,' he said, in a belated attempt to erase the hurt look from her face, 'there is absolutely no reason why you should not qualify. I mean,' he went on, 'you are as well born as many of the debutantes my female relatives keep urging me to consider.' Whenever there were no daughters of dukes available, that was. Although their mamas took pains to keep their pure little doves well away from his grimy paws these days.

Just as Lady Bradbury was attempting to protect Miss Mitcham.

'Perhaps,' he conceded, 'I can see why she felt she needed to save you from my evil intentions.'

'I got the impression it was the other way round,' she pointed out.

'Possibly,' he conceded. She was very attractive. There was something about her that made him want to visit this property far more frequently than was absolutely necessary. It wasn't that she was particularly pretty, in the conventional way. But then she didn't make any attempt to make the most of herself. She scraped her hair into a most unattractive style and wore clothes that concealed her figure. At least, she thought they did. When she was moving about, or bending down, or reaching up, however, he hadn't been able to help noticing that she had a curvaceous, yet trim figure beneath the unflattering garments she chose. He placed his hands on his hips as he looked her up and down. He'd never really considered it before, but with a new hairstyle, and clothes designed by a London modiste, clothes designed to flatter her rather than make her fade into the background, she could easily take her place at any function in London, and be described as handsome.

'The only thing you lack, in point of fact, is money,' he mused. 'And land.'

'That's two things,' she pointed out pedantically, making him chuckle.

'That's the thing about you,' he said. 'You amuse me. Even when I'm furious, you manage to make me see the lighter side of things.' And hadn't he just been thinking how restful she was to come home to at the end of the day? 'I have always enjoyed our conversations. Even when you were so tongue-tied by my magnificence you could barely string two words together.'

She blushed.

All of a sudden, a solution came to him. A solution so dazzlingly brilliant he didn't know why it hadn't occurred to him before. He'd always known he *ought* to marry, for the sake of the succession. The prospect had hung over him like a black cloud ever since he'd learned that his primary function in life was to sire the next generation. But the prospect of marrying a 'suitable' girl, for dynastic reasons, had always seemed cold and cheerless. The alternative, marrying for love, had been equally repellent, because he'd seen what marrying for love had done to Seb. The cheerful boy who'd naively believed he could find heaven on earth with his pretty little wife was now living in a hell from which there could be no escape until one of them died. He had no intention of letting any woman break him like that. So he'd declared, loudly and often, that he would never marry.

But what if marriage was not based on either of those two alternatives? What if he could find a middle way? What if he married a girl he liked? A girl like Miss Mitcham? A sensible, decent girl who would see all the advantages of marrying for practical reasons. A girl who wouldn't make outrageous demands upon him.

'Yes, why not?' It felt as though that black cloud lifted off him as he gazed down at Miss Mitcham's puzzled countenance.

'Why not what?'

And then another aspect of things sprang to mind.

'Why not make Lady Bradbury's worst fears come to pass?' That would teach her to think she could interfere in his private life.

'In…er…what way?'

'Don't be stupid.' She wasn't usually this slow on the uptake. She must know what he meant. 'By marrying me, of course.'

Chapter Three

'What?' Eleanor's heart squeezed at hearing her first proposal of marriage coupled with an insult to her intelligence. Besides, from the wicked gleam in his eye, it looked as though he was joking. 'That isn't funny.'

'It isn't? Oh, I think it is an excellent jest, as well as being one in the eye for Lady Bradbury,' he said, stepping closer and taking hold of her upper arms. Not tightly, the way he'd done before, but gently. Almost as though he was handling fragile porcelain which he didn't want to damage. 'Wouldn't you like to take some revenge upon my great-aunt?' he said, caressingly, running his thumbs up and down her arms in an equally caressing manner. 'She's always treated you like some kind of medieval serf, even though you come from as good a background as she did.'

'I don't think revenge is a good reason for getting married,' she said, although her heart was pounding as fast as if she'd been running. Because he was tugging her closer to his body until she could feel the heat blazing from him. And smell his scent. Something citrusy and warm, mingled with the smell of outdoors.

'And I,' he was saying, as though he hadn't heard her say anything, 'would be able to put a halt to all the complaints from the female members of my family about doing my duty.'

'But you don't really wish to marry anyone,' she reminded him. 'Let alone me.'

'Why not you? You are as well born as most of them that get paraded about town as being eligible brides. And just as pretty,' he said, causing her spirits to soar. 'At least you could be,' he added, 'if you had as much money to spend on clothing and such.'

Her spirits plunged back to normal. And her practical, sensible side reasserted itself. 'But I don't believe you are ready to…er…take such a drastic step. You give no appearance of being ready to…er…settle down.'

He chuckled. 'What a coy way of referring to my reputation for enjoying the pleasures of the flesh,' he said, bringing a flush to her cheeks. 'I suppose Lady Bradbury has been regaling you with tales of my amorous exploits?'

It felt as if her cheeks went from rose pink to beetroot red.

'Damn the woman,' he said with a scowl. He let go of her upper arms. Ran his fingers through his hair. The curls, she noted with resentment, immediately fell back into place. 'Look here,' he said. 'There is no use denying that I've been very active in that regard. But no more than any other healthy male of my age, I promise you. And I'll make you another promise.'

Oh? Something that felt rather like hope began to

unfurl from the knot of confusion and disbelief which had taken up residence in her insides.

'I will be completely faithful to you,' he said, making hope prick up its ears and raise its head. 'For the first month or so of our marriage. And during that time I will, in public, make the whole world believe I am totally smitten.'

'A month or so?' Hope flinched.

'Make the whole world believe?' Curled up and died.

'Everyone will be stunned by me looking smitten for that long,' he said, with a twisted smile. 'I don't normally…er…feel anything very much, for any of my lovers.'

She supposed he expected her to feel flattered that he was going to pretend to be *smitten*. For even a month or two.

'But here's the beauty of it,' he said, with what, previously, she would have thought of as a winning smile. 'After those few months, at the time when most married couples begin to despise each other, we might still remain friends…'

Friends? Did he think she could become friends with a man who could treat her with such little respect?

'Since we are going into this arrangement with no unreasonable expectations,' he carried on, that smile still on his face. 'You can choose whichever of my properties you like best to make your home,' he said, as though he was making another great concession. 'And I will make you an allowance that will enable you to live like a…well, a countess, which is what you will be.' He stuck his hands on his hips and grinned at her, as though he'd just said something extremely clever. 'Though of course, if I haven't got you with child, I will have to visit you from time to time, to… er…expedite the matter.'

Expedite? The matter?

'Well, Miss Mitcham, what do you say? Would you like to become Countess of Lavenham?'

Peter would have expected his great-aunt's rather dowdy little companion to have flung herself into his arms with gratitude at this point. For what woman would not wish to become his Countess? Especially as he'd just told her he would give her the means to live pretty much as she liked. That he wouldn't be making any excessive, or unreasonable demands.

Miss Mitcham, however, did not appear to appreciate the enormous honour he'd just done her in finally offering to become a tenant for life.

'Why on earth,' she said, reeling back with an expression of utter horror on her face, 'would I wish to do anything so…dishonest?'

'It is not dishonest,' he flung back at her. 'It is more honest a bargain I am offering you than most men of my station make to the women they intend to make their wives. I am not trying to convince you that we will ever know what is commonly called *wedded bliss*.' He couldn't help sneering over the words, for they were just a euphemism, intended to account for the way a man and a woman could be together during the first flush of passion. Before they began to know each other as people and wondered what on earth had made them want to become intimate with them at all.

But of course, being an innocent, she wouldn't understand about that kind of thing. About how, to start with, the arch of a neck or the flutter of an eyelid could induce such pangs of lust that nothing else mattered. Or how, for a few weeks, passion could make him overlook the irritating laugh or the vapid conversation of the current beauty whose bed he was visiting. Or how, after a few weeks more, the very way the woman breathed induced such revulsion that he could barely stand to be in the same room with her, never mind the same bed.

'Look,' he said, seeing that spelling out the way relationships between men and women invariably went was not going to persuade this particular woman to bend to his will, 'why don't you consider the practical benefits?' As he had. 'For spending a couple of months in my bed, and providing me with an heir, you will get a title, a generous allowance and a position so far above Lady Bradbury's in society that you will have plenty of opportunity to pay her back for the way she's treated you.'

'I have no wish to *pay her back*,' she retorted, flinging her chin up proudly as though such behaviour was beneath her, making him see that he'd made an error in bringing that aspect of things to her notice. She was not, essentially, a vindictive woman. 'Especially not by entering into an arrangement which you have made sound so...horrid.' She wrinkled up her nose. 'Like a kind of...refined prostitution.'

'Well, is that not what marriage is?' He flung that at her, stung by her inability to see how generous his offer truly was. 'An arrangement whereby a woman agrees to provide a man with children in return for gaining access to his purse?'

She gasped. 'No! That is not what marriage is. Not what it should be, anyway.'

'I am probably going to regret saying this, but what, in your opinion, should marriage be about then, if not the obvious?'

She stood up straight and clasped her hands at her waist, like a governess about to give a lesson to a particularly unruly class. 'Marriage should be about two people wanting to spend the rest of their lives together, in companionship and harmony. They should be like a team, who always defend each other and face down the rest of the world, and all its hardships, together.'

My God. Could anyone really be that naive? 'That sounds idyllic,' he said, 'but the truth is that nobody can ever trust anyone to always defend them.' Or, in his case, ever. He'd learned in the nursery that when faced with possible punishment, not only children, but also the people supposed to be looking after them, would invariably put their own interests first. Before truth, before justice, before compassion.

But then what else could anyone expect, when the master and mistress of the house had been setting the example they had? 'Especially not the person to whom they are married. Betrayal, that is what a husband can expect from a wife. Or,' he put in swiftly as he saw her indignant reaction to the slur on her own sex, 'vice versa.'

'That is not true!'

'Believe me, little innocent, it is. I have never seen a married couple attain anything like the state of harmony you have just described.'

'Well, I have,' she retorted. 'My own parents were

friends right up to the last. No matter what troubles beset them, they never turned on each other. They were always glad, they said, that, in the midst of what life threw at them, they had each other.'

'To the exclusion of everyone else, apparently.'

She frowned. 'What do you mean?'

'Why, that in the midst of all this grand coping with whatever life threw at them, they did not take steps to provide for their daughter.' His own parents had actively hated each other, yet neither of them would have dreamed of leaving him to make his own way in the world. 'Their lofty ideals did not extend to making sure you didn't end up so impoverished you had to take employment with a woman as uncongenial as my great-aunt, did they?'

'That's nothing to do with it! Whether they were poor or not doesn't alter the fact that they were happy with each other. That they loved each other right up to the end. That there was never a cross word spoken between them—'

'They sound dull,' he said cutting through her rapturous encomium for two people who sounded as though they'd taken notice of nobody but each other. Not that his own parents had been any better with regard to child-rearing. Children, as far as they were concerned, were merely pawns in their ongoing battles. Whenever he, or either of his brothers, had been caught out in some misdemeanour, one would claim it was a trait of the other's family.

'A typical Harford,' his mother would sneer when he'd been accused of poaching fish from a neighbour's stream.

'The kind of behaviour I would expect from a Trafford,' his father would sigh when he'd been sent down from Oxford for involvement in a romp that had not even been of his own making.

'I am not interested in them. What I am interested in is your answer to my proposal.' Which was the first he'd ever made. And one he'd thought he never would make.

She lifted her chin again. 'I want no part,' she said loftily, 'of what you propose.'

Peter could have let it go, with a laugh. Told her she didn't know what she was missing, flicked the tip of her nose and gone off to dress for dinner.

But for some reason, perhaps because he'd just remembered the way his own parents had always rejected him, or because his honour had been called into question by Lady Bradbury, or perhaps because he was annoyed by being denied not only the company of this woman as a dinner companion, but also having her turn down his offer without even really considering it, he was in no mood to laugh it off.

'You're a hypocrite,' he said, making her coffee-brown eyes widen in surprise and outrage. Although they were going to widen even further in a moment. 'There is one part you most definitely want. I've seen the way you look at me sometimes. The way that probably put Lady B. on the alert.'

'I don't look at you in any way that—' she said, guiltily.

'Yes, you do,' he said, stepping far closer than any chaperon would permit were they on a dance floor, never mind when they were alone in a room with the door closed. 'You want me. Just admit it and you can have me, with the advantage of a wedding ring on your finger since that is the only way a little prude like you would ever give way to your natural impulses.'

'I will admit to no such thing,' she said indignantly, although her face was flushing and she was having trouble meeting his eyes.

'Then I will prove you a liar,' he said ungallantly, before drawing her unresisting body into his arms and kissing her.

She stiffened in surprise, but only for a second. Then she melted into his embrace like ice cream the moment it was served up on a summer's day.

And then, she put her arms round his neck and pressed as much of her as she could against his body, with an enthusiasm that surprised him. Because, although he'd noticed the way she'd looked at him with hungry eyes, and he'd just teased her for doing so, he'd never guessed that she was this ravenous. She'd hidden it well. Or she'd fought it valiantly.

But she wasn't fighting it now. If he had the inclination, and if he was truly the kind of man his mother's aunt had accused him of being, he could steer her over to one of the sofas and take his fill of her. And she wouldn't put up a single protest.

Not until it was over.

But that was *not* the kind of man he was.

And so, before things could go too far, he gentled the kiss, broke away and gazed down into her flushed face with what felt remarkably like a thrill of conquest.

'I shall inform Lady B., then,' he purred with satisfaction in gaining such an easy victory, 'that we are betrothed, shall I? And set the cat among the pigeons.'

'No.' She pulled out of his hold. 'No!' She put her hands to her cheeks. Her hair, he noticed, was coming down out of its neat arrangement. He hadn't been aware that he'd been plunging his fingers through it, though he'd sometimes wondered what it would look like, down. And how long it was. And whether it would riot into a mass of curls once allowed to go wherever it wished instead of being wrapped up into the severe bun her position in life demanded.

'I won't marry you,' she was insisting, pushing one stray dark brown lock from her forehead and tucking it behind her ear with a hand that was trembling. With thwarted passion, if he was any judge. 'And have you think of me as some kind of...prostitute, simply because I...you...we...' She waved that hand between their two bodies to refer to what had just happened when they'd kissed. The errant strand of hair slid from its moorings, making her look like the very wanton she was denying she could become. 'Knowing that two months after you've put a ring on my finger you will be back to your old ways and expect me to live in the country like a...a nun!'

'Ah, is that all that is bothering you?' He sighed. He didn't know why he should have felt so disappointed. That had been one of the bones of contention between his own parents, after all. For some reason, though Father believed he had the right to keep a mistress in Town, he took a very dim view if ever he discovered Mother had taken a lover. And Peter suspected that she took most of them with deliberate intent to cause him as much inconvenience and embarrassment as possible. The older she got, the more unsuitable her bedfellows became until not even his own friends, so-called, were safe from her predations if they came to visit.

'I am a fair man. I won't object to you having your own affairs, once you've provided me with an heir that I can be sure is my own...' That was not too much to expect, was it? That a man should see his own flesh and blood inherit all that was his?

He frowned. Until now, he'd told anyone who tried to impress upon him that he owed it to the family to sire that child that he had two perfectly healthy, married brothers who could keep the family line going. Even though, given the fact that Seb's wife appeared to be sleeping with everyone but Seb, and Gerald had taken a commission in a regiment serving overseas, leaving his wife in England, the chances of either of them providing that heir was minimal. Still, he kept saying that he didn't care who would inherit, for he wouldn't be there to see it. But the moment he'd spoken about giving Miss Mitcham children, something shifted inside. A feeling that perhaps, with her at his side, he might not necessarily follow in his father's footsteps. That he might, possibly, become a tolerable sort of parent.

Miss Mitcham, however, did not seem to appreciate the fact that he had no intention of featuring as a jealous, controlling, hypocritical sort of husband. And a father who would see his children only as pawns. She reeled back as though he'd struck her.

'I would rather die,' she cried, then darted past him and fled from the library.

Without whatever it was she'd been searching for in the desk drawer.

Chapter Four

Eleanor didn't bother going to Lady Bradbury's rooms to see if there was any tea left. She hadn't got any writing paper to hand over and she could not face explaining just what, or rather who, had prevented her from finding any.

Apart from the embarrassment factor, Lady Bradbury would be bound to carry out her threat to dismiss her, if she found out that not only had she spoken to Lord Lavenham against her express wishes, she'd let him kiss her.

Oh, be honest with yourself, Eleanor, she scolded herself as she reached the set of stairs which led up to the section of the attics that contained her room. *You kissed him back. And flung your arms round his neck and rubbed yourself up against him like...like ivy trying to send tendrils into any little crevice so that it could take a permanent hold.*

Though permanence was not what he was offering. Not by any means. The proposition he'd made, which she would not dignify by describing as a proposal, was the most cynical, jaded, pessimistic statement she'd ever heard. He'd even used the *tendre* she'd begun to develop for him against her!

She reached the turn in the stairs and went pounding up the last half-flight to the upper landing, her fists clenched at her side. Yes, she found him physically attractive and, after that kiss, that sizzling, bone-melting kiss, she had no doubt he'd be able to make the marriage bed a feast for all the senses. For the few months he planned to spend with her in it, that was. But then what?

She scurried along the uncarpeted landing to her room, darted in, shut the door behind her and leaned back against it, her chest heaving. A few months of exquisite pleasure would never, ever compensate her for the lifetime of humiliation that would follow. How could he think it?

Oh, yes, because he assumed that once he'd commenced her sensual education, she'd be perfectly happy to continue experimenting, with other men.

She shuddered. How could he imagine she'd ever do such a thing?

Because he didn't believe in love, that was why. He'd hotly repudiated her suggestion that he was romantic. Had sneered at her account of how deeply her own parents had loved each other, then proposed the kind of marriage that would make her feel like a temporary mistress. Had told her, with perfect candour, that he would only *pretend* to be smitten with her for long enough to get her with child and that, when he'd achieved that noble duty to his family, he'd resume his raking ways with a clear conscience.

He'd spelled it all out to her, in detail so that, if she agreed to become his wife, he would be able to point out that by accepting his proposal she'd agreed to it all.

Which meant that she could not possibly marry him.

How on earth could he think that agreeing to such a demeaning relationship would be an improvement upon working for Lady Bradbury, anyway? Lady Bradbury might be a bit cantankerous, but then who wouldn't be, when riddled with arthritis? She was in a great deal of pain most of the time and didn't sleep well. Eleanor could easily let her waspish comments slide off her like water off a duck's back, knowing she didn't mean the half of it.

But Lord Lavenham had meant every single word he'd said.

Well, so had she. She wasn't going to marry him. She…

But what if he persisted in trying to persuade her? What if he kissed her again? And somebody caught them at it? Her hands flew to her face. Her lips were still burning with the echo of his mouth on hers. She pressed her fingers to them, then relived the feeling of his tongue, sliding into her mouth…

Oh, lord. Just thinking about it made her feel all hot and bothered. And sort of hungry inside for more than kisses.

What was she to do? Just stay firm in her resolve to refuse his offer? Hah! She might as well try to…to stop a coal from catching light after tossing it into the fire.

He'd only just arrived at Chervil House. He normally stayed at least a week. She would never be able to resist him, if he decided he wasn't going to take no for an answer. Not that she believed, for one moment, that his heart was set on marrying *her,* particularly. Not after letting her know exactly how he planned the course of their marriage to develop. But he might not want to abandon his outrageous plan to get even with Lady Bradbury by elevating her paid companion to the position of his wife. He might even take it into his head to regard her in the way he did those birds he spent so long hunting for, for the mere pleasure of shooting them. He was a natural hunter, a man who enjoyed stalking prey…

She pictured him lurking in wait for her in various rooms of the house. Or merely following her with his eyes as she went about her legitimate business. There were all sorts of ways he could get round Lady Bradbury's orders, since he owned the house and paid the wages of every servant in it. And if he were to kiss her again…

She placed her hands on her lower abdomen, which was pulsing and tingling, even though he hadn't touched her anywhere near there. But which wanted him to. Which yearned for him to do.

That settled it. She'd have to leave. And then she'd be free from the temptation of his kisses and the threat of dismissal. Lady Bradbury couldn't dismiss her if she gave up her position!

She looked round the cheerless, bleak little room. She'd never managed to make it feel homely. She still kept most of her possessions in her trunk, since it had more space than the slender wardrobe, which was the only item of furniture up here, apart from the narrow bed. So it would take her hardly any time at all to pack.

She might as well do the packing now, while waiting for her dinner. It would give her something to do since the room was too small for her to pace back and forth, wringing her hands, which was what she really felt like doing.

She crossed the room to her trunk, which she'd wedged in between her wardrobe and her bed, and which doubled as a bedside table.

Now that she'd taken the decision to leave, she couldn't see why she'd put up with working for Lady Bradbury for as long as she had, really. She knelt beside the trunk to remove her hairbrush, comb, bible and towel from its surface and lay them on the bed. It wasn't as if she didn't have other options. She lifted the lid. It was true that her parents had not left her financially well off, but she had plenty of uncles and aunts and cousins, all of whom had offered her homes with them when she'd become an orphan. She had just preferred to support herself by doing paid work, that was all, so that she'd feel she was not a burden, or a drain on anyone else's finances. But she wouldn't mind spending a short while with any one of them while she was looking for another post.

'So there,' she said out loud, although there was nobody to hear her. Though of course she would not have dared say it if there had been. It wasn't in her nature to be rude, especially not to an elderly lady who was in pain. Not that it had ever stopped Lady Bradbury from saying exactly what she thought, in the frankest of terms.

Which led her to imagine the scene at dinner, when Lord Lavenham informed Lady Bradbury what he planned to do. She shuddered. Thank heavens she wouldn't be there to witness it. Thank heavens Lady Bradbury *had* ordered the housekeeper, Mrs Timms, to have a tray sent up to her room while Lord Lavenham was in residence. Eleanor would gladly have saved everyone the trouble and dined with the rest of the staff in the servants' hall, but Lady Bradbury was not having any of that.

'Class distinction must be maintained,' she'd insisted, *'or else where will it all end? In a revolution, like the French have endured, like as not.'*

Eleanor sighed as she dug down through her gowns and under-things for the little portmanteau in which she'd carried the essentials for her journey here: night things, brushes and combs, toothpowder, spare handkerchiefs and so on. It had meant that she never needed to unbuckle the strap holding her trunk shut, the entire journey, in spite of changing coaches several times. It only took her a few minutes to place the same items into it and then there was nothing to do but sit there, imagining the scene she would have to face the next morning, when she told Lady Bradbury she was leaving.

Her stomach turned over. Mrs Timms was always saying she had the patience of a saint, because she'd lasted so much longer than any of Lady Bradbury's previous paid companions, but it was probably more accurate to say that Eleanor shrank from confrontation. Besides, in the past whenever Lady Bradbury had shouted at her, Eleanor had known that it wasn't her fault. Her father had taught her that bad temper nearly always stemmed from a logical reason, for which she only had to search. And it was no great feat to see that Lady Bradbury was angry at the world, and her pain, not Eleanor. But tomorrow would be different. Tomorrow, Eleanor would deserve every ounce of Lady Bradbury's anger because she had been alone with Lord Lavenham, even though she should not have been. And had kissed him. And enjoyed it.

Her cheeks burned. Whatever names Lady Bradbury called her, they were nothing to how Eleanor felt about herself, at this moment. She would want to curl up and die of shame when Lady Bradbury said them to her.

And what of Lord Lavenham? What if, after Eleanor came out of the interview with Lady Bradbury, he *still* wouldn't take no for an answer? Well, she'd already considered that. And faced up to her complete inability to resist him.

But what, a tiny voice from somewhere deep in the depths of her suggested, if he *did* finally take no for an answer? What if, by tomorrow, he'd thought better of his impulsive proposal and was relieved to hear he wouldn't have to go through with it?

A pain struck her in the middle, like a knife to the heart.

Oh, lord, but tomorrow was going to be unbearable. However was she to face it?

She squeezed her eyes shut. A single tear escaped and ran down her cheek. She brushed it away, opened her eyes and reached for a handkerchief.

As her gaze alighted on the fully packed portmanteau, an outrageous idea popped into her head. Why not leave right now?

Because it was already dark outside, her sensible, cautious side replied.

Hummph. She was far less afraid of the dark than she was of the horrible scene she'd just imagined, which she was going to have to endure tomorrow.

On a rush of an impulse she'd never experienced before, but thought was probably what people described as panic, Eleanor went to where her coat hung on a hook on the back of the door and put it on. If she left right now, she was pretty sure she could reach Burton-in-Steane before nine o'clock, which was the earliest anyone was likely to ask after her. Mrs Timms didn't have her dinner tray brought right up here, but had the maid leave it on the table at the foot of the attic stairs. And nobody ever came up to collect it until the staff had finished seeing to the rest of the family's needs for the evening.

As Eleanor rammed her bonnet on her head, she did wonder, for a moment, if she was being a bit selfish to run off like this, without telling anyone.

Though it wasn't as if anyone was going to *worry* about her, was it? Lady Bradbury would be cross, of course, but then, when wasn't she cross about something? And as for Lord Lavenham…he might feel a touch of pique. A slight dent to his pride. But nobody could convince Eleanor that he cared tuppence about her. Or he would never have suggested that she would… *sell* herself to him like some kind of…well, she couldn't judge the kind of women that did. They probably had their own reasons. Some of them pretty compelling, from what she'd gleaned from her Uncle Norman, who was the vicar of a little town just outside Newmarket.

And come to think of it, Uncle Norman would be the very person to whom she should go. He could always do with an extra pair of hands, to judge from his most recent letters. His wife, Agatha, was currently expecting her fourth child and, reading between the lines, was struggling to keep up with all the demands of the household, her lively children and parish affairs.

Having made this decision, she spent a few moments scooping the rest of her possessions from the wardrobe into the trunk, to save Mrs Timms the bother of having to pack for her. She could send for the trunk once she'd got wherever she was going, should Uncle Norman, for some reason, be unable to house her at present.

Satisfied she'd done all she could to mitigate the crime of running away while everyone was busy with dinner, Eleanor draped a warm woollen shawl about her shoulders, picked up her portmanteau and shoved her gloves into her coat pocket.

It was only when she was shutting her bedroom door, for the last time, that she gave any thought to how she was actually going to leave the house without running into the two people she most wished to avoid.

She rapidly reviewed the layout of the house. The family rooms were at the front, overlooking the sweep of the driveway that led down to the lane. If, while they were getting changed for dinner, either Lady Bradbury or Lord Lavenham happened to glance out of the window, they might see her trudging along that lane, case in hand, and...well, she couldn't imagine either of them coming after her. But they might send one of the staff to bring her back.

So, she'd go out of the back door.

No. The back door led out from the kitchens. She had no more wish to run the gauntlet of the staff who'd be busy there than she had to have one of them sent after her. They'd all be terribly sympathetic, if she could bear to relate what had happened this afternoon, but they'd probably advise her to be sensible and leave in the morning, when it was light, and one of the male staff could see her safely on to a coach.

The trouble was, she didn't want to be sensible. No, more than that, she *couldn't* be sensible. She hadn't been able to form a single sensible thought since bursting into flames in Lord Lavenham's arms. He'd catapulted her into a state where all she could do was act on her emotions. Her father would have been terribly disappointed in her complete inability to behave in a rational manner. But...she had tried to argue, rationally, with Lord Lavenham and he'd countered by kissing her. She'd defy even her father to apply rational arguments to kisses of that sort. At least, not that Lord Lavenham would ever have kissed him like that, but...

There, you see? Her mind was getting tangled up in knots instead of thinking straight. So, back to what she ought to do next, not what she should have done half an hour ago. Which was to find the best—that was, the most discreet route out of the house.

The morning room. That would provide the best way out. It was not at the front or the back of the house, but at the side, with a pair of French doors which gave access to a small formal garden. Beyond that garden was a ha-ha, to keep the sheep away from the bedding plants, but there were places where she could scramble down and up the other side. She'd done so plenty of times when she'd wanted to take a walk across the hills on her days off. And, from the tops, she'd seen the road that led, eventually, to Gloucester, by way of Burton-in-Steane. She'd be able to get some form of transport from Burton, which was within walking distance, to Gloucester, surely, since it lay on the main road. And from there, she'd be able to change for London, where she could find the inn from which coaches left for Newmarket.

Pleased to discover that her wits had not been completely scrambled by Lord Lavenham's kiss, she ran down both flights of stairs and across the hallway to the morning room before she could think better of it. Nobody saw her crossing the hall, and the key to the French doors was in the lock.

The cold slap of the damp night air almost brought her to a halt as she stepped outside. But she couldn't stay. It would mean facing two people whose characters were much more forceful than her own. People who would not be prepared to reason things out in a calm, rational manner. They'd shout and berate her until she ended up doing as they bid her, just to silence them.

So she shut the door behind her and set off across the terrace and into the formal garden.

She just wasn't used to arguments; that was the trouble. Her parents had never raised their voices to her, or each other. If she had been naughty, they would explain why her behaviour was displeasing and discipline her by withdrawing treats or simply their own attention from her. That had always been enough.

She sighed as she reached the lip of the ha-ha and saw a thick mist was swirling down from the tops of the hills. As if things weren't difficult enough already. At least her shawl was large enough to drape over her bonnet and wrap round her waist where she could tie it, the way working-class women did. Which she did, before tossing her portmanteau across the ditch.

Oh, dear. Running away in the middle of the night like this made her feel like a criminal. She'd have to write a grovelling apology to Lady Bradbury. She could add it to the letter she'd have to write anyway, providing her forwarding address, so Mrs Timms would know where to send her trunk.

Dare she also request a reference? Because, by the time she reached Suffolk, Lady Bradbury might have calmed down. She might even be grateful to Eleanor for putting herself beyond Lord Lavenham's reach. After all, she'd *said* that she was keeping them apart for Eleanor's benefit. To save her.

Although, now that she'd seen how concerned Lord Lavenham had been over the implication he could behave with impropriety to someone who was in his employ, it made her even more inclined to think that most of the stories Lady Bradbury had told her about him were either exaggerated, or completely untrue.

Hadn't he sworn that he was no worse than any other healthy male of his age?

Yes, but that made no difference. She'd already thrown her portmanteau across the ditch, both figuratively and literally. There would be nothing to lose now by asking Lady Bradbury for a character reference. The worst she could now do would be to refuse. She couldn't shout at her, she couldn't make her run stupid, pointless errands, or forbid her from talking to anyone. Anyone at all.

So Eleanor made use of a couple of strategically placed boulders to make her own way across the ditch.

And then she was free.

Chapter Five

Crossing the hills as night drew in, with the temperature steadily dropping and the fog growing thicker by the minute, was a completely different experience from wandering about aimlessly on a sunny afternoon off. By the time Eleanor reached the dry stone wall which ran along the main road that wound through the valley, she was so relieved she could have kissed it. She'd lost count of the times she'd been convinced she was lost, or that she'd stumble and fall into some hidden gully.

She was pretty soon glad she hadn't yielded to the impulse borne out of sheer relief, though. Although it wasn't all that high, the wall was slippery with fog-dampened moss and she was shivering with a combination of cold and anxiety. She'd also missed her dinner, as well as tea. And had as much success getting over the wall as a fish would have had mounting a horse.

She tossed the portmanteau over the wall, to leave her hands free, and had another go at scaling it herself, rather than wasting time searching for a stile. Once she made it into the lane, she would have no trouble reaching Burton-in-Steane, that was what she had to fix her mind on. And the inn, which would have a roaring fire, in front of which she could sit cradling a cup of steaming hot tea to thaw her frozen fingers.

By the time she slithered clumsily into the lane she'd torn her gown and skinned her knee. And down there, between the stone walls, the fog was even thicker. She could see no sign of her portmanteau through air that had the consistency of meringue. In the end, she had to drop to her hands and knees, and crawl about, feeling for it with outstretched hands. She was on the verge of tears by the time her fingers finally brushed up against the familiar straps, and had to simply crouch there, cradling it to her chest for a few moments, before regaining enough composure to stand up and continue her journey.

At that point she realised that while she'd been crawling about searching for her portmanteau, she'd probably turned round several times. She had no idea which of the two walls bounding the lane she'd just climbed over. Not that she could actually see either of them, anyway. She flexed her fingers on the handle of the portmanteau and peered into the fog. Which way was she facing? There was no way to tell. In fact, if she didn't know she was standing in the middle of the very road she'd been making for, she would have absolutely no idea where she was.

Next time she took it into her head to avoid an awkward situation, she would remind herself how much worse just running away could turn out to be. If she'd only held firm, she could have left Chervil House tomorrow morning in a carriage and gone to Gloucester in comfort, rather than frightening herself silly stumbling about in freezing fog as night was drawing in, grazing her knee, ripping her dress and ending up totally disorientated.

Yes, but she hadn't been able to imagine herself holding firm in the face of Lady Bradbury's disapproval, or the blandishments of the handsome and attractive Lord Lavenham, that was the trouble.

If only she had more backbone with people. Or if only she hadn't missed afternoon tea as well as dinner. If only the weather wasn't so atrocious…

But it was no use standing there wishing things were different. She still had a great way to go. In one direction along this road, or the other.

She peered to the right, then to the left, and blinked when she saw a sort of golden glow which appeared to be hanging in mid-air.

For a second, visions of pearly gates and heavenly beings flashed through her mind. Without her volition, her feet began to move in the direction of the light. Or lights, she discovered after only a few more paces. With, floating just in front of them, two ghostly white shapes. And…could she hear the low murmur of voices?

Eleanor had not been brought up to fall prey to superstitions. Knowing there must be some perfectly logical explanation for what looked like angels appearing in an English country lane, she gripped the handle of her portmanteau tightly, lifted her chin, and walked purposefully forward.

Hearing the distinct sound of a horse, stamping an impatient hoof and whinnying, she almost laughed out loud. Of course she wasn't anywhere near the pearly gates. Father was right about there always being a logical explanation for everything, no matter how strange it looked. There was a coach, pulled up right in the middle of the lane, that was all. The white shapes were the heads of the greys in harness and the golden glow emanated from nothing more unearthly than the carriage lamps. And the voices, which were more distinct now, must be the coachman and groom, discussing whatever calamity had caused them to stop right in the middle of the road.

After a few more paces, she could make out the dark bulk of the coach itself.

As she drew level with the lead horse, the massive shape of a man condensed out of the fog and moved to bar her way. From the powdered wig he was wearing and the fancy lacing on his caped coat that she could make out as she drew closer, she guessed the occupant of the coach must be someone of consequence. This was most definitely a footman of the type that served the upper classes.

'Pardon me, miss,' he said, making a half-bow that somehow managed to stem the slight apprehension that the size of him had engendered. 'But we seem to have missed the road to Oxford. I don't suppose you could point us in the right direction, could you?'

'Oxford? No. I have no idea how you might get to Oxford from here.' From studies she'd made of coaching timetables, some years ago, when she'd first considered taking a post out here, she had a vague inkling that it lay on the other side of the Cotswolds.

The footman gave her a look of disdain, the kind of

look they no doubt taught all footmen of his status to cultivate when confronted with idiot girls.

It made her hackles rise.

'This road leads into Burton-in-Steane.' Which was true. Even though she wasn't sure which direction she was facing, now, it did run between Burton-in-Steane and the hamlet of Chipping on Hay. Whichever way they went, they'd reach one or other of them. 'You can ask the landlord of the inn, when you get there—' wherever *there* happened to be '—for directions.'

'Which inn might that be?' came a voice out of mid-air. No angel, though, but likely the driver of the coach, since the place from which his voice emanated was about where the driver of such a vehicle would sit.

Eleanor thought about how to answer. She had no idea what the name of the coaching inn was in Burton-in-Steane. She only recalled, from her studies of the coaching timetables, that it was a place where several routes crossed.

But before she could admit to even further ignorance, the window of the coach slid down and a lady poked out her head.

'Gordon, have you found a local who can tell us the way?'

'Ah, not exactly, Your Grace,' said the footman, turning his back on Eleanor to go the coach window. 'The girl says this lane leads to somewhere called Burton-in-Steel. And that there is an inn there where we can find someone who might be able to guide us.'

The lady, who must be a duchess if the footman addressed her as *Your Grace*, leaned a little further out of the window.

'I cannot make out a thing in this fog,' she complained. 'Young lady, would you mind stepping closer so that I can see you?'

Eleanor could scarcely refuse such a reasonable request, having just found it most disconcerting to hear the voice of the driver without being able to see him. As she drew closer, she could see that the Duchess was not, as one might expect from someone who bore such a weighty title, a fat, bulldog-faced woman of advancing years. She was not young, either, but bore the appearance of a woman who had once been a great beauty and who still took great pains to stave off the advancing years.

'I have had such a horrid day,' the lady complained.

She'd had a horrid day? Eleanor almost snorted in derision when she thought of the day she'd had so far.

'It wanted only getting lost in the fog,' the Duchess complained. 'Are we very far from Oxford?'

'I am not perfectly sure,' said Eleanor, dipping into a curtsy. 'I am not a native of this area. But I seem to recall, from my study of maps, that it lies on the other side of the Cotswolds.'

'Bother,' said the Duchess. 'We must have come down on the wrong side, somehow. Though, of course, I cannot blame Richard,' she said, tilting her head to the front of the coach where the driver must be sitting. 'This fog came down so quickly, and these little roads all look the same. And I had urged him to go as quickly as possible. Which only goes to prove that saying about more haste meaning less speed. Are you heading to this Burton Steel place?'

'Burton-in-Steane,' Eleanor said, before wondering whether it was good manners to correct a duchess, even one as enchanting as this one. 'Yes, I am, Your Grace,' she said, dipping another curtsy just to be on the safe side.

'And is this inn you speak of tolerable? Because I think we may have to break our journey overnight after all. And we may as well stay there as anywhere, now that it has got so late. And the fog is so thick. If we try to push on, we are bound to get lost again.'

'I cannot say, Your Grace,' said Eleanor, apologetically. 'I have never even been to Burton-in-Steane before.' They always made for Chipping on Hay for their shopping, since Lady Bradbury had accounts with all the traders there. 'I only know, from looking at coaching timetables, that several routes to larger towns, such as Oxford, cross there, so that it is a handy place to change.'

'It sounds as if it will do, don't you think, Gordon?' The Duchess looked past Eleanor to the massive footman who'd looked at her with such disdain. 'A coaching inn on the juncture of several routes is bound to be full of all sorts of interesting people, too.' The Duchess clapped her hands in a rather childish fashion. 'It will be such fun. Just what I needed to take my mind off...'

She petered out, and cast her eyes on Eleanor. 'And you, dear girl, I cannot possibly leave you standing here in this horrid weather. Gordon, do open the door so that... I'm sorry, my manners! I have not even asked you your name.'

'It is Miss Mitcham, Your Grace,' said Eleanor, dropping yet another curtsy. And wondering how her knees were going to cope with all this bobbing.

'Miss Mitcham,' said the footman, opening the coach door with a flourish and a sneer, as if daring her to set foot inside. Which made up her mind about the wisdom of getting into a coach with a total stranger. She was not going to permit a servant to browbeat her, no matter how lofty he considered himself. Besides, it would be much warmer in the coach than outside. And she could put the portmanteau, which felt as if it had grown heavier the longer she carried it, down on the seat beside her and start nursing her cramped fingers back to life.

It was only once she'd climbed in and taken a seat facing the Duchess and with her back to the horses, that she remembered that she was, in truth, a servant herself. Or at least, had been until a couple of hours ago.

'This is very kind of you, Your Grace,' she said.

'Oh, think nothing of it,' said the Duchess with a smile as the coach lumbered into motion. 'I couldn't possibly leave you standing in the lane in such frightful weather.'

Why not? Most people of her rank would. The footman certainly seemed to think she should have done.

'Besides,' the Duchess continued, 'I have been cooped up in here, on my own, for what feels like for ever and I am so bored I could scream. So, you can repay me for getting you out of the weather, if you like, by telling me all about yourself and how you came to be walking along this particular road, at such a time of night, in search of an inn. It will help to while away the next few hours, or however long it will take Richard to plod to this inn you have promised lies at the end of this road.'

'Er...' Eleanor's mind flashed back to that searing kiss, in the library, and her subsequent cowardly flight from Chervil House. And felt her cheeks grow warm.

'Perhaps it would help if I told you a bit about myself first,' said the Duchess, eyeing Eleanor's face with amusement. 'I am the Duchess of Theakstone. Widow. Thank heaven!' She gave a rather wicked chuckle. 'I have been visiting my older daughter. The Lady Twickenham. I had hoped it might be possible to make my home with her, because my stepson wants me to remove from his town house in London, which I suppose I really ought to do. Though I would never, ever admit that to him. You won't tell him, will you?' The Duchess placed one hand on Eleanor's knee. Right above the rent in her skirt, which that footman had probably noticed. No wonder he had looked at her with such disdain. There were smears of something green on her coat, as well, probably acquired when she'd crossed the ha-ha. Or when she'd been crawling about feeling for her portmanteau. She still had the shawl wrapped round her bonnet and tied at her waist, too, making her look like a peasant woman.

'Of course I won't,' Eleanor answered the Duchess's plea. For when was she ever likely to meet this woman's stepson? And why would she betray this confidence, uttered in such an open manner, when the lady had been kind enough to offer to take her up in her carriage even though she looked like a gypsy?

The Duchess beamed at her. 'But it won't do. Living with Jane, that is,' she said with a moue of distaste, as Eleanor began to untie the shawl in an attempt to make herself look a bit more like the kind of person who had every right to be travelling with a duchess.

'So, I am going back to Town, before Theakstone returns from wherever he has spent Christmas, so that I can be in possession of the ground, so to speak. Or at least, that was my plan. Only now I am wondering if perhaps I should have waited until Maud recovered. My personal maid, that is, who took it into her head to contract a chill. Well, you must have wondered why I am travelling without one? A maid, that is, not a chill, of course!'

It was only then that Eleanor realised that it *was* a bit odd for a lady of rank to be travelling without a maid.

'I am far too impulsive, sometimes,' the Duchess said with a rueful shake of her head. 'And this is what comes of it. Lost. In the middle of nowhere.'

'I know what you mean,' said Eleanor. Then bit her lip. 'Er...that is...'

Rather than appearing annoyed that Eleanor had interrupted her, the Duchess giggled.

'You, too? I wonder...' The Duchess eyed Eleanor from top to toe. 'I don't suppose you have any experience working as a lady's maid, do you? I didn't think I would miss Maud and, indeed, I don't in many ways. But I must confess the prospect of staying in some public inn, without the services of any sort of maid at all, fills me with horror.' She shuddered.

'I am sorry, I haven't ever worked as a lady's maid,' said Eleanor. But then, seeing the Duchess's look of disappointment, added, 'But I have recently been working as a companion to an elderly lady. So I have observed the kind of things her maid did.'

'Then you could fill in for tonight, couldn't you? How marvellous!' The Duchess clapped her hands again, just like a little girl who has been handed a basket of sweets. 'It doesn't even matter if you don't know exactly how to do things. The most important thing is that you are *there*, keeping me company. And I am sure you could do that very easily because if you were working as a companion you must be from genteel stock. I suspected as much from your voice, to start with. You do not speak like a member of the lower orders.'

Ah. So that was why the Duchess hadn't hesitated to offer her a ride. She wasn't as foolish as she appeared, with all her girlish mannerisms and apparently artless, open conversation.

'No. My father was a scholar. My mother the daughter of another.' Was it any wonder that neither of them had been particularly practical? They had lived for their books. She had always assumed her arrival on the scene had been a bit of a surprise to them, although she'd never doubted they'd loved her very much. But Lord Lavenham had been correct about them leaving her without a feather to fly with. Even after she'd sold off all their books, it had not left her with enough to live on. Oh, and how it grated to admit he was right about even *one* thing.

'And you said you had been working as a companion. Did your employer die? Is that why you are out here in the dead of night, seeking an inn? Did some dreadful lawyer turn you out, or some such thing?'

'No, it was nothing like that. It was all my own fault. I...'

To Eleanor's surprise, she felt her eyes begin to

smart. She fumbled in the pocket of her coat for a handkerchief to blot at them before tears could start trickling down her face. It was the strain of the day's events, that was what it was. The creeping anxiety of that flight over the hills, the fear of being lost, or dying all alone, and then the unexpected kindness of this high-born lady, after suffering nothing but insults and neglect for…well, for months.

'It's a man, isn't it,' said the Duchess with a knowing look. 'Some relative of your employer tried to take advantage. It is the only thing to account for you being out here, at such an hour, in such vile weather.'

Eleanor opened her mouth to deny it. But instead of managing to say a single thing, she burst into embarrassingly noisy sobs.

Chapter Six

'Ask Miss Mitcham to come to the library after breakfast, would you, Mrs Timms?'

There. That would show Lady Bradbury who was in charge here. Besides, he really did need to talk to Miss Mitcham to thrash out a few things, not least of which would be to reassure her that she had nothing to fear from Lady Bradbury. He wasn't going to allow the woman to bully her, ever again.

'I am sorry, sir, she appears to have gone.'

'Gone? What do you mean, gone?' Peter set down his tankard of ale next to his plate of eggs and ham. 'Gone where? At this time of the morning?'

Mrs Timms twisted her hands together at her waist and, though she was facing him, she couldn't meet his eye.

Lady Bradbury must be making one last attempt to assert her authority over her companion before he raised her status to one where she'd be untouchable. She must have sent poor Miss Mitcham out on some futile errand, to show that she was still in charge this morning, even if she wasn't going to be by the end of the day. He might have known she'd do something like this, after the fuss she'd made last night when he'd informed her of his plans. Not that it would make any difference in the long run. It had taken him years to stumble across a woman he could imagine marrying and, now he'd proposed, he wasn't going to let anyone…

'Oh, we don't think it was this morning, my lord,' said Mrs Timms nervously. 'We believe she left last night, for her bed was not slept in and her tray was untouched.'

'Her tray?'

'The one Maisie took up to her room, for her dinner, my lord.'

Ah, yes. Because she was not allowed to eat at the same table as him.

'Why did nobody say something before?'

'Well, nobody noticed she'd gone, my lord, until Maisie went to collect her tray this morning and saw that it hadn't been touched. Then, of course, she went up to see if Miss Mitcham had been taken poorly in the night, only to find her bed untouched.'

Up? It sounded as though they left a tray somewhere for her to collect, rather than go all the way to her rooms.

'Where, precisely, are her rooms?'

After a token objection about it not being appropriate for him to go there, Mrs Timms led him up to a tiny garret room which was utterly devoid of comfort. The ice on the inside of the window was so thick he couldn't see out. And every breath he exhaled sent out a plume of mist. He could totally understand her wishing to leave such a place, now he'd seen it. The only surprising thing was that she'd put up with it for as long as she had. But to leave the house entirely, without eating her dinner? That had all the hallmarks of someone coming to the end of their tether.

With a growing sense of unease, he went across to the tiny wardrobe and opened the door.

'It's empty,' said Mrs Timms, from somewhere behind him. 'That is how we knew she must have really gone. Her coat and bonnet aren't in her trunk, either, we looked.'

He lifted the lid of her trunk, seeing a rumpled mess of clothing that looked just as if half the household had gone through them, searching to see what she'd taken.

'The only things she seems to have taken are her brushes and a few toiletries, as far as we can ascertain.'

That was the moment when it hit him, right between the eyes, that she really, really must not have wanted to marry him.

She'd said so, of course. But he'd mocked her feeble protestations, assuming she hadn't really meant them, because of the way she'd kissed him.

If she hadn't wanted to marry him, she had no business kissing him the way she had! With such enthusiasm, even if it had been inexpertly. A heady mixture of innocence and eagerness that had made him think that perhaps getting married might not be such an onerous fate. Not if it was to a girl like Miss Mitcham. So certain had he been that he would soon be off buying a marriage licence that he'd told Lady Bradbury, with a feeling of satisfaction, that she was going to have to look for a new companion.

Well, she would still have to do so. But it didn't look as if he was going to be buying any licence. All of a sudden, her flight felt like a slap to the face. The one she should have given him, he reflected angrily, when he'd hauled her into his arms. She'd misled him, kissing him like that. No wonder he hadn't taken her words of rejection seriously.

Yet he couldn't argue with this. Rather than escape her bleak living conditions by taking his name, she'd turned her nose up at the only proposal he'd ever steeled himself to make. And rather than confront him, or Lady Bradbury, she'd sneaked away in the middle of the night.

Although, if he was honest, he could hardly blame her for wishing to avoid Lady Bradbury. He'd had no idea, until last night, that she could be so…vicious. She must have always reined herself in, with him, before, but last night it was as if a veil had come off, revealing her true nature. The nature Miss Mitcham had been contending with on a daily basis.

But *he* wasn't an ogre. Surely she knew she could have come to him and discussed her decision to turn him down rationally…

He spent a moment or two imagining how that conversation might have gone. How, in fact, he'd planned the meeting in the library, after breakfast, to go. And honesty compelled him to admit that he wouldn't have paid much attention to any objections she might have raised. Not after that kiss. Not after the way not only she, but he, too, had gone up in flames. He'd intended to use every weapon in his arsenal to bend her to his will.

Had she known it? Did she understand his nature

so well that she'd predicted that he wouldn't have listened to any rational argument? That he would have just kissed her again? Kissed her into submission. Married her. And then, probably before the ink was even dry on the marriage lines, he'd have proceeded to make her miserable. Because she'd spelled out what she wanted from marriage and there was no way he could have given her the kind of sickly-sweet relationship she'd described her parents having, so wrapped up in each other that they barely noticed they had a child. If a man became a father, then he had a duty to his child. Children. To provide for them. Teach them how to survive in what was a hard and often cruel world.

He would never want to be so dependent on another person for his happiness, either. He'd have had to demonstrate, right from the start, that he'd meant what he said about both of them having their own lives, their own interests, their own social circle, so that they weren't always in each other's pockets.

Or, rather, at each other's throats. Because that was what happened when people expected too much from marriage. Especially people in his family. Pretty soon, one of them would start to feel as if they'd got a pebble permanently lodged in their shoe. A pebble they could never shake out. And then the other would start feeling hurt, and resentful, and before you knew it…

In fact, why was he standing here feeling ill used? She'd probably done the best thing, for both of them, by ensuring there would be no marriage. He'd never wanted to marry anyone, anyway. He'd only proposed to Miss Mitcham last night because he'd been so angry about the way his female relatives kept on interfering, and criticising, when he was doing his best to support the indigent ones like Lady Bradbury.

And because he'd had a brief flare of something like hope that it might not get too messy if he married a sensible girl like Miss Mitcham. A girl he liked and could actually imagine living with, for some time to come, if only she…

But she hadn't been sensible at all, had she? First of all she'd gone up in flames in his arms, then she'd run away without…

And why had she felt the need to do that? Why couldn't she have…?

Idiot. He was an idiot for thinking she could snap her fingers at both him *and* Lady Bradbury. She was rather a timid little thing. The kind that wouldn't say boo to a goose, or she wouldn't have been able to put up with Lady Bradbury's temper for as long as she had. And that being so, of course she would rather run away without a word to anyone, than trying to stand up to two rather more forceful persons, persons who were also of higher status and to whom she owed her living. He could just picture her, standing with her head bowed, hands clasped at her waist, denying she had any ambition to marry him, while Lady Bradbury flung vile accusations at her and he mockingly refused to admit she meant a word she said.

Wasn't hindsight a wonderful thing?

He slammed the lid shut on the trunk, as well as on the faint hope he'd harboured, had been harbouring all night, that he had finally found a woman he could forge…something with.

Mrs Timms cleared her throat. 'The front door was

locked this morning, which, if it hadn't been, would have raised suspicions. But when we had a look round later to see if she was anywhere in the house, we found that the door of the big windows in the morning room were unlocked. So she must have gone out that way, while we were all busy serving dinner, though why she should want to sneak out like that I cannot imagine,' she finished saying, giving him the kind of look that told him she had her suspicions, but it wasn't her place to voice them.

Ironically, for the first time since he'd reached adulthood, a woman was wrong about what she suspected him of doing. The proposition he'd put to Miss Mitcham had been entirely honourable.

'And in such weather, too,' Mrs Timms added. 'I do hope no harm has befallen her.'

A chill ran down his spine. 'What do you mean?'

'Well, only that if she went out of the drawing room, it meant she would have gone through the formal gardens and up on to the hills. That is a walk she would often take on her days off, you see, my lord. Only not at night of course. And not with that freezing fog coming down so thick. We are all a bit concerned about her. Should we send one of the lads to Chipping on Hay to see if she is come safely to the Dog and Pheasant, my lord?'

He glanced again at the ice on the inside of the one small window the room possessed. And thought back to the breakfast table where he'd been able to see nothing but a wall of fog where the gardens should have been. Nobody should be out in this weather. And certainly nobody should have been out in it last night, either.

'No.' This was his doing. It was his responsibility to check that she'd reached her destination safely and, as she was quitting her job as well as her home, to ensure she had sufficient funds to get to wherever she was going.

It wouldn't hurt to show her that he didn't care about her rejection while he was at it. That she *hadn't* hurt him by doing so. Angered him, yes, because he'd offered her a position which most women of his acquaintance would have grabbed with both hands.

But then she wasn't like most women, was she? Or he would never have dreamed of proposing marriage, not even to spite Lady Bradbury. She wasn't vindictive enough to take lovers to spite a husband for disappointing her. She wasn't unkind enough to drive a man from the country by constantly belittling him, in public as well as in private. She wasn't mercenary, either. She'd never used her feminine charms to try to entrap him, preferring to work for her living and maintain her independence instead. Were she any other woman, he would also have accepted her rejection with a shrug of the shoulders, if not with downright relief, blamed Lady Bradbury for pushing him to the bounds of sensible behaviour and cut back on his visits to Chervil House in future.

Only, the thought of never again seeing Miss Mitcham's face light up with that shy, welcoming smile of hers whenever he stepped over the threshold, of seeing her intelligent face mask her amusement at one of the jibes that went right over Lady Bradbury's head, of just watching her capable hands arranging flowers, or twitching a shawl round her ungrateful employer's shoulders…no, that was something he hadn't been prepared to face.

Only now it looked as if he was going to have to.

'Tell Norbert to saddle my horse,' he said irritably. 'But not one for himself. I won't send anyone, not even my groom, out in weather like this.' Besides, he didn't want anyone else present when he spoke to her again. Because he had a few choice words he needed to say. About how he had no intention of ever repeating a proposal she'd found so offensive she had to run off like someone fleeing the scene of a crime. About encouraging him to hope, for the first time in his life, that he had found someone who…

But he hadn't. 'I will go in search of Miss Mitcham alone.'

Alone. As he always had been. There had never been anyone to take his part or give him the benefit of the doubt. And now that she'd gone…

'You think she will have made for Chipping on Hay, do you?'

'Yes, my lord. It is the nearest town, once you reach the high road. And Lady Bradbury shops there, so the tradesmen there know her. Which means there will be plenty of people who she could ask for help about finding a stage to get to…' she gave a shrug '…well, wherever it is she's thinking of going.'

Well, that was something, he supposed. No matter how angry he was with her for spurning him, he certainly didn't wish her to come to any harm.

Chapter Seven

The Duchess was an absolute delight to work for, Eleanor reflected as she went to join her in the private parlour where they were about to take a light luncheon. Although she supposed any employer who said please and thank you occasionally would be an improvement on the way Lady Bradbury had ordered her around as though she was a medieval serf.

But then the post of companion to Lady Bradbury had been Eleanor's first paid position. She hadn't had a clue how to choose where, or for whom, to work. It was a great pity, she decided as set her hand to the latch, that employers didn't have to provide references, the way servants had to.

'Oh, there you are, dear,' said the Duchess with a smile. 'And I can see you found it. What a clever girl you are.'

'It wasn't very hard,' said Eleanor as she crossed the room to hand the Duchess the shawl that had somehow been packed right at the very bottom of the third trunk Eleanor had searched.

'Thank you,' said the Duchess with what sounded like genuine gratitude as Eleanor draped it round her shoulders. 'This inn is so draughty.' She gazed round the rustic room critically, even though the landlord had gone to some trouble to make it fit for her use. He'd clearly got out the best tablecloth, an enormous expanse of white damask which had once probably been magnificent, but which now showed evidence of poor laundering and exposure to moths. 'And I see you found something for yourself while you were searching my things.' She looked Eleanor up and down with approval.

It had been far harder to find something among the Duchess's clothing that Eleanor felt she could borrow than it had been to locate the precise shawl she'd described. But the Duchess had insisted she could not go about in a torn, stained gown. Not if she was going to pass as her personal maid. Seeing the sense in that, Eleanor had searched until she discovered this high-necked, long-sleeved morning gown of kerseymere.

'There now,' said the Duchess. 'Don't you feel better for having a clean gown?'

'Yes, I do, thank you very much,' said Eleanor.

The Duchess waved her hand as though it was nothing. 'You may as well keep it. I never liked that gown very much anyway. And don't say you couldn't possibly, which I can see is what you are thinking of saying. It is one of the perks of being a lady's maid, you know, to have the clothes your mistress no longer wishes to wear for one reason or another. Besides, I am so grateful that I have your company, while I'm stranded in this dreadful little place, that I would willingly give you a dozen of my gowns.'

'You don't need to do that. I'm just as grateful I'm not staying here on my own.'

If she hadn't met up with the Duchess, Eleanor would have been extremely uncomfortable. The inn, when they reached it, was absolutely crammed with dozens of other people who'd decided to break their journey on account of the fog which was making driving hazardous. All of them male. And all of them disgruntled. Eleanor wasn't even sure the landlord would have let her perch in a corner of the taproom if she'd turned up alone in a gown that looked as if she'd waded through a ditch, tramped through the woods, climbed over a wall and then crawled about in a road, clutching only one, rather scuffed and grimy portmanteau. As it was, however, she'd rolled up in a coach with a crest on the door panel, accompanied by two superior footmen and a coachman who were more than a match for a provincial innkeeper. Within ten minutes, they had a room with a truckle bed for Eleanor and use of this private parlour for their meals.

'Now what?' The Duchess sighed as the sound of raised voices came from the direction of the lobby. 'It sounds just as though a fight is about to break out.'

It did. The door rattled and there was a thump, as though two men were striving over gaining entry. But what alarmed Eleanor most was the fact that she recognised one of the angry voices, even though she'd never heard him use exactly that tone before.

It was Lord Lavenham!

Heaven alone knew what he was doing here, but one thing she did know. And that was that she did not want him to find her. Not when he was in this mood.

She gazed frantically round the room for somewhere to hide. There were no cupboards and the single window was high up in the wall and didn't have a sill, let alone the benefit of curtains to dive behind. The tablecloth, however, was far too big for the little table where they were taking their meals, pooling on the floor all the way round.

So Eleanor lifted one corner and, to an exclamation of surprise from the Duchess, dived beneath it, drawing her knees up to her chest.

Peter was at the end of *his* tether now. He'd been riding about in this freezing fog all morning without catching the slightest scent of his quarry. And now, far from wishing her no harm, he could cheerfully have wrung her neck. What did she think she was about, swanning off without as much as leaving a note behind to let anyone know where she intended to go? Didn't she realise they'd worry about her? Come after her to make sure she'd made her way safely over the hills to the nearest town?

Not that she'd headed for the nearest town. Oh, no. Nobody in Chipping on Hay had caught as much as a glimpse of her. And he should know. He'd spoken to just about the entire populace. It was the landlord of the Dog and Pheasant who'd suggested she might have made for Burton-in-Steane. Either deliberately, since there was a coaching inn which served routes that went north and south, as well as east and west. Or by accident, if she got turned round in the fog and mistook her way.

Which was likely. The fog was now so thick that

he'd had to dismount to make out what was written on the last milestone he'd been able to see at the verge of the road. He could easily imagine her losing her bearings, going over the hills, in the dark.

So here he was, arguing with a bellicose and rather stupid landlord.

'Look, I told you, guvnor, there's no females here but one. And she's a lady who won't want to be bothered by the likes of you.'

'And I told you, I don't believe you. You can easily have overlooked one small insignificant female in that mob of travellers seeking shelter here...'

'Oh, no, I couldn't! Think I don't know what guests I have in my own ken? There's but the one female and she's a gentry mort, I tell yer!'

As the landlord's vocabulary descended into the vernacular, Peter suspected that a girl like Miss Mitcham might easily appear very ladylike to a ruffian of this sort. 'In here, is she? I think I'll just take a look at her with my own eyes, if you don't mind.'

'Well, I do mind! And so will she! Promised her she wouldn't be bothered by nobody, I did,' said the innkeeper, stepping in Peter's way and folding his arms across his ample stomach.

Peter had been itching for a fight for some hours. And since this fellow seemed disposed to give him one, he cheerfully set to. It didn't take Peter long to discover that the innkeeper wasn't as easy to overcome as his girth had led him to believe. He had clearly had a lot of practice at dealing with troublemakers. But either none of them had been sober, or Peter had more determination to get his own way than the innkeeper's regular sparring partners, because, after a short scuffle, Peter emerged victorious, if with slightly sore knuckles, and was able to step over the slumped form of the landlord and into the parlour where he fully expected to find Miss Mitcham.

'Aha!' he cried, flinging open the door. And immediately felt like a third-rate actor making an entrance on to the stage. Because, far from finding Miss Mitcham cowering in a corner, he saw an elegant lady of a certain age, sitting at a table, a cup of tea halfway to her mouth.

'What,' she said, regarding him with the kind of froideur that only ladies of rank ever managed to pull off successfully, 'is the meaning of this?'

'Beg yer pardon, Yer Grace,' said the landlord, staggering to his feet and holding a grubby cloth to his bleeding nose. 'I tried to tell him you couldn't be the young lady he was looking for, but he wouldn't take no for an answer.'

'Go at once and fetch my footmen, you stupid man,' she said. '*They* will know how to deal with this blackguard.'

'There will be no need for that, Your Grace,' said Peter, sketching a bow. 'I have clearly been labouring under a misapprehension. Please accept my apologies for the unseemly intrusion.'

'You know me?' She raised her fair brows and looked him up and down with chilling disdain.

'By sight, Your Grace,' he admitted. And by reputation too. The Duchess had set the *ton* by the ears last Season by not only taking a lover who was young enough to be her son, but by introducing a mill-owner's daughter into society under the pretext of launching her own goddaughter. 'I am Lavenham.'

'Ah,' she said, with a slight wrinkle to her nose which suggested that she had not only heard of him, but didn't think much of what she had heard. 'And you are searching for a young lady. I did hear that aright? Lost her in the fog,' she said with heavy sarcasm, 'did you?'

'Ah, in a manner of speaking...' Why was it that ladies of her sort could always manage to make even a man of his age and experience falter and resort to excuses with one haughty glance and a couple of disdainful words?

'How extraordinary,' she drawled, giving him a pointed look. 'I cannot think why any young lady should take it into her head to go wandering about in the kind of weather that came down last night,' she said, setting her cup down in its saucer in a way that somehow expressed her utter contempt for him. And the devil of it was that he had not a single word to utter in his defence. He had been responsible, or at least partially responsible, for driving Miss Mitcham out into the night. In the fog.

'I believe, that is, there were circumstances which...'

The Duchess raised her hand, a pained expression on her face. 'Please, say no more. I have no wish to listen to the sordid details.'

'Sordid? I can assure you, Your Grace, that—'

She lifted her chin and looked down her nose at him. 'I said, I did not wish to hear your excuses. Though it is clear you are suffering from remorse this morning, it does not alter the fact that you have obviously acted in a manner that drove some poor, defenceless, innocent female to believe she had no recourse but to flee from what should have been the safety of her home—'

'Now, look here. That is grossly unfair. You have no right to assume—'

'That you have acted in character? Please!' She uttered a harsh little laugh. 'You are a notorious rake. Your escapades are the talk of the *ton*. Now, if you would not mind...'

She made a dismissive gesture with her hand just as he became aware of the presence of not one, but two enormous footmen in the doorway.

'Your servant, Your Grace,' he said through clenched teeth as he made his bow and withdrew, feeling like a schoolboy who'd just endured a painful interview with the head of house. But he had no intention of attempting to exonerate himself. Not only was it none of the woman's business, but whatever he said she was bound to think the worst.

Besides, it was his own fault she believed he was a rake. He'd fostered the reputation he'd inherited, since it had suited him to keep marriage-minded females at a safe distance, while giving him licence to enjoy the basic pleasures that women without marriage in mind were keen to offer. He wasn't about to shed that armour now, in front of this woman, particularly. Who knew what capital she'd make from it?

He clapped his hat on his head and strode to the exit. That was two excruciatingly awkward scenes he'd endured, at the hands of two matrons, in the space of under twenty-four hours. On account of Miss Mitcham.

You see? That was what happened to a man who started to care...no, who started to be too concerned about a woman's welfare. A woman who clearly didn't want any man to look after her, or she'd have accepted his proposal gratefully, not gone running off to make her own way in the world. He'd ended up riding all over the countryside in freezing weather, asking questions that had raised eyebrows and would probably set tongues wagging in towns where previously he'd been held in regard.

If he ever saw her again, wringing her neck was going to be too good for her. He wouldn't be satisfied by anything less painful than slow roasting over open coals.

Chapter Eight

'You can come out from under the table now,' Eleanor heard the Duchess say.

She wasn't ready. Oh, she might now be safe from Lord Lavenham, who had clearly stormed out of the inn and galloped away. But she shrank from facing the Duchess, and explaining her extraordinary behaviour.

But the longer she stayed down here, the more ridiculous she would appear when she eventually did emerge. And so, red-faced, Eleanor came out on her hands and knees, wondering what on earth she was going to say.

'I knew,' said the Duchess, with a satisfied smile, 'that you must have undergone some horrid experience, for you to be walking down that lane, with just the one small bag and not even a change of clothing! And…' her face sobered '…that some man's vile behaviour was at the root of your distress.'

Incredibly, the Duchess appeared to be more pleased about being right than shocked by what Eleanor had just done. And, although Eleanor had been silently cheering the way the Duchess had routed Lord Lavenham, she didn't want her to think ill of him. So far the Duchess hadn't pressed her to provide details, but she couldn't go on letting her assume the worst. That wouldn't be fair to him. Somehow she garnered the courage to say, 'It wasn't that vile. Truly. He kissed me, that was all.'

'And you were so afraid he would go further that you felt you had no choice but to run away.'

'No! Well, I did feel I had no choice but to run away, but it wasn't the way it sounds. You see, he asked me to marry him. I suppose you now think me very stupid for not accepting his offer.' How could she not? It was the main ambition of most women to marry well and Lord Lavenham was quite a catch. Chervil House was only one of his many properties. His principal seat was, according to Lady Bradbury, mentioned in every travelling guidebook, with recommendations to visit on days when it was open to the public. She'd made it sound like a richly carpeted palace, stuffed to the rafters with priceless antiquities. Coupled with the way she'd just dived under a table, the Duchess must now think she was a complete zany. She hung her head, clasping her hands at her waist.

'I think,' said the Duchess firmly, 'you did very right. No girl should marry a man if she as much as *suspects* he will not make a good husband. For once she has taken that step, she is tied to him for life. And *nobody* will help her escape him. No matter how tyrannical, or even violent he may turn out to be.'

Eleanor lifted her head, stunned to hear the Duchess saying something so unconventional with such vehemence. Although, she had announced the fact she was a widow with the rider of *thank heaven*. Now it sounded as though she'd been very unhappily married to a cruel man, and had had nobody to turn to. Her heart went out to her.

'I could,' Eleanor said, addressing her second-most pressing concern, 'have just stood my ground, though, couldn't I? It was just I was afraid that if he'd kissed me again, I might weaken. Because I couldn't think when he kissed me, about anything apart from—' She broke off, blushing.

'You have no need to tell me what happens to a woman's brain when certain men kiss her,' said the Duchess tartly. 'It is as though they cast a magic spell, which removes the power of logical thought and renders her helpless to his wishes.'

'Yes, it was exactly like that!' Eleanor moved a little closer to the Duchess. 'But when I was able to think about it rationally, I was so certain he wouldn't be a good husband—well, not for me, anyway. Perhaps, to some woman who only cared about rank or wealth…' She spread her hands.

'Do you know what I think?'

'No, Your Grace.'

'I think you should travel with me all the way to London. You did say at some point that it was your intention, didn't you?'

Eleanor frowned as she tried to recall exactly what she'd told the Duchess about her plans, last night, as she was helping her settle into bed. There had been a lot of chatter about the perfume Eleanor sprinkled all over the inn's rather musty pillows, which was expensively created for the Duchess alone from some exclusive perfumier, which had led to discussion about the Duchess's favourite shops and the perfidy of tradesmen who would not allow long lines of credit. As she was still frowningly trying to remember if she'd ever actually got a word in edgeways, the Duchess continued.

'You need a job and it won't be easy to get another post without a reference. And it doesn't sound to me as if you are likely to get one from the place you have just run away from.' She raised her eyebrows pointedly. 'But if you work for me, as my personal maid, then I can give you such a glowing recommendation that the lack of one from the employer before won't matter. Besides...' she stretched out a hand in entreaty '... I would so value your company on the road. It is so dull being cooped up in a coach with nothing to look at but muddy fields, for mile after mile, and nobody to talk to. Do say yes,' she finished saying with an appealing smile.

Eleanor hardly had to think about her answer at all. Travelling to London with the Duchess would save having to dip into her own pocket for coach fares. It would be far less awkward than travelling as a lone female. And she could repay the Duchess's generosity by making her as comfortable as she knew how, en route.

'Thank you, Your Grace,' she said, dropping a curtsy. 'I would love to accept the position. Just until we reach London, of course. I do assure you that I am fully aware that a lady such as yourself will want a properly trained lady's maid...'

The Duchess raised her hand to stop Eleanor saying anything further. 'What you lack in experience you make up for in intelligence. I don't have to spell anything out to you, do I? I am sure we shall get along splendidly, for the time you are in my employ.'

Which settled the matter.

The trouble was that, although the landlord kept urging them to wait until the fog lifted before setting out, it didn't lift. If anything, it seemed to grow thicker.

Eventually, the Duchess could stand no more.

'That's it,' she said, sitting up in bed one night when the noise from the other stranded travellers, who were making the most of the local brew in the taproom directly below their room, grew to an uproar. 'I want to go home where I can go to sleep in a comfortable bed, without having to stick my fingers in my ears, between sheets that have been laundered properly, and where Dawes, that is my butler, would *never* permit rude men to burst in on me during tea. I don't care how bad the fog is in the morning. We can surely hire some local person to walk in front of the coach so that we don't get lost again. Can't we?'

As it turned out, they could. In spite of the landlord telling them it was not possible, the Duchess's footmen procured a guide in next to no time. And kept on doing so, day after day, from a succession of carters and drovers and farmers, until they reached the outskirts of London itself, where the roads were familiar enough to the coachman that he could get by with only their own footman walking ahead of him.

'Home at last,' sighed the Duchess, craning her neck out of the window as the coach finally lumbered to a halt. The footman who'd been walking ahead of them came to open the carriage door and let down the steps, and through the swirling fog Eleanor perceived the stone-clad frontage of a building. She heard a door opening and, as she followed the Duchess up a set of broad steps, eventually saw the door itself. A butler was standing just inside, holding it open, and smiling at the Duchess in what, to Eleanor, looked like a rather avuncular fashion.

'Dawes,' trilled the Duchess, holding out her hands and clasping both the butler's in her own. 'I cannot tell you how glad I am to see you again. To be in my own home. Even if…' At this point, her lower lip wobbled. And the butler, to Eleanor's astonishment, raised her hands to his lips and kissed them in a manner that was not the least avuncular.

'On behalf of all the staff, may I say how glad we are that you have arrived home safely. There have been no end of tales of travellers getting lost in the fog. Even people out on foot have had accidents. Lord Eldon,' he said, lowering his voice, 'claims that it was because of the fog that he walked into the Opera House so hard that he suffered an injury to his head.'

The Duchess laughed, as the butler had clearly intended her to do.

'The worst that happened to us was that we got lost. Fortunately, Miss Mitcham here came to our rescue,' said the Duchess, turning and smiling at Eleanor. 'And then we hired a whole succession of locals to lead us down stretches of road they knew.'

'Very wise. Would that the Prince Regent had taken similar precautions. We heard that he had to turn back from a visit to the Marquess of Salisbury and one of his outriders fell into a ditch in Kentish Town.'

'No!' The Duchess laughed again.

'May I be the first,' he went on smoothly, 'to wish you a happy new year?'

'Good heavens, is it January already? I must have lost track of time on the road.' She moved deeper into the hall and to one side, to make room for the footmen who were carrying in the first of her trunks. 'Well, never mind. I am heartily glad to see the back of 1813. Nothing but trouble and woes... Oh, by the by, Dawes,' she said, as one of the footmen set down Eleanor's battered portmanteau at her feet, 'Miss Mitcham will be staying with us for a short while.'

The butler gave her a half-bow. 'Welcome to Theakstone House, Miss Mitcham,' he said, just as if she were an honoured guest, rather than a temporary lady's maid. But then the Duchess hadn't explained her position properly, had she? He then looked beyond Eleanor, through the still-open front door, then turned to the Duchess, who was drawing off her gloves. 'Maud?'

The Duchess wrinkled her nose. 'Took ill. I had to leave her behind. Please, tell me there is a fire lit in the drawing room.'

'Indeed there is, Your Grace. We have kept everything in readiness against your return. I shall have some tea prepared.' He then turned to a side table and handed the Duchess a stack of papers and cards.

'Thank you, Dawes. Heavens, what a lot of invitations. I shouldn't have thought anyone would be back in town just yet.'

'London is very thin of company. However, the people who are here are making the most of it,' he said with a wry smile.

'So I see,' replied the Duchess, flipping through the thick pile of correspondence as she made her way across the hall, apparently having forgotten Eleanor was there. But the butler, seeing her dilemma, gestured to her that she should follow. Again, just as if she were a guest, rather than an employee, who ought probably to go to the kitchens for her own tea.

So Eleanor followed the Duchess into the beautifully appointed sitting room, so that she could ask what she ought to do, in private. The Duchess had taken a chair by the fire and lifted her eyes from her pile of post only briefly to indicate a chair on the other side of the fireplace. She obviously wanted to go through her post before considering what to do with her, so Eleanor sat down, grateful for the warmth of the flames.

She was just beginning to feel as though she might wish to remove her gloves and bonnet, when the Duchess suddenly uttered a shriek.

'The beast!' she cried, leaping to her feet, her eyes riveted to the sheet of paper she was holding at arm's length, as though it were a coiled snake. 'Oh, how… how dare he?'

She whirled on Eleanor, as though only just recalling she was there.

'It is my stepson. He has the gall to write and offer his condolences on the defection of Captain Bucknall, and his marriage to Miss Mollington, *the heiress*—' She grimaced, waving the sheet of paper in such a way that Eleanor could tell she was quoting from the letter. 'And then, not content with rubbing my nose in that misfortune, he goes on to inform me that he will be considering marriage this Season and expects me to throw open this house—' she gestured wildly round the room in which they were sitting '—and act as hostess while he goes about selecting a *suitable candidate*.' She waved the letter again for good measure.

'Um…' Eleanor said, since she had no idea why the Duchess was so upset.

'This is all part of his plan,' said the Duchess, without Eleanor having to ask her for an explanation, 'to get me out of this house, that is what it is. He tried it last year and I wouldn't go. He even threatened to turn off all the staff if I didn't, but when I told them about it they all vowed to stay on without wages. But now he's decided to take a wife,' the Duchess continued, without appearing to need to pause to draw breath, 'I won't have a leg to stand on! She will become the mistress of this house. And I will have to move aside. Oh, I can't bear it!' She flung herself back on to her chair and covered her face with her hands.

'Um…' said Eleanor again, completely at a loss.

'I will become a *dowager* duchess,' the Duchess moaned. 'Do I look like a dowager to you? Do I?'

'Not at all,' said Eleanor, relieved that at last she knew exactly what to say.

'No. Dowagers have double chins and crow's feet. I have neither. Nor will anything induce me to wear a turban. Besides, I am not going to go tamely to live in the Dower House. I swore, when Theakstone banished me from Theakstone Court, that I would never set foot on the estate again and I won't. Do you hear me? I won't!'

Eleanor suspected people in the street outside could

have heard her, but decided it wouldn't be tactful to say so. Instead, although she didn't believe there was anything she could really do to help, she uttered what, later on, she would consider to be the fateful words, 'If only there was something I could do.'

The Duchess, who'd thrown herself into a chair and put her hand to her brow, sat up straight and stared at Eleanor, wide-eyed.

'Of course,' said the Duchess. 'That's it! What a clever girl you are. And such a godsend. Not only materialising out of the fog just when we despaired of finding our way out of the maze of stupid little lanes that litter the countryside, but also for being here now.'

'Well, I'm glad you think so. But I'm not sure what I can really do...'

'You can make my horrid stepson fall in love with you, that's what you can do!'

'What? No! I mean, I wouldn't know how to do such a thing.'

'You got Lavenham to propose to you, didn't you? If you can get a proposal out of such a notorious rakehell, then I'm sure you can do the same for a duke who is actively *seeking* a bride.'

'No, I really don't think I could. You are making it sound as though I deliberately set out to wrest a proposal out of Lord Lavenham, but I didn't. Truly. He just sort of...pounced. I honestly would have no idea how to make another man wish to marry me, when I don't know the first thing about what goes on inside a man's head, or what on earth induced Lord Lavenham to suddenly consider me as a bride.' Apart from a momentary whim, brought on by irritation with Lady Bradbury, his pensioner. 'Besides, I don't have any ambition to get married, just for the sake of it, or I wouldn't have run away, would I?'

'Well that just makes you even more suitable! You can keep the Duke dangling all through the Season, blind him to any other woman, and then...disappear! Then he won't be able to evict me using the excuse that this house is the domain of his wife, because he won't have one. And I,' she said with a delighted grin, 'won't be a dowager, either.'

'Your Grace, I am very sorry, but you don't seem to understand that what you have suggested is simply beyond my capabilities. I have not the first idea how to keep a man dangling...' Even if she wished to do such a thing, which she most emphatically did not. Toying with the Duke's emotions, even if it was to help the lady who'd been so kind to her, sounded like a rather mean thing to do.

The Duchess sighed and slumped down into a despondent attitude. 'I suppose you are right. It was a very foolish idea,' she said, her lower lip trembling. 'And why should you go to such trouble anyway, for a woman you have known only a few days?' She reached into one of the hidden pockets of her gown and extracted a handkerchief, with which she dabbed at eyes that were brimming with tears. 'It is over,' she said with a sniff. 'I must just accept my fate, and say farewell to this house, which has been so much more than a home to me for the past few years.'

She looked around the room with such a tragic mien that Eleanor felt dreadful. She recalled the way each and every landlord along the way had bowed and scraped and given them the best rooms, and urged them to stay for a second night rather than risk some mishap in the dreadful weather that seemed to have fallen upon the entire southern part of the country. How the Duchess had shaken her head and charmingly insisted she was prepared to take any risk, if it meant getting a few miles closer to home. By which she meant this house.

The bleak expression in the normally ebullient Duchess's eyes, as she gazed round the room as if silently bidding it farewell, tore at Eleanor's heart. What was more, her drooping attitude highlighted the fact that she was nowhere near as young as she acted. It would have been unkind to say she had crow's feet, but there were, definitely, traces of advancing years beneath the carefully applied cosmetics. Traces of a lifetime of suffering. At which she'd hinted.

'Perhaps,' said the Duchess, 'it won't be so bad, living in the,' she shuddered as she uttered the words with eyes closed, '*Dower* House at Theakstone Court. Perhaps, now that Theakstone is dead, I can build new memories. Happier ones.' She smiled bravely at Eleanor.

'But I am being a terrible hostess,' she said, dabbing at her eyes briefly with a little lace handkerchief which she produced in the manner of a magician. One minute her hands were empty, then next they contained a little scrap of lace. 'Instead of moaning about my woes, I should be discussing what you would like to do while you are staying in London with me.'

'Um, I am supposed to be filling in for your lady's maid, am I not?'

'Oh, no. We agreed, only until we reached London,

and,' she said, waving her hand about, 'here we are. You must think of yourself as a guest. There are,' she said, dipping into the pile of correspondence Dawes had handed her, 'a few invitations here from people you would probably enjoy meeting.'

Eleanor shook her head. 'It is very kind of you, but I am not the sort of person you should take about as if I am someone…'

'Why not? You are the daughter of a gentleman, are you not? And if you'd had a mind to marry Lord Lavenham, you would have become a countess. And moved among such people…' she waved her hand at the invitations '…by right.'

'Yes, *if* I had married him, but I didn't, did I? And, Your Grace, I don't think you have considered, that, well, grateful though I am for your kindness and your willingness to take me about, if you introduce me to people as Miss Mitcham, then Lord Lavenham will know that you concealed me from him.'

'Pooh! What do I care?'

It was all very well for the Duchess to discount Lord Lavenham. But…how could she put this tactfully?

'I am sure you would be able to stand up to him. But if he were to find a clue as to my whereabouts, and where I plan to go next, he might…'

'Goodness gracious! I had not thought of that. It would be just like the beastly man to chase after you, wouldn't it? Well, he's already done so, hasn't he? Hmmm…' She tapped her chin with her finger. 'What we need is some way for you to be able to stay in town without anyone knowing who you are.'

'It is very kind of you, but really, I do need to make

arrangements to leave. I had planned, I think I explained to you, that I would write to my uncle and ask if I may go and stay with him until I find another suitable post.'

'Oh, I do so admire you,' said the Duchess, clasping her hands at her breast. 'If only I'd had the backbone, at your age, to earn my own living, rather than depending on some fickle male. And of course you don't want to get tangled up with Lord Lavenham again, I quite understand. But what do you mean to do while you are waiting to hear from your uncle? Have you thought of that? You will have to stay *somewhere* until you hear from him, won't you? And you would enjoy yourself far more if you stayed with me than if you went off to some dreary lodging house and hid indoors all the time in case Lord Lavenham took it into his head to come to London, which I shouldn't think he would, not until Easter, because he rarely does. To my knowledge. And I am sure, if we put our heads together, we could come up with some way of explaining your presence in my house, without telling anyone anything about you.'

In the midst of that tangled speech, the Duchess had made one good point. Eleanor was going to have to stay in London until she had made firm plans. And the prospect of going off to some dingy lodging house really didn't appeal.

'I could just stay here and work as your maid,' she suggested.

'Absolutely not! You need to have a little fun before going back to a life of servitude,' said the Duchess contrarily, after having just said she envied Eleanor's determination to work. 'And we agreed that you would only work for me until we reached town. You are now my guest,' she said firmly.

'Then I am shall be a guest who will not stir out of doors,' said Eleanor sadly.

The Duchess sat up straight. 'Never tell me that you mean to cower indoors, as though you have done something wrong, simply because you spurned a man you could not marry!'

'No, it isn't that…not only that…'

At that point, the door opened, and the butler came in with the tea tray.

'Dawes,' cried the Duchess, leaping to her feet. 'We have to come up with a plan so that my young friend here can stay in town and go about and enjoy herself, without anyone ever finding out who she is.'

The butler raised one eyebrow.

'I should have thought the solution was obvious,' he said. 'She will have to adopt an alias. And a disguise.'

Chapter Nine

Eleanor had never heard anything so ridiculous in her life. But the Duchess, far from telling Dawes not to be so silly, clapped her hands with glee.

'You are brilliant,' she cried.

'Um...' Eleanor said, while she tried to think of some way of explaining why the butler's idea was far from brilliant.

'It will be such fun, taking you about and introducing you to people as...' She turned to Dawes. 'Who ought she to be, do you think?'

Dawes gave Eleanor a measured look. 'With a little work, Miss could easily pass for a foreign princess. From a tiny principality, naturally, that nobody has ever heard of.'

'Because we will have invented it,' said the Duchess.

'Precisely so,' said the butler, setting the tray down on a little table. 'There are many such people in London lately, having been driven from their palaces by the depredations of Napoleon's armies.'

'No,' said Eleanor firmly, making them both start,

as though they'd forgotten she was there. 'I cannot possibly pose as royalty. It would be unethical to go round telling everyone I am a princess, when I am not.'

'Oh, there will no need for that,' said the Duchess. 'On the contrary, I shall tell everyone that you are *not* a foreign princess, newly fled from the Continent. That there is *no* truth to the rumours that you have fallen victim to Bonaparte's ambition.' She burst out laughing. 'The rumour will then fly on its own.'

Eleanor could just see it. The more she protested that she was not a princess, the more everyone would believe the opposite.

'And we could always refer to you as Miss Smith,' suggested the butler. 'A name so ordinary that it will be easy to suppose it is an alias.'

'Which it will be,' said the Duchess, 'just not in the way everyone thinks.'

'Just a minute,' said Eleanor, becoming irritated by the way they were continuing to make plans even though she had told them she had no intention of going along with them. 'For one thing, nobody will believe I am anything but an out-of-work companion, when I have only my night things and the gowns you gave me on the way here...'

'Oh, but that is soon remedied,' said the Duchess, seizing her hand. 'Come with me and I'll show you.' She tugged a by now completely bewildered Eleanor from the cosy drawing room, up two flights of carpeted stairs and then an uncarpeted one. Dawes, who'd calmly picked up the tea tray, followed behind at a stately pace.

'There,' cried the Duchess as she flung open the

door to what looked like as though it had been a lumber room before somebody had filled it with dozens of bolts of fabric in all sorts of rich colours, making it resemble a draper's shop. 'Your wardrobe,' the Duchess declared, letting go of her hand, striding over to a bolt of spangled gauze, and pulling out a length of it with a flourish.

Eleanor gasped as the Duchess flung the length into the air and it came floating down, soft as thistledown. She had never seen any fabric so delicate, or so beautiful. It really was the kind of thing a princess would wear. She couldn't resist holding out her hand as the gauze floated down, so that it sifted across the palm of her hand.

'Oh!' She sighed. 'How lovely it is.'

'Yes, and I haven't known what to do with it all until now. My goddaughter, who was staying with me last year...but that is another story. The point is, we could make an entire wardrobe fit for a princess out of all this. If nothing else, dear, it would give us something to do while this weather is so dreadful and we cannot go out.'

An entire wardrobe? No...she mustn't...

'Just look at this amber satin,' said the Duchess, pulling out another bolt of fabric and laying a swathe of it across Eleanor's hands. Hands which had reached out of their own volition to touch the sumptuous material. 'You would look lovely in a gown of this colour. Even if you don't want to stay in London long enough to go out and about as a princess, there is no reason not to have just one ball gown, is there? Even if you never get to wear it outside?'

Eleanor bit down on her lower lip. One gown. There

really wouldn't be any harm in making up just one gown from this gorgeous satin, could there? And adding an overdress in the delicately floaty gauze? She'd always secretly wanted to know what it would be like to wear a satin gown. Or a silk one. When she'd been a very little girl, she'd found some clothes that had belonged to her grandmother in a chest in the attic, where she'd been playing on a rainy day, and had draped some pieces of the slightly moth-eaten silks and damasks around her. And put on some elbow-length evening gloves, of the softest, most supple kid leather, which had come up to her armpits. She'd played at being a fairy the entire afternoon. Very happily. Until her mother had found her trying to cast spells with a ruler wrapped round with silver lace and frowned, lecturing her about the dangers of believing in ignorant superstitions and how much better it was to use the rational part of the brain to examine the facts. Mama had thrown away the contents of the trunk and bought Eleanor a microscope, so that she could study the marvels of the unseen world that were really there, rather than existing only in the imagination. And ever since then she'd worn durable fabrics in plain, unobtrusive colours.

Eleanor forgot whatever second point it had been she'd intended to make to the Duchess. All she could think about was how wonderful it would be to make up the amber satin into a totally impractical gown.

'We will have to create something a touch exotic,' said the Duchess, as Dawes set down the tea tray across the top of an open packing case and began rearranging the cups and saucers as though it was perfectly normal to serve tea in an attic. 'Something that looks as though it might well have come from a foreign country, where the fashions are a little different.'

Something that looked like the kind of thing she'd imagined a fairy would wear…

The Duchess darted over to another bolt of fabric, a deep scarlet shot through with threads of silver, as Dawes handed Eleanor a cup of tea.

'Thank you, miss, for playing along with Her Grace,' he said quietly as he bent down. 'It will do her no end of good to give her something to think about, apart from her troubles.'

Yes. Yes, that would be a jolly good reason for making a ridiculously impractical gown. A gown with a train…

'Now this material,' said the Duchess, holding out the scarlet silk, 'would look lovely on you, too. For going out to dinner, or a card party, or something of the sort…'

If they'd been in a formal room Eleanor might have summoned the common sense to stop the Duchess right there. But up in this attic, which resembled a sort of Aladdin's cave, with a butler setting out tea and cakes on a packing case, and urging her to go along with the Duchess to help cheer her up, she couldn't help getting carried along with the fantasy. Before long, she was putting in her own suggestions about what sort of gown could be made from the vast array of choices. It was all only make-believe, after all. She would never actually go anywhere in any of the gowns they were talking about. She'd probably only be in London for a few days. Just long enough to write to, and receive a reply from, her uncle.

And if playing along with the Duchess's determination to use some of these gorgeous fabrics to make fantasy gowns would help to keep her spirits up, there could be no harm in it. Could there?

'If I might make a suggestion,' said the butler, as the Duchess pulled open a box which contained a selection of intriguing objects wrapped in tissue paper. 'Nothing would more strongly suggest that Miss is a royal refugee than a male body servant of military aspect. Someone with a distinctly foreign accent.'

'And do you think you could find such a person?'

This was the moment when Eleanor really should have made an objection, but she'd started unwrapping one of the intriguing packages and become distracted when she found that it contained yards and yards of velvet ribbon in a shade of gold that would be perfect to provide trimmings for the amber gown.

It was like…a sign…

Not that she believed in signs…

'I do,' she dimly heard Dawes saying, as she excitedly reached for the next package. 'He is currently lodging with the sister of our own housekeeper and is having difficulty finding the money to pay his rent. Whenever anyone tries to help him gain useful employment, he has always insisted that he is a foreign nobleman and that, when Bonaparte is defeated, he will go back to his country—a place that nobody I know has ever heard of—and will then be able to reward Mrs Bateman amply for housing him.'

'He sounds to me,' Eleanor said, in what she hoped was a withering manner, because bringing another person into this game of make-believe would make it real, 'as though he's touched in the upper works.'

'We believe he may be exaggerating his importance, certainly,' Dawes replied, calmly. 'But he has such finicky ways and such courtly manners, and such fine clothes to hand that he is likely to have experienced life in some form of royal court. Perhaps as a body servant to someone of rank.'

'If he wants everyone to believe he is a foreign prince,' Eleanor put in, determined that nobody else should be dragged into a game she had no intention of playing beyond a certain point, 'he isn't likely to wish to pose as the servant to an impostor princess, then, is he?'

'It has come to the point where, if he does not take up some form of employment, Mrs Bateman is going to have no alternative but to evict him. I should think he would prefer to take up residence in the servants' quarters here, which are far superior to the rooms he currently inhabits, by the way, and take on the task of accompanying a young lady about the place, rather than go to debtors' jail.'

'Yes, but,' the Duchess said, 'how are we to pay him?'

Eleanor could scarcely believe that the Duchess could consider anything so practical. But it sounded as though she had come up with the one obstacle that might yet prevent her from getting in too deep, without her having to take a stand.

'We cannot,' the Duchess continued, thoughtfully, 'very well put him on the wages book which goes to Theakstone's man of business, can we?'

The butler cleared his throat. 'Last year, although His Grace threatened to withhold our wages, he did not actually do so. And, since Mr Mollington also paid us, we all have a tidy sum put by. We could all chip in a small amount. Enough to pay him for as long as he stays here, without it going through the official account books.'

'Dawes,' cried the Duchess. 'You took two lots of wages last year? And never let on? You old rascal!' But she didn't look the slightest bit cross. If anything, she looked impressed.

'Shall I proceed,' said the unflappable Dawes, 'with arranging an interview with the gentleman, then? And, while we are speaking of staff, should I also engage a person to take on Maud's duties? Or would you prefer not to bring in strangers, while you are engaged on such a...' he coughed, and glanced at Eleanor '...delicate mission?'

'Good point,' said the Duchess. 'We don't want to bring in too many strangers when we are going to be playing so many games, do we? How about promoting Sukey, temporarily?'

He nodded his head, conferring his approval on the Duchess's suggestion, leaving Eleanor wondering just exactly who was in charge here. The Duchess certainly treated Dawes more like a co-conspirator than a menial. In fact, she was beginning to feel as if she'd stepped out of the real world and into one where none of the normal rules applied. Or on to a stage, where some unseen playwright was manoeuvring all his principals into the opening scenes of what was going to turn out to be a farce.

* * *

However, over the next few days, she certainly had a lot of fun designing a couple of dresses fit for a princess, cutting them out and sewing them up, and trying them on. The Duchess, it turned out, could sew a seam at an impressive rate, while the maid, Sukey, had a talent for creating little knots and ruches, and other complicated finishings.

Then, one afternoon, the Duchess declared that Eleanor was ready to go out.

'Mrs Broughty has invited us to one of her informal suppers. You would enjoy that, I'm sure, since she has three lively daughters and two sons who have a wide circle of friends, among whom are a few with some intelligence and wit.'

'Oh, no, I couldn't possibly.' It was one thing playing along with the Duchess and keeping her spirits up, and dreaming about going out dressed like a fairy princess. It was quite another deliberately hoaxing other people that she was something she was not.

'But what is the point of having such a beautiful gown, if you don't go out in it?'

'I... I have been thinking,' said Eleanor timidly. 'I admit, I got carried away when I saw all the beautiful fabric. And who can resist fashioning a new gown out of such gorgeous satin,' she said, fingering the amber satin, which lay across the arm of the chair in a nest of silver gauze. 'But I have been thinking about what will become of me later. I mean, once I leave London. If I have been going about everywhere in the guise of a foreign princess, how am I ever going to find another job? Nobody will hire me. I shall be notorious.'

'But it's not as if you were planning to stay in London, was it? I have a considerable circle of friends, with whom I keep in touch by letter, who must know of somebody who needs a companion, or something of the sort. Somebody who has never been to London. Besides, you are talking about what would happen if you were found out. And you won't be found out. I have made sure of it. Sukey,' she said, turning to the maid. 'Go and fetch the wig.'

'The wig?'

'Yes,' said the Duchess. 'I have been thinking, too, and talking to Dawes about your fear of discovery. And we decided that you needed to do more than go about under an assumed name. Which we decided would be Miss White, by the way. Like a blank page, do you see?'

Eleanor shifted in her seat, a touch irritated to hear that the Duchess had been discussing her with Dawes and making plans without consulting her. 'This is all very good of you, I'm sure, but…'

'But you don't want anyone to be able to furnish a certain rake with clues, which might enable him to find you. And if people talk about the mysterious young lady who went about London with me who fits your description, it might rouse his suspicions. But if the mysterious young lady who stays with me has black hair and eyes, and a regal bearing, then he will never put two and two together, will he? And you have lived in such obscurity that nobody else will suspect a thing, will they?'

'Black hair?'

'Yes. I took the liberty of getting that hairdresser

who came to give you your fashionable crop to measure you for a wig.'

Oh. She'd wondered why the man had done all that measuring before cutting her hair. She'd thought it must be the sort of thing London hairdressers did to try to make themselves look more proficient, or something.

'Black, as I said,' the Duchess continued. 'And we can very easily darken your brows and lashes, so that your eyes will look much darker than they really are.'

'But...'

'Don't you want to go out? Really?' The Duchess sighed and drooped like a wilted flower. 'I am sure I don't wish to make you uncomfortable. Very well,' she said with one of her brave smiles. 'We shall find some other way to amuse ourselves this evening.'

'Oh, but there is no reason why you should not go...'

'What! Do you think I am such a poor hostess that I will go gadding about and leave my guest to mope alone at home?'

It was at this moment, while Eleanor was feeling like the most ungrateful guest, as well as the most selfish one, that Sukey came back in with the wig.

'Put it back,' said the Duchess mournfully. 'Eleanor does not wish to go out.' She heaved a sigh. 'And I was so looking forward to taking you out and about. We get on so well, you and I, that it would have been great fun taking you to balls and card parties, and so on, and having someone intelligent to talk to about them afterwards.'

The Duchess, Eleanor suddenly perceived, was a very lonely woman.

A very unhappy one, as well.

Oh, dear.

'It isn't that I don't *want* to go out,' said Eleanor, smitten to think she'd caused this lady any further hurt, when she'd been so kind. When nobody else had really cared tuppence about her, for so many years…

'But…having to use a false name to conceal my identity…convincing people I am a princess…' She shook her head. 'I am just not brave enough…nobody would believe it, anyway…'

The Duchess leapt up, came to Eleanor's side and took her hands in her own.

'My dear, you will not need to do anything much, apart from being yourself. You have perfectly charming manners—indeed, you behave more like a lady than many who actually bear the title. During the days we spent on the road, you were never ruffled, or ill tempered, were you?'

'Well, no, I have never been one for making a fuss…' Her parents had always taught her that it was better to consider things rationally, and work out solutions by discussing them, rather than flying off the handle over every little trifle. And she supposed she had become used to disguising her deepest feelings while working with Lady Bradbury. Her temper had been sorely tested, on many occasions, and she had managed to stay calm. Well, until that final day and that hadn't been down to anything Lady Bradbury had done.

'But that doesn't mean I have the skills to fool the entire populace that I am of royal birth.'

'But you won't be doing so, will you? You will be hotly denying it! Listen, dear, it is not all that hard to persuade people you belong in a certain social sphere.

I had to learn how to act as if I belonged, very quickly, when I married the late Duke. I come from a background much like yours, you see. My father was a gentleman, merely. But I had a friend who taught me a few mannerisms that made all the difference. What you have to do to persuade people that you are a grand lady, even when you don't feel like one, is to raise one eyebrow at them as if you cannot believe how vulgar they are being. As if you expect deference from others.'

'You make it sound so simple, but...'

'Here,' said Sukey, bringing over a little hand mirror. 'Have a go.'

'Yes, that's it. Like this,' said the Duchess, giving a demonstration.

Eleanor lifted one brow, pulled her mouth into a flat line and let her nostrils flare slightly. The Duchess broke into a fit of giggles and made her try again.

Before she knew it, Eleanor was rigged out in amber satin, wearing cosmetics and a black wig, and getting into a carriage, feeling as if she'd abandoned just about every principle she'd been brought up to hold dear.

And not caring anywhere near as much as she probably ought.

Chapter Ten

Peter's feelings of hurt and resentment had settled down by the time he got back to Chervil House. In fact, he couldn't believe he'd actually considered wreaking vengeance on her. The only kind of man, he muttered under his breath as he handed the reins over to his waiting groom, who'd consider such action was a man who'd allowed a woman to dig her talons into his heart. And he'd always guarded his own heart carefully.

Besides, Miss Mitcham didn't have talons. She wasn't the sort to latch on to a man and smile as she watched him bleed.

Unfortunately, he found he couldn't just put her out of his mind altogether, either, because the next newspaper that reached him was full of lurid stories about calamities which had overtaken anyone who'd been out of doors since the fog had wrapped England in a smothering shroud.

It made him wonder if perhaps he hadn't been able to find her at either Chipping or Burton because she'd never made it across the hills. With visibility being so poor, she could easily have stumbled into a ravine and broken her leg, and been unable to crawl back to a path…

Or slipped, crossing a stream, and struck her head on a stone, and drowned as she lay face down in the water…

Or…

That was it. In spite of the freezing fog still pressed up against all the windows, he grabbed his coat, slapped on his hat and went out through the French doors so that he could have a go at following in her tracks. Albeit rather belatedly.

But it was no good. There was no sign of her. No sign of anyone up there. Because anyone with any sense was staying indoors, in the warm. Not stumbling about in the fog, searching for…

He stopped and stood completely still for a moment, taking stock. It was eerie, up there, with fog muffling all his senses. And must have been even worse for Miss Mitcham, with night drawing in.

He shouldn't have made her feel she had no choice but to face…all this. But who could have predicted she'd run off like that? Women wanted to catch earls in their snares. Wanted marriage and money, and rank. Especially, he would have thought, women who had to work for a living.

Only… Miss Mitcham wasn't like any woman he'd ever met before. It was what had made it possible to propose to her. Because a part of him, a very small part had hoped…or had thought it just possible…

Not that he'd allowed that part of him to make the

proposal. Oh, no, he'd let the cynical, worldly-wise part of him do all the talking. So that he'd ended up offering her a lot of things she didn't really care about. He'd acted out of his long-ingrained habit of preserving his own dignity, of not letting anyone guess how important the question he'd asked was to him, glossing over any hint of emotion with a hefty dollop of cynicism.

But standing up here, wherever here was, he could no long gloss over the fact that his actions might have brought harm to an innocent woman.

No, he refused to believe it! She *had* to have reached the road. She wasn't an idiot. All she'd have to do was keep on going uphill until she reached a crest and then down again the other side. No matter which direction he struck out in—and he'd struck out in several, just in case she didn't have a good sense of direction—he always ended up facing the drystone wall that bordered the entire length of the lane. She *must* have reached it.

Only, if she had, then why hadn't he been able to learn any news of her in either Chipping or Burton?

Or, if she'd reached some other destination safely, why hadn't she written to request they forward her trunk? It contained all she possessed.

But she hadn't.

Or had she? And had her letter been delayed by the fog?

Or had it simply taken her far longer to reach her destination than anyone might expect?

Or had she broken her journey somewhere between here and...wherever it was she was going, because of the weather. There could be any number of reasons to account for her silence that didn't involve the worst.

But even if she was safe, it would make little difference to him. He kept on hearing the words of the Duchess of Theakstone, about him driving a girl from the house, where she had been at least safe, if not very happy. And he realised that if anything really bad had happened to her, he would never, ever forgive himself.

Even if the worst hadn't happened, he didn't think he'd ever be quite the same again.

Because he'd learned that his actions had consequences. Potentially serious consequences. He'd learned that life wasn't a game of chance, through which he could stroll, giving the occasional shrug of his shoulder when the dice didn't fall his way.

Then, on January the third, a cold northerly wind blew the fog away, bringing with it a heavy fall of snow. That night he hardly slept at all, for visions of shivering figures huddled against flimsy shelters, or buried entirely in drifts of snow.

And he woke up feeling as though he'd murdered her.

He'd already reached the point where he could barely endure sitting across from Lady Bradbury over the dining table. Although she never expressed any concern for Miss Mitcham, he could tell that she blamed him for making her leave. And why shouldn't she? He blamed himself.

And every room in Chervil House carried memories of Miss Mitcham. In the morning room he recalled the way the sun's rays would bring out copper lights in what was normally a wispy head of indeterminate brown. An empty vase on the sideboard reminded him of the deft way her fingers would arrange autumnal flowers in it. Worst of all was the place at table, where her chair had been, at which he often used to glance to try to catch her in the act of repressing a smile at something particularly fatuous Lady Bradbury had said.

It was as though she haunted the place.

That was the day he realised that he'd have no peace of mind until he'd found out what had become of her. Even though she didn't want to be his wife—and why should she when nobody else had ever found anything in him worth loving?—he had to make sure she was safe and well. Because the thought that there was no longer a Miss Mitcham, somewhere in the world, was insupportable.

He also realised that he was going to have to get some help. It was going to be impossible for him, on his own, to locate one nondescript woman of average height and retiring nature, in a country the size of England. So he'd have to go to London, even though the roads were barely passable. Because in London, he'd be able to enlist the aid of the Bow Street Runners. They'd know how to find her.

Surely.

After the Duchess of Theakstone had persuaded Eleanor to go to Mrs Broughty's card party it felt pointless trying to avoid going to other events. Especially since the Duchess had already employed the impoverished émigré Dawes had recommended and all the servants were chipping in to pay his wages. It would have been churlish of her to disappoint them all when they were all going to so much trouble on her behalf.

Besides, there weren't that many people of note in London. The awful weather, and the dangerous conditions of the roads were keeping them all tucked away on their estates in the country.

'Not many ever return much before Easter anyway,' the Duchess had reassured her, 'when the theatres open.'

And so Eleanor succumbed to all the temptations offered her. The Duchess had been correct, she decided, in saying that it would be silly to hide away indoors, while awaiting a reply to the letter she'd written to her uncle, when she could be making the most of an opportunity she'd never expected to have. Not that it was exactly the same as having the kind of Season debutantes had. She wasn't going to be presented at court or seek vouchers for Almack's. But there were plenty of other amusements to which she'd never had access, either as a girl growing up with scholarly parents, or later, as the paid companion to an elderly lady who lived in the middle of nowhere. In the evenings, there were card parties and suppers, and gatherings that started out soberly, before somebody would call for dancing and they would push aside the furniture and roll up the rugs. And by day there were all the sights to visit. St Paul's Cathedral and Westminster Abbey, and the Tower. She'd never enjoyed herself so much in her life.

Occasionally she felt guilty, when the Duchess did something like buy accessories to match the gowns they made up. But the Duchess waved her objections aside as though they were nothing.

'If you really were a foreign princess, you'd have

arrived with several trunks filled with fripperies such as this,' she'd say.

Eleanor wasn't so sure that a foreign princess, escaping from Bonaparte's army, would have escaped with very much more than the clothes on her back, into which she'd sewn some jewels to fund her flight. But she daren't say so, because that might have prompted her generous benefactress to go out and buy some jewels as well. Instead, she accepted the gifts of shoes and gloves philosophically, since it was evident that buying them, so that she could take Eleanor out and create a bit of a stir, was making the Duchess happy.

At least, this morning, the Duchess was only lending Eleanor a fur coat and hat which she'd unearthed from her own wardrobe.

'You must wrap up warmly,' the Duchess had said when Eleanor might have protested, 'because they are going to lead an elephant across the river, just below Blackfriars Bridge. I don't care what anyone says, we simply must see that!'

Every day since the Thames had frozen over and some enterprising souls had set up all manner of booths on the ice, the Duchess had wanted to go to what was generally being called the 'Frost Fair'. And so had Eleanor. There were booths selling all sorts of refreshments, as well as various games and things in which to take part. For a very modest sum, according to the various flyers being printed, you could go sledging, or play skittles, or even dance on the barge which had frozen in place right in the middle of the river. Though what she'd really like to try was skating.

'If they think the ice is thick enough to bear the

weight of an elephant, it is bound to be safe enough for one tiny little Duchess,' she said defiantly, as both Dawes and Herr Schnee, the foreign gentleman who was posing as Eleanor's body servant, took breath to voice their usual objections. While Dawes was concerned for the Duchess's safety, Herr Schnee kept on insisting that it was a vulgar spectacle, fit only for the entertainment of the lower orders.

Really, Eleanor reflected as she sipped her tea, he was the greatest snob she'd ever encountered. He considered just about everyone beneath his notice. Apart from, for some unaccountable reason, the Duchess herself. He'd only raised a few objections before falling in with all her plans, even though he clearly thought it well beneath his dignity to take on the job of a servant. He was, she reflected with amusement, in spite of all his airs and graces, as susceptible to the Duchess's charm as Eleanor was herself.

'Mein Gräfin,' said Herr Schnee, his iron-grey brows drawing down with disapproval, 'you can surely not wish to expose you to the rough persons who will be drinking of grog all day long.'

'I am sure I shall be perfectly safe,' she said, giving him a melting look, 'with you to protect me.'

Herr Schnee puffed out his chest. 'Certainly I know how to keep you safe. Only…the rabble…' He subsided, shaking his head. 'I have seen a mob. It acts like a mindless animal. No lady would be safe should the mob take it into his head to riot.'

'I am sure that may be the case in foreign parts,' put in Dawes, who'd unaccountably taken a dislike to the man from the day he'd moved in, considering he'd been the one to suggest hiring him in the first place. 'But Englishmen have no cause to riot.'

'Not when they're having as much fun as it sounds as though they can have at the Frost Fair,' put in the Duchess. 'Anyway,' she continued, 'I am in charge. It is for you to do as I bid you, not the other way round.'

'Of course, Your Grace,' said Dawes, chastened.

Herr Schnee did his funny half-bow, during which he clicked his booted heels at the same time, to acknowledge his place, though his face was like thunder.

Eleanor went to her room, where a maid helped to fit her black wig over what was left of her hair. Eleanor was beginning to suspect that the reason the barber had cut it so short was because the Duchess had already been planning to furnish her with a wig. It made it less likely that any of her own hair might peep out and spoil the illusion that the wig he'd also created was real. Though to be honest, she didn't really mind. Not that much. She'd only suffered a momentary pang when she'd seen the first hank of hair fall to the floor. It wasn't as if it had ever been glossy enough, or curly enough, or an interesting enough colour for her to consider it her crowning glory. Besides, the barber had cut it in a gamine style which she thought rather suited her face and made her look different. Rather fashionable. And almost pretty.

By the time Eleanor was all bundled up against the weather in the luxurious furs the Duchess had loaned her and the thick boots she'd bought her, the carriage was ready to set off. Eleanor, the Duchess and Herr Schnee climbed inside. Eleanor had to suppress a giggle as Dawes, having tenderly handed the Duchess into the carriage, instructed the two footmen, who were mounted up behind, not to let her out of their sight. And Herr Schnee bristled at this slur on his own ability to protect the Duchess.

There was never a dull moment in the Duchess's household. It was a pity she'd agreed to pose as a mysterious foreigner. It would be lovely to have been able to stay on as companion to the charming, irrepressible lady. Though that would have meant staying in London and probably coming face to face with Lord Lavenham when he returned for the opening of Parliament. Which she did not want to do, even though the Duchess had coached her as to how she ought to behave if, by some strange chancc, he did surprise everyone by returning before her situation was settled. It was, in a nutshell, as though she'd never seen him before in her life.

Eleanor wasn't sure she could perform such a feat of acting, although she was getting the hang of some of the little mannerisms which the Duchess was saying would convince people she was a grand lady, without having to say so. With the help of a mirror, she'd practised the lift of one eyebrow to express disdain so often that she no longer looked like a horse which had found a wasp in its nosebag, but just like a high-ranking person who expected better.

When they had reached the river, the larger of the two burly footmen, Gordon by name, paid the required pennies to the watermen for the privilege of walking across a few planks on to the ice and into the fair.

Eleanor was rather alarmed at first by the number of fires and furnaces she could see, upon which cooks were roasting everything from larks on spits to whole oxen. She was beginning to think Dawes might have a point about their safety and hoped the Duchess wouldn't venture too far from the banks, into the middle of the river, where the ice was bound to be at its weakest.

But everyone else was behaving as if it was a public holiday. Well, everyone but Herr Schnee, who was wrinkling his nose in disgust.

The tents where publicans were selling hot grog looked particularly popular and through the partially open flap of one Eleanor spied people dancing to the music provided by fiddles. Herr Schnee dragged them past the display of vulgarity, indicating the more genteel places providing tea, coffee and hot chocolate.

Lord Lavenham, she reflected, wouldn't have led her past the tent where everyone was dancing. He might be a rogue, but he would have noticed her wistful glance and would have whisked her inside and whirled her round the floor without a moment's hesitation. Might even have let her sample the drink advertised as 'Mum', which smelled of all the spices that usually went into a Christmas cake, too. It was funny, but ever since she'd come to London, a place she knew Lord Lavenham visited frequently, she kept wondering what he would make of every event to which the Duchess took her. He'd certainly be making the most of the revelry going on around them today.

Just then a woman with a tray of baked apples approached, but the Duchess waved her away. 'I would much rather have some of that gingerbread,' she said, pointing to another vendor who had her own stall. The Duchess bought slices for herself, Eleanor and the two footmen. Herr Schnee, predictably, refused to do anything so common as eating in public without the benefit of a plate. Eleanor grudgingly had to admit that he might have a point, after a moment or two, because she had to remove the glove from one hand to properly handle the crumbly slice of cake and her fingers quickly became cold. Also, whenever she dropped a crumb, it fell to the floor and was lost for ever. If she'd had a plate, she wouldn't have wasted a single morsel.

Her fingers might be cold and fumbling because of it, but at least her head and neck were lovely and warm, thanks to the wig she was wearing.

She caught Herr Schnee giving her a disdainful look as she dropped a cascade of crumbs down the front of her borrowed coat. She lifted her chin. What right had he to look at her like that? Lord Lavenham had never looked down his nose at her, not even when she'd been a servant and he her employer, which was the opposite to the situation here.

She was just licking her fingers, with a touch of defiance, since she was sure it was the kind of thing that would revolt him, when, just as if she'd conjured him up by thinking about him, she spied Lord Lavenham. Standing not three yards away, in the central street of the village that had sprung up on the river.

And in spite of the furs and the wig, and the cosmetics darkening her lashes and brows, she could tell he knew exactly who she was.

For he was glaring at her, his hands working at his sides as though he'd like to strangle her.

Chapter Eleven

It was her. Finally. She wasn't lying frozen to death in a ditch after all. Which was a relief, of course. But the resentment, which he'd thought he'd managed to bring under control, rose up and shoved all other considerations rudely aside. He'd spent days tramping over the hills in all weathers, lost hours of sleep imagining various horrible fates befalling her and suffered nightmares involving a pair of reproachful brown eyes gazing up at him the way they'd done after he'd kissed her, except glazed over with ice.

He'd even felt the stirrings of a guilty conscience, because of her. A guilty conscience which had spurred him to travel to London in the most horrendous weather so that he could seek the help of Bow Street Runners. It hadn't been until he was mounting the front steps of his London town house, pulling gloves off fingers he was sure were going to turn out to be blackened with frostbite, that it occurred to him that he had no idea about her family network, let alone who else she might go to at short notice. Worse, he had absolutely no useful information he could impart to the Runners, not even the means by which Lady Bradbury had employed her in the first place. He'd meant to ask her, but in the end the atmosphere in Chervil House had become so unpleasant that he'd decided walking out into the blizzard was preferable to staying there one hour longer.

And what had happened next, when he'd accepted the fact that he'd come to London on a fool's errand? That he was never going to be able to find her? That he was going to have to give up? He'd started imagining he saw her, that was what. Every bloody where.

First, it had been the tilt of a woman's head he'd seen over the top of a crowd which had reminded him of her so strongly that he'd run after her, caught her arm and spun her round. Which had meant he'd had to offer his apologies to an outraged and rather scared stranger. The next day almost the same thing had happened, except that this time he'd had the sense to overtake the woman in question and then turn round so he could watch her pass rather than repeating his behaviour of the day before and ending up gaining a reputation for accosting random women on the street.

He'd been starting to feel as if he was losing his mind. He'd become reluctant to go outside again, in case he did something so irrational that he wouldn't be able to explain it away. Which meant that he'd spent the last few days hunched over his fireplace, wondering what his life was going to come to, if he couldn't somehow lay the ghost of Miss Mitcham to rest.

Even the novelty of visiting the fair upon the Thames, which had frozen over, hadn't roused him from his chair. Not until he'd read about the elephant. If roasting an ox over an open fire hadn't caused the ice to give way, he shouldn't think walking an elephant across would cause disaster. But if there was a disaster, he'd thought that perhaps he would be able to rescue someone. Because if he happened to be able to pluck some other female from an icy death, it might, perhaps, go some way to assuaging the guilt that was gnawing away at his entrails.

But far from being a ghost, she was very much alive, gazing round with bright, amused eyes at the entertainment while eating gingerbread. Decked out in furs, to boot. When he'd believed she was *poor*. So poor she'd had to accept a position with Lady Bradbury.

He was just trying to work out how on earth she'd achieved the transformation from dowdy, put-upon servant to this height of fashionable elegance, when the other woman in the group laughed. And he dragged his eyes away from Miss Mitcham and saw the Duchess of Theakstone.

The Duchess of Theakstone! He was almost certain he growled out loud as his mind flew back to that encounter in the inn at Burton-in-Steane and what she'd said about driving a girl from her home. Which had pierced him to the core, making him writhe, night after night, in shame. Hah! No wonder she'd managed to say exactly what was most likely to sear his conscience. She'd known exactly what had happened. Miss Mitcham must have told her. Why hadn't he noticed it before? He hadn't said anything about looking for a girl who'd gone missing the night before. She was the one who'd brought that aspect of things into it.

And after he'd gone, no doubt they'd had a good laugh about the way he'd retreated, cringing and apologising...

My God. He'd spent all this time practically tearing his hair out, because she hadn't bothered sending them as much as a brief note to let them know she was safe and sound.

He clenched his fists. He was going to kill her.

With nothing in mind but making her pay for the days of anguish she'd put him through, he strode across the ice. She saw him when he was less than a couple of yards away and, with an expression of horror, dropped the last of her gingerbread.

Before he could get his hands on her lying, cheating throat, however, one of the males in the party stepped in front of her. Not that he would have posed much of an obstacle, despite his military outfit and bearing, for he was no longer a young man and Peter had several weeks of pent-up feelings that needed relief.

But then the Duchess, too, stepped forward.

'Lord Lavenham,' she cooed. 'I wouldn't have expected to see you in Town at this season. Are you not usually too busy shooting things on one of your estates at this time of year?'

He wished he had a fowling piece with him now. He would dearly love to shoot something. Or rather some*one*.

'But I suppose,' the Duchess prattled on, 'that if anything could tempt you back it is a spectacle such as this one.' She waved her hand round, indicating the revelry going on all around them, as though attempting to distract him from the sight of Miss Mitcham, who was gazing at him, wide-eyed. As well she might. She must have known he'd been hunting for her. A man didn't propose to a woman and then dismiss her from his mind overnight. Well, not if he cared about her, the way he—

He pulled himself up short. He felt responsible for Miss Mitcham, that was all. He didn't *care* for her. He'd be a fool to do so, when she clearly didn't care tuppence for him.

And he was nobody's fool.

'Oh,' said the Duchess, with an artful start. 'I can see you are wishing for an introduction to my young friend.'

An introduction? He tore his eyes from Miss Mitcham's guilt-ridden features and turned them on the Duchess with disbelief. Why would he need an introduction? She knew full well that he and Miss Mitcham had previous knowledge of each other.

'This is Miss *White*,' said the Duchess, waving her little hand at Miss Mitcham. 'Newly come to Town from...' She gave a bright little smile. 'And Herr Schnee—' she indicated the older man of military bearing '—her major-domo.'

Her what? Since when had Miss Mitcham needed anything so grand sounding as a major-domo? And why was she going by the name of Miss White?

Hold on. Schnee. Wasn't that the German word for snow? *Two* fake names if ever he'd heard them.

The German bowed ever so slightly, as though he was of far higher standing than a mere earl, but was in a mood to be gracious. Miss Mitcham lifted her chin and wiped her face of all expression. The way she'd so often done when Lady Bradbury launched into one of her lengthy diatribes about the uselessness of female servants.

'Miss White, I should like you to meet the Earl of Lavenham.'

She, too, gave him a regal little nod, as though being gracious to a social inferior.

'Miss White?' He approached and stared at her, hard. What was her game? Why was she going under a false name? For false it was. He hadn't spent hours and hours going over every moment they'd spent together without ending up with her features seared into his brain. This was Miss Mitcham. Same height, same nose, same little mouth that had flowered with passion under the onslaught of his lips. Her eyes looked darker, it was true. And he couldn't tell much about her figure, swathed as it was in bulky furs. But it was her. Without a shadow of a doubt.

Miss Mitcham returned his challenging stare by riposting with a lift of her chin, as though daring him to expose her lie.

He was tempted. Oh, yes, he was tempted to grab her by the shoulders and shake her until she admitted who she was and what she'd done.

But he wasn't the kind of man who went round accosting females in broad daylight. At least, he hadn't been before she'd turned him inside out. And even then it hadn't been on purpose. Anyway, he *wasn't* that kind of man.

So, what was he to do?

He eyed her up and down, seething with so much emotion he didn't know how to describe it. Then he glanced with fury at the Duchess and finally swept his gaze over the three men, hovering with barely concealed anxiety, as though expecting to have to defend their ladies from potential danger. From *him.*

He'd probably feel a whole lot better if he had a set-to with the pair of them. And the military fellow, if the old charlatan didn't take to his heels in fright.

However, a small part of him still retained enough sense to remind him that while he'd feel better for knocking a few people down, he'd regret starting a brawl, in the long run. It might look as if he'd lashed out in a rage, because she'd hurt him. And he never, but never, allowed anyone to suspect they had the power to do that.

There was always a better way to deal with any emotion that threatened his equilibrium. He just had to find it.

He took a deep breath and tried to think, instead of just reacting.

The Duchess, for starters. What was she up to? He could see she was playing some deep game of her own and had probably dragged Miss Mitcham into it. He couldn't see Miss Mitcham concocting a fake name and *asking* to be decked out in furs. Besides it was the kind of thing the Duchess was infamous for doing. But even if this was yet another of her madcap schemes to set the *ton* on fire with gossip, it made no difference. It was Miss Mitcham who'd caused him all the sleepless nights, whose disappearance had made him look deep inside himself and find certain aspects of his behaviour…questionable. While it seemed she'd been gallivanting about Town eating gingerbread and shopping for furs!

What he ought to do, he supposed, was walk away. Put this whole episode down as a lesson in what a woman could do to a man if he started believing she might be something special.

Only...how could he let her get away scot free? Didn't she deserve to suffer for what she'd put him through?

Before he'd come to any real conclusion, the two burly men in livery, the Duchess's footmen, he'd wager, began to shift from one foot to another. They'd all been standing, until then, in a tense silence. He suddenly realised they were all waiting to see what he was going to do, because, for the moment, he held their fate in his hands. One word from him about Miss Mitcham's real identity would bring all their plans to an abrupt halt.

It would be a form of retribution he could inflict on her and her companions, he supposed. But it would all be over so quickly. And Miss Mitcham had put him through several weeks of such soul-searching that he'd started to think he'd never be able to live a normal life again.

It would be much more satisfying if he could make her suffer the same kind of torment, for the same amount of time. He could do this by letting her know, at some point, that he knew she was not who she claimed and that he could expose her for the impostor she was, at any moment.

That would be fair retribution. As long as he only kept up the game for the same length of time that he'd been worrying about what had become of her. Plus one day, for good measure.

'Miss White,' he said, allowing his mouth to form a

smile, though nobody seeing it, he was certain, would mistake it for one of anything but that of a predator toying with its prey. She blinked, the only sign that he'd surprised her. Oh, yes, he was going to enjoy exacting his revenge by keeping her guessing. 'Charmed to make your acquaintance.'

She looked a touch uncertain. Had she expected him to shout at her? To expose her? She knew he'd recognised her. Well, of course he had. Did she think he'd so quickly forget the only woman to whom he'd proposed? Especially when she had turned him down as though he'd offered her a gross insult? And that after kissing him like a wild creature?

'Been long in Town,' he drawled, 'have you?'

A frown flitted across her brow. Though what had she expected? Wasn't she trying to pretend she'd never met him before? Didn't she know that two could play at that game?

But she rallied swiftly. 'Only a few weeks. So charming a city. So full of interest.' She attempted a social smile which was little more than a brief baring of the teeth before it vanished.

'You have visited many cities, then, have you?' He pounced on what sounded to him like a rehearsed speech. Even the words she chose, and the way she used them, were not the way she normally spoke. It was as if she was trying to sound like someone who had learned a very correct form of English as a foreign language.

'Miss White does not like to speak of her past,' put in the Duchess hastily. And then lay one hand to her breast, in the manner of an actress in a tragic play. 'Too, too, upsetting.'

Miss Mitcham lowered her head, which he supposed was meant to indicate she was sorrowful, though there was more than a touch of unease about the performance.

'Miss White is starting out afresh in London,' the Duchess continued. 'With a clean slate.'

And a new name.

'And you are providing her with the chalk with which to write on it,' he observed.

'Yes,' said Miss Mitcham, holding up her head once more. 'I am most truly grateful to Her Grace for coming to my rescue. For taking me in when I had nobody.'

That, he surmised, was intended to rouse his sympathy. But he didn't have any for her. The only reason she'd had nobody was because she'd chosen to run off into the night rather than accept a perfectly honourable proposal of marriage. She hadn't even had the courtesy to hand in her notice before leaving.

'But,' he put in smoothly, indicating the so-called Herr Schnee, 'you had your...major-domo, surely?'

She looked flustered. Before she could launch into any sort of explanation, the Duchess stepped forward once again.

'Lord Lavenham, it has been a pleasure to see you, but really, we cannot stand about here on the ice gossiping all day. It is too, too, cold,' she added with an artificial shiver. 'Come, Miss White, bid his lordship farewell.'

As they made to depart, he bowed to Miss Mitcham. 'I had not hoped to meet such a delightful and mysterious young lady when I came to Town on, ah, pressing personal business. I do hope to see more of you, now that I have made your acquaintance.'

He would make sure of it. There were only a few people of note in Town at the moment and all of them were taking it in turns to host various impromptu events to while away the evenings. Which, he wondered as he watched them scurrying across the ice in the direction of the banks of the Thames, would the Duchess be most likely to attend? Not that it mattered, he'd go to them all. His rank meant that any hostess would welcome him with open arms, whether she'd sent him an invitation or not. So that was where he would go. Everywhere. He would pop up where Miss Mitcham was least expecting him.

And not only would he dog her footsteps, but he would also discover what it was that the Duchess was hoping to achieve while he was at it—and prevent her from being able to do it. Because Miss Mitcham was not the only one with whom he was angry. That Duchess had a lot to answer for.

Chapter Twelve

'He recognised me,' said Eleanor, the moment she and the Duchess were alone. 'I know he did.'

'Hmm?' The Duchess was leafing through a pile of correspondence which had arrived while they were out and wasn't paying much attention.

'What's more, he knows that I know he knows,' she said, wringing her hands.

'I beg your pardon? Whose nose?' the Duchess said, distractedly, wrinkling her brow.

'Nobody's nose,' said Eleanor in exasperation. She'd accepted the Duchess's decree that they should not discuss the encounter while they were still on the river. She'd been too shaken to speak rationally anyway. It had been such a shock, seeing him standing there, looking as though he was barely restraining himself from strangling her. Even more of a shock when he'd started to play along with the charade of her being a total stranger to him. And once they'd gained the relative safety of the coach, she hadn't argued much when the Duchess had insisted that it would be better to wait until they were home and in the warm because she'd naively assumed that the Duchess must be thinking about what their next step should be.

But now it appeared the Duchess was not prepared to talk about it *at all*. Which might be because Herr Schnee was still in the room, standing as if to attention, by the door.

'I am speaking of Lord Lavenham,' said Eleanor, in a lower tone, in the hopes that the man might be a touch hard of hearing. 'And what he means to do about me.'

The Duchess waved one hand dismissively. 'I am sure he doesn't mean to do anything. Or he would have said something straight away, wouldn't he?'

So that was it. The Duchess thought that Lord Lavenham didn't care. But Eleanor knew better.

'I beg to differ. That smile of his, when he accepted an introduction to me as though we were strangers—well, it boded ill.' She shivered. 'And you may not have seen the way he looked at you, as we were leaving, but I did and I know what it meant. He is furious with us both and, if he can do either one of us an ill turn, he will.'

The Duchess finally looked up from her pile of mail. 'Even if that is true, my dear, there is nothing he can really do, is there? Apart from telling everyone that he knows who you are. If he does that, then we can counter with the unpleasant truth that you were working for a female relative of his and his behaviour obliged you to flee the house. And,' she continued, inexorably, 'people will think that you are so afraid of him that that is why you are living with me, under an assumed name. It will not do his standing any good, let me tell you.

No, on the whole, I don't think he will say anything about what he knows.'

'But—'

'No, no more of the tiresome man, dear, not now. I am already in danger of being made a dowager and losing my London home,' said the Duchess, straightening her spine and putting on a brave smile. 'It is of no use cringing and looking over our shoulders all the time, while we wait for the axe to fall. Let us just put all vile men from our minds and enjoy ourselves while we can, hmm?'

'Yes, that is all very well, but don't you think we should be making some sort of…plan? In case…'

'Well, now you come to mention it,' said the Duchess, thoughtfully, 'you could do worse than reconsider my suggestion you attempt to make my stepson fall for you. He is powerful enough to shelter you from any revenge you think Lord Lavenham might attempt. And I wouldn't mind *you* being my daughter-in-law at all, since—'

For once, Eleanor decided she simply had to stop the Duchess, even though she was in full spate. 'I am sorry, Your Grace, but that won't work. Even though I would love to be able to shield you from his plans, before I actually married *anyone*, I'd have to tell him the truth about myself, wouldn't I? I couldn't carry on pretending to be a princess for the rest of my life…'

'Oh, but it need not come to that. You only need to keep him dangling long enough to prevent him from marrying anyone else.'

'No, that wouldn't work, I'm afraid,' said Eleanor

firmly. 'For one thing, I don't have any idea how to make a man fall for me and—'

But as usual, Eleanor never got to make her second point, which would have touched upon the morality of the scheme, for the Duchess sighed and said, 'Yes, I suppose you are right.' She leaned across and patted Eleanor's hand. 'It was just an idea. Oh, do let us put aside thoughts of both those beastly men and think about what we are going to wear tonight, instead.'

And that was the end of that. The Duchess, Eleanor saw as they planned where they were to go, and how they would dress later that day, was one of those people who refused to dwell upon difficulties. She was probably the kind of person who put all her bills in a drawer out of sight, when money was tight, rather than working out a way to pay them.

She truly envied the Duchess her ability to put aside problems and simply enjoy herself later that night, because she couldn't help flinching every time the door to the salon opened, in case it was another guest arriving. One specific guest in particular.

When the butler finally announced him, it was all she could do to stay sitting on her chair. All her instincts were screaming at her to leap up and run as far and as fast as she could.

She lost a trick she should have won easily, because she was listening to her hostess, Lady Gowan, greeting him in an effusive manner rather than concentrating on her hand. And scarcely knew what cards she picked up in the next deal, because she was watching him scanning the room. Searching…searching…until his eyes snagged upon hers.

She didn't imagine the way his face hardened. So, she'd been right. He was angry—and intent on exacting some form of retribution by the looks of it. Not that he'd find it all that difficult. Just walking into the same room, knowing who she was and having the power to expose her ridiculous behaviour at any moment was enough to make her wish she'd never agreed to humour the Duchess.

Her mother had warned her about the perils of dressing up and playing make-believe. Why hadn't she listened and been more obedient? Then she wouldn't have…

'I say, Miss White,' said her partner in this game of whist, Mr Spenlow, 'are you not feeling quite the thing?'

She looked across the table blankly to where the normally care-for-nothing young man was eyeing her with concern.

'You have gone as pale as milk. You know,' he said, leaning forward, making one brown lock of hair flop across his forehead, 'it doesn't matter to me, at all, losing a few shillings at play…'

She tried to smile, but her lips felt wobbly and wouldn't oblige.

'I dare say,' said another voice, the voice of Lord Lavenham, who was now standing right beside her, 'that Miss White is merely overheated, and would benefit from some fresh air. It is much cooler out in the hall. Permit me to escort you there,' he finished on what sounded to her like a rather implacable note.

She fought desperately to find some reason to refuse, but nothing came to her.

'Shouldn't someone inform the Duchess,' put in Mr Spenlow, as she continued to dither. 'Or that servant chappie of hers?'

'They are both deep at play,' said Lord Lavenham smoothly. 'And I am sure Miss White would not wish to disturb them for what is, I am sure, a fleeting malaise easily dealt with by a few moments spent in cooler surroundings.' He held out his arm.

Eleanor decided it would probably be better to go with Lord Lavenham, listen to whatever it was he clearly wanted to say to her and get it over with. Besides, this might be the very chance she needed to explain to him how she'd ended up wearing a wig, and a silk gown, and adopting an assumed name.

So she got to her feet and placed her hand on his arm.

'Thank you, Lord Lavenham,' she said meekly. 'So kind.'

She noticed, as he began to lead her away, another girl darting up to take the chair she had just vacated. A rather delicate-looking blonde who'd been hovering close by, watching Mr Spenlow with hungry eyes for some time.

Lady Gowan fussed over Eleanor a little as they reached the drawing-room door, and went out into the hall with them to make sure she had a chair on which to sit before sending a footman off to fetch a glass of wine. She returned to her place in the doorway, from which vantage point she could watch over all her guests. Which meant, to Eleanor's relief, that she would not be entirely at Lord Lavenham's mercy.

He sat down beside her, leaned back and crossed his legs, eyeing her with a smile so hard, so taunting, that she felt as if she ought to fall to her knees and beg forgiveness.

But Mrs Gowan was watching. Oh, not all the time, but she was bound to notice if Eleanor did anything as dramatic as that.

'Last year,' said Lord Lavenham, in a conversational tone of voice, 'the Duchess, with whom you are now living, attempted to pass off a mill-owner's daughter as a lady. Introduced her to everyone. Took her everywhere.'

Yes, Eleanor knew about that. But it wasn't as bad as he was making it sound. The Duchess had only agreed to sponsor the girl into society because the mill-owner in question had agreed to meet all the Duchess's expenses for the Season. And she'd only sought help for those expenses because her stepson had threatened to stop paying the servants.

'It only ended,' he carried on, before she could think exactly how to phrase her defence, when Lady Gowan might be able to hear what she said, 'when her lover, a captain of the guards who was young enough to be her son, ran off with the girl…'

Oh. So that explained why the Duchess had been so angry about the comment in the letter from her stepson about that Captain marrying an heiress. The Captain had been the Duchess's lover first. Naturally, she hadn't been able to spell it all out to Eleanor, who was unmarried and almost totally innocent. But it did make sense of the remarks she'd made about women losing their heads when certain men kissed them. As she'd lost her head when Lord Lavenham had kissed her.

She couldn't help stealing a glance at his mouth, the hard, uncompromising mouth which had set her body on fire and robbed her of the ability to think rationally.

'I suppose the military man who is posing as your—what was it she called him?—your major-domo is her latest lover. And your presence in Grosvenor Square is intended to fool everyone into thinking he has a legitimate reason for living there openly.'

'No!' His wildly inaccurate guess finally jerked her out of her silence. 'It is nothing of the sort. Herr Schnee—' She pulled herself up short, as she noticed a footman approaching, bearing a glass of wine on a silver tray.

'No?' Lord Lavenham didn't seem to mind that the footman might overhear. 'Ah well, never mind. I shall hit upon the truth eventually,' he said, taking the glass of wine and holding it out to her.

She found that her hands were shaking so much she had difficulty raising the glass to her lips.

'You do well to be nervous,' he said as the footman turned away and began walking across the hall. 'After what went on in Grosvenor Square last year, someone is bound to write to the Duke to tell him what his stepmother is up to now.'

'You wouldn't!'

His face tightened. 'I am not, and never have been, a bearer of tales. I am merely giving you fair warning,' he said, with a smile that was very far from being friendly, 'that there are plenty of people who are tattletales. And, moreover, that the Duke of Theakstone is not a man to cross.'

Her stomach plunged. Up to this moment, she realised, she hadn't really believed the Duke would be a problem. Because she hadn't thought he'd come to London before she left.

But then she hadn't thought Lord Lavenham would return, either, since travelling was so difficult at the moment. But here he was.

'If you—'

But she never discovered what he'd been about to say next because the Duchess came bursting out of the drawing room, arms outstretched.

'Darling girl,' she cooed. 'I am so sorry to hear you are unwell. We must get you home at once. Thank you so much, my lord,' she said to Lord Lavenham, 'for taking care of her…'

And in the ensuing bustle of calling for a coach, and their coats and outdoor shoes, the Duchess somehow managed to manoeuvre Lord Lavenham to the sidelines.

It had been an immense relief to get back to Grosvenor Square, though she found it very hard to get to sleep later on, even when she pulled the covers right over her head. For her mind kept going over and over all the things that had happened that day.

Well, all the things concerning Lord Lavenham, anyway. She could see the expression of utter disbelief on his face when he'd first seen her at the Frost Fair. And the look of fury which had swiftly followed. Then the vengeful smile he'd smiled when he'd called her Miss White. And remember every word he'd said to her at the card party.

Had he been trying to frighten her, by telling her someone was bound to inform the Duke about his stepmother's activities? Or was it, as he'd said, a warning? Whichever it was, she didn't want to be around when the Duke came back to London. If he did come. And even if he didn't, she'd had enough. It was time to leave. Past time.

She'd played at being a princess long enough. It was time to get back to real life. To her real self. To being plain, practical, drably dressed Miss Mitcham, who needed to work for a living.

And she'd do so, the very next day.

The moment she'd reached that decision she was able to roll over, heave a sigh of relief and slide directly into sleep.

The next morning, the moment she entered the breakfast room, she told the Duchess what she'd decided.

'I have to leave London. At once,' she said, waving to Herr Schnee, who'd sprung to his feet when she'd come in, indicating that he might sit down and continue with his plate of steak, potatoes, eggs and mushrooms. Even though he was posing as a servant, he was taking his meals with them, as though he was an old family retainer who'd won such privileges for long and faithful service. It was also a way of pandering to his pride. He had almost baulked at taking the job as what he termed a menial, until the Duchess had suggested this compromise. The only time when he would not sit down with them would be if they were invited out to dine, at which point he would take the role of body servant to Eleanor and stand behind her chair.

The Duchess looked up from her plate of toast. 'But where will you go? You have not had a reply from your uncle yet, have you?'

'No.' Which was hard to understand unless her letter to him had gone astray. There were all sorts of tales in the newspapers of coaches overturning, after all. The mail bags might have fallen into a drift somewhere and the letters been soaked, and the address could have become illegible. 'I had better write to him again, in case…'

'That is an excellent idea. And while you are waiting for a reply, you may as well stay here as anywhere. I do so enjoy your company.'

'Oh, thank you. Well, I have enjoyed staying here, too, very much. You have made me feel like a friend, and equal, rather than merely a sort of paid companion,' said Eleanor, feeling rather emotional, as she took the place at table where the footman was holding out a chair for her.

'Well, it would be very silly of me to look down my nose at you when we both come from similar backgrounds and the only reason I have a title was because I married one.'

Most women of her rank wouldn't think so. It was one of the things that made Eleanor like the older woman so much.

'You are still looking a little peaky, dear. Have you not recovered from whatever ailed you last night?'

No. Because what ailed her was comprised of a mixture of Lord Lavenham, and living this lie.

'Well,' said Eleanor, as the footman draped a napkin tenderly across her lap, 'I hardly got a wink of sleep last night, for worrying about what Lord Lavenham might do.'

'Oh, my dear,' cooed the Duchess. 'You really mustn't let him scare you. I have known him, by reputation, for years, and he has never managed to do anything of note about anything.'

'Yes, but—'

'No buts, my dear,' said the Duchess as one footman poured her tea, while another placed a rack of toast done exactly the way she liked it next to her plate. 'He really isn't going to be the biggest of our problems. That, I would remind you, comes in the form of my stepson, who is bound to turn up when we least expect him. And to that end, I really must ask you not to emerge from your room without your wig.'

Eleanor instinctively put one hand to her closely cropped hair. Fortunately, she hadn't yet put her knife to the butter dish.

'Yes, I know it hasn't mattered before, since we are all friends here,' she said, beaming round the room to include the footmen, the butler and Herr Schnee. 'But we cannot risk my stepson catching you unawares. We would all be in the suds,' she said with a little laugh. 'So it would be tremendously helpful if you could just keep up the disguise for as long as you remain here…'

'That's a good point,' said Eleanor soberly, recalling Lord Lavenham's warning that someone was bound to tell the Duke about his stepmother, which would make him come hotfoot to London to see if it was true that she was brewing up another scandal.

'Wonderful! I shall send Sukey to you first thing every morning...'

'Oh, but isn't Sukey acting as your own maid while Maud is out of action?'

The Duchess made a dismissive motion with her hand, scattering toast crumbs across the tablecloth. 'She can see to me after she has made sure you are looking the part. Nobody will be surprised if I don't come down to breakfast early. Or if I suddenly start taking a tray in my room, once my stepson is in residence.'

Eleanor went cold inside. The Duchess intended to leave her to deal with the Duke all on her own? First thing every morning? No, no, it wouldn't come to that. She'd already decided to write to her uncle, again, the moment she'd finished breakfast. Pray heaven that this time her letter got through and he would write back immediately, agreeing that of course she could go and stay with him.

And if he didn't, then she'd have to start making other arrangements. Because there was no way she could spend any great length of time deliberately deceiving a duke. Particularly not when she came to the breakfast table bleary of eye and mind because she wasn't sleeping properly over worries about what Lord Lavenham was planning. It was all very well the Duchess saying he'd never done anything of note. But Eleanor was certain he could do anything he set his mind to and it was just that, so far, he hadn't really exerted himself to do much more than flit about enjoying whatever pleasures his rank and wealth could procure.

There was no telling what he might do now. He must have been terribly insulted when she turned down his marriage proposal. Once her departure had forced him to see that she really, really meant it, that was. And he was evidently furious to discover she'd taken up with the Duchess. Which wasn't so surprising, given the withering set-down the Duchess had given him when he'd walked into the taproom, searching for her.

He'd searched for her. He'd gone riding out, in all that horrid freezing fog, to try to find her. Which meant he must have been concerned. She hadn't known him to put himself out for anyone all that much before. No wonder he was furious.

Not that anyone would have guessed it, from the friendly greeting he gave her that night, not five minutes after he'd strolled into the crowded front parlour of Mrs Broughty's house.

'How are you this evening? Fully recovered, I trust? Miss...er... White, isn't it?' He smiled down at her where she sat, rigid with tension, on one of the many chairs their hostess had crammed into the room. 'I do have the name correct, don't I? So hard to recall names, don't you find? I confess, I often have to be reminded of a person's name several times before it lodges in my brain. Although,' he added, his smile turning hard, 'I never forget a face.'

Nobody else would have noticed there was anything amiss with what he'd said, she was certain. Only she heard the veiled warning that he knew she was using a false identity.

'And yours,' he went on, before she could think of anything to say in response, 'is truly unforgettable. Your eyes are unique.'

She blushed, just as though he was flirting with her, which was what it must sound like to anyone else.

'They fairly sparkle with intelligence.'

'I… I do not know what you mean,' she said, utterly confused by this approach.

'Oh, I am sure you do. I think you are a very clever, not to say cunning woman.'

She gasped. Behind her, Herr Schnee bristled. 'You think to insult my lady?'

'Not a bit of it,' said Lord Lavenham airily. 'I admire intelligence in a woman. So many young ladies who come to Town are such silly things. Not a thought in their heads beyond fashion. Whereas Miss… White's own head is clearly full of all sorts of things that a mere man could never start to guess at.'

Golly. If she didn't know better, she'd think he was sincere. He sounded as though he really did admire her mind. Well, when she'd been Lady Bradbury's companion, she'd often thought the same. His face had often changed from the bored, aloof expression he normally wore, when he'd chatted with her, as though he was enjoying her company. And then there were those jests he made, which only she and he could share, since they went straight over the older lady's head.

Which, actually, only went to prove that he had a

streak of cruelty. A man couldn't make sport of an elderly lady without being something of a beast.

'You need not try to guess at anything that is going on in my head,' she said, tartly. 'I am sure none of it would interest you.' Not really. He was only paying her so much attention because she'd annoyed him.

'Well, we will never know, will we? Since you are so determined to remain a mystery.' He glanced round the room with what looked like cynicism, before looking down at her once more. 'There is nothing more intriguing to the jaded members of society than a woman of mystery, did you know that? Since I met you at the Frost Fair, I have been hearing all sorts of tales about you. Everyone is desperate to know where you come from. And how you came to be taken up by the Duchess of Theakstone. Half of them think you must be from a junior branch of one of the noble houses and the rest declare that, if it were so, then somebody would be bound to recognise you. But, as nobody yet has done, they are beginning to speculate that you hail from a foreign royal house.' He eyed Herr Schnee. 'And they are citing this chap's accent, and his military style of clothing, as evidence. But of course, you would not do such a thing as impersonate a member of a royal family, would you, Miss White? That would be such an outrageous, not to say *criminal* thing to do.'

Eleanor did not know what to do with her face. Fortunately, Herr Schnee was not at such a loss for words.

'You are impertinent, sir,' he said. Or rather growled between his teeth. 'I hear there is a code for the English gentleman. But you,' he spat, 'are not that.'

'No,' replied Lord Lavenham lazily. 'I am not much

of a gentleman. But then,' he added, provocatively, 'nor, I dare swear, are you.'

With that, he sauntered off, looking vastly pleased with himself, while Eleanor just wanted to sink through the chair cushions and into the carpet. Everyone was looking at her. Surreptitiously, for the most part. But they'd all seen, and many of them must have heard, Lord Lavenham's challenge.

There was only one thing for it. She lifted her chin and began to fan herself lazily, as though she didn't care. It was either that, or run from the room like a coward, which would be to admit that everything he'd accused her of was true.

And even though it was, she'd only make things worse by giving in to the urge to run from the room in tears. Not only would she be making a spectacle of herself, but she'd be letting the Duchess down, too. The Duchess, who'd gone to so much trouble and expense on her behalf.

Anyway, she'd never have come to London at all if he hadn't forced her to run away in the first place. Yes, it was *his* fault she'd ended up here. His behaviour that had forced her to run away. If he hadn't kissed her...

She plied her fan a bit faster. Because even thinking about that kiss still had the power to make her feel hot all over. She couldn't believe he could have turned her from sensible, practical Eleanor into a wild, passionate creature in the space of two seconds. Just by taking her in his arms. But he had.

The Duchess was wrong about him. He was a powerful man. A man who had the power to destroy Eleanor, anyway, in any number of different ways. If he chose to.

The question was, would he choose to?

And if he did, which of the various methods at his disposal would he employ?

Chapter Thirteen

'I believe you feel I owe you an apology,' said Lord Lavenham, two evenings later, at a small gathering of the *ton* hosted by Lady Fewcott, whose husband's work at Horse Guards meant they lived in London all year round.

Eleanor eyed him warily. He wasn't apologising. He was challenging her by stating that he thought she thought he owed her one.

'It was Herr Schnee,' she pointed out, after considering the number of *he thoughts* and *she thoughts* for only a moment or two, 'who accused you of being impertinent.'

'So it was,' he said cheerfully. 'What a good memory you have, on the whole. But then I dare say you need it.'

She refused to rise to the bait and ask what he meant by that. Because he was obviously implying she'd need a good memory to keep track of all the lies he thought she was telling. And as for the *on the whole* portion… no, she wasn't even going to try to unravel what he might mean by that.

'And where is your, ah, major-domo tonight?'

'He is,' she replied frostily, 'as I'm sure you have already discovered, partnering Her Grace at the whist table.'

'Leaving you all alone and unprotected, yes,' he said, taking the chair next to hers without asking her permission. 'So naturally, I mean to take advantage of the opportunity. To...' He paused, eyeing her challengingly.

After his pause became so lengthy her nerves were almost at screaming point, she broke the deadlock.

'To what? What do you want with me?'

'I think you know,' he said, a wicked glint in his ebony eyes putting her in mind of the moment just before he'd taken her in his arms and kissed her so ruthlessly. 'In fact, I'm certain of it. But let us put it this way. You consider me a rake, with a jaded appetite. Didn't you expect your air of mystery to pique my curiosity?'

'No. That aspect of things had never occurred to me.' Well, she hadn't expected to see him ever again. She'd hoped he wouldn't return to London until after she'd left.

'No? Nevertheless, I have to tell you,' he said, lowering his voice to a seductive purr that warmed its way right down her spine, 'that I cannot stop thinking about you.'

'I don't see why.' Was that her voice? All breathy and uncertain?

'Perhaps it is the way you have burst upon society like...like Athena, the day she sprang fully formed from the head of Zeus.'

The absurdity of that statement brought her back

to reality. She was no goddess. Especially not one of wisdom and warfare. Besides, he knew exactly who she was and where she'd come from. 'No, that is definitely not it,' she said, her voice sounding much more satisfyingly brisk.

'No? Then...it must be because you are so captivating.'

'Oh, please,' she said in disgust. He didn't find her captivating. If anything, she would say he was more likely to find her irritating than anything else. 'If there is one thing I dislike above all others, it is false flattery.'

He raised one eyebrow. 'What if it is not false?'

She almost blurted out the truth, which was that she knew he was angry with her and was trying to make her nervous. But that would be to admit to a prior knowledge when she was supposed to have only met him a few days ago at the Frost Fair. 'What else,' she managed to say, even if it was with a hint of desperation, 'can it be?'

He half-smiled, Then leaned back, tapping one lean forefinger against the back of her chair. 'Allow me to tell you,' he said, his lids lowering over his dark eyes, 'that I have never had to resort to flattery, false or otherwise, when it comes to women. They tend to fall into my arms without the least little bit of encouragement.'

Her face flamed at the reminder she'd done precisely that. Worse, she'd done it immediately after insisting she wanted no part of him.

'Your vanity is offensive,' she managed to choke out.

'It is my honesty that offends you, I think,' he said calmly. 'Unlike the vast majority of your sex, who profess one thing with their mouths, while their bodies sing a different tune, I have never attempted to hide what I want.'

'I…no—I… I don't know what you mean!'

'Tut-tut-tut.' He shook his head reproachfully. 'You know exactly what I mean. And by denying it, you are proving my point. At least, while looking offended at the same time. Because if you were really an honest, innocent woman, who didn't know what I meant,' he said, clasping his hands on his knees and leaning forward to make his point, 'you would simply look puzzled. Ah, and now I come to think of it,' he continued, with a hard smile, 'I now know why it is that I cannot stop thinking about you.'

He paused. But she was too wary of the answer he might give if she admitted to being curious.

'It is,' he continued, 'because you remind me, very forcibly, of a girl I once knew.'

Oh, lord, what was he going to say next?

'A girl I believed was kind and intelligent, and, above all, honest.' His mouth twisted into a sneer. 'I thought so highly of her that I asked her to marry me. She'd encouraged me to believe, you see, that she returned my feelings. But it turned out that she was capable, like all your sex, of dissembling.'

No! That wasn't how it had been. She stared straight ahead, gripping the struts of her fan as she sought some way of explaining that she hadn't been dishonest, only rather cowardly. That she had returned his feelings…

His feelings? No, that wasn't quite true. She hadn't believed he'd felt anything much for her at all.

She tried to look back at him, her heart pounding. Was he saying that he had truly wanted to marry her?

Because of what she was, rather than all that flannel about doing his duty to the family name and putting Lady Bradbury's nose out of joint?

A cynical smile was playing about his lips. 'Ah, yes, much better.'

'What?'

'That expression you have adopted now. Two parts bewildered and one part wounded. Very affecting. Or it would be,' he added, the smile vanishing, 'if I did not already know it was all an act.'

Without giving her a chance to deny it, he got to his feet and sauntered away, leaving Eleanor shaky and sweating, and writhing inside with a whole host of unpleasant feelings, the dominant one being a horrid suspicion that she'd hurt him. Something she'd never dreamt possible before.

There was worse to come. When they arrived back at Grosvenor Square that night, Dawes gave them the news that the Duke of Theakstone had arrived while they were out.

'Bother,' said the Duchess. 'I was sure that the condition of the roads would keep him away.'

They might have done, if someone hadn't written to tell him about her presence, and that of Herr Schnee, in Grosvenor Square. Just as Lord Lavenham had predicted, the Duke must want to see for himself exactly what his stepmother was up to. Eleanor only just barely resisted the temptation to pelt up the stairs and hide in her room. It was bad enough having just learned that she'd made such a terrible, erroneous assumption about Lord Lavenham. She really, really wasn't in any state to start trying to deal with the Duke, particularly not when he sounded such a formidable man.

'His Grace said that he took advantage of what seems to be the beginning of a thaw and has already gone to his room,' said Dawes, perhaps sensing Eleanor's nervousness at the prospect of meeting him. 'We do not expect to see him until the morning. It is his habit,' he said to Eleanor, 'to breakfast early.'

'Thank you, Dawes,' said the Duchess, 'for warning us. Eleanor, I mean Eve—oh, bother, I really must be more careful about using your new name, mustn't I? But anyway, you will be prepared now for your first meeting, won't you? And all the staff will back you up, won't they, Dawes?'

Dawes bowed in a way that conveyed the meaning that, of course, Eleanor would have the support of all the staff in hoodwinking their employer.

'Thank you,' said Eleanor shakily, wondering what kind of man the Duke must be for all his staff to collude with his stepmother in this deception. How on earth, she wondered as she made her way up the stairs while the Duchess, Dawes, and Herr Schnee all went into the drawing room for a nightcap, and what she suspected would turn into a council of war, had she got embroiled in this situation? She'd planned on spending her life in a quiet country backwater, as a companion to an elderly lady, not living in London with a duchess, trying to pass herself off as a foreign princess. All under the watchful, mocking, cynical gaze of Lord Lavenham. Poor Lord Lavenham, who'd just confessed he'd been on the verge of perhaps developing something like a *tendre* for her. But…

Oh, if only Uncle Norman would write back to let her know that he was willing and able to let her stay with him for a while. Nothing like this could possibly happen to her in Suffolk. Perhaps she should write to a few of her other uncles and aunts? None of them had such roomy houses, or the means to support an indigent niece, but really, it might be better to have some bolthole ready, for when the Duke found out that she was an imposter.

As soon as Sukey had helped Eleanor out of her disguise, and bustled away with the wig under her arm so that she could tidy it up and generally make it ready for the next day, Eleanor sat down at the little writing desk in her room and began writing to every relative she thought might be able to squeeze her in. She burned several candles down to the sockets while she did so, only pausing to wrap first a shawl round her shoulders, then a blanket round her knees as the room grew steadily colder.

For once she didn't care how late she sat up. She wasn't going to get any sleep anyway for worrying about one thing and another. By the time she'd finished writing to every relative she could think of, she was so tired it was all she could do to keep her eyes open. She drifted off to sleep almost at once, soothed both by the knowledge that she'd done what she could to effect an escape, should one become necessary, and by the sound of rain pattering against her windowpane.

Next morning, there was no ice on the inside of her windowpane for the first time since she'd reached London. A thaw had definitely set in.

With the weather, that was. But most definitely not between the Duke of Theakstone and his stepmother. Both of them were already sitting at the breakfast table when Eleanor went down, surprisingly, considering the Duchess had warned her that she might have to face the dour Duke alone. And the atmosphere was positively chilly.

'Good morning, dear,' said the Duchess as Eleanor began walking to the table. 'This is the young lady I was telling you about, Theakstone,' she continued, as the Duke, very correctly, got to his feet.

What had the Duchess said about her? How was she to avoid betraying the fact she was none of the things she was supposed to be, if the Duchess didn't keep her up to date?

'Good morning, Miss White,' said the Duke, running a pair of snapping brown eyes over her entire form, making her feel as if he'd seen through her disguise right away. The way Lord Lavenham had done at the Frost Fair.

'Good morning, Your Grace,' she replied, stopping to bob a curtsy before stumbling her way to the chair one of the footmen was holding out for her.

Goodness, he'd never believe she was a foreign princess if she acted so nervously around a mere duke. *Mere?* Heavens, when had her priorities become so disordered that she could attach the word *mere* to a man of such high rank? Besides, there was nothing *mere* about his person. He had deep, straight, no-nonsense eyebrows and a beak of a nose that made him look like some great, dark bird of prey.

It was just as well that he was the kind of man who

was taciturn at breakfast, because Eleanor didn't think she could have strung more than two words together. And they would have come out in a high-pitched, nervous squeak.

The only thing keeping her spirits on any sort of even keel was the hope that one of her aunts or uncles would reply with good news. Within a day or so.

She could last that long, couldn't she?

Chapter Fourteen

Peter's stomach clenched as he read the account of the catastrophe. In spite of clear warning signals, almost a thousand people had gone on to the ice. It had broken apart, the whole mass surging in a great tumult through the arches of Blackfriars Bridge, sweeping everything along with it. It was a wonder there hadn't been more casualties. He lowered the paper and gazed at the lovely warm fire blazing in the breakfast-room grate, remembering his earlier impulse to be there, should anything dreadful happen, so that he could rescue anyone who was in danger.

But he hadn't rescued anyone. People had died while he'd been sitting at home, plotting ways to spoil Miss Mitcham's fun. People had plunged beneath the broken ice and drowned. It made him feel almost as bad as he had during those sleepless nights of imagining Miss Mitcham, frozen to death somewhere out on the hills.

He flung the newspaper in the fire. Or, at least, that had been his intention, but the newspaper, being large and light, took an erratic course and ended up half-draped over the fire irons. Which seemed to sum up the course of his whole life, of late.

Nothing had been the same since the day Miss Mitcham had run away from him. And now, to cap it all, he was concerned about other people, people he'd never even met. Was it because he'd been to the Frost Fair himself? Walked on the very ice which had given way?

He suspected not.

No, he *knew* he would never have reacted with such horror to a story in a newspaper before Miss Mitcham. Before Miss Mitcham, he'd read of far worse tragedies befalling people he'd rubbed shoulders with, and done little more than raise one brow. With perhaps a slight sneer at whoever it was for being stupid enough to have got caught up in it. For instance, he would have scoffed at these particular people for ignoring all the warning signs. Hundreds of them had been stupid enough to venture out on to the ice, even though it was emitting loud cracking sounds.

So why wasn't he sneering at them? Why hadn't he been able to turn the page to see what news was coming from the Continent regarding the war, while congratulating himself for being a sensible, practical, wealthy Englishman?

It was all Miss Mitcham's doing. She'd…she'd… caused the carapace that grew round his heart to crack, just like the ice, that's what she'd done. Or woken up his conscience. Or whatever that tender part of a person was that made him care about what happened to anyone but himself.

Well, however anyone might describe it, the fact was that, somehow, she'd changed him. He could no longer be the kind of man who just sat here, drinking ale and eating sirloin and not *doing* something about the tragedy he'd just read about.

He rang for his butler and asked him to send in his secretary. While he was waiting for Pettigrew to come, he paced up and down while considering what, exactly, he *could* do after the event, only pausing to pick up the recalcitrant newspaper, wad it into a ball and consign it to the flames. And holding it over the coals with the poker to make sure he destroyed the damn thing.

'You wanted me, sir?' Pettigrew hovered in the doorway, tugging at his neckcloth as though he half-expected to learn the butler had made a mistake in asking him to attend his employer at breakfast. Peter had never sent for him this early in the day, not in all the years he'd been working for him. They normally met at the same time, in the study, to trawl through the torrent of paperwork that flowed across his desk. Most of it irritating, routine stuff for which Peter had neither the time nor the patience.

'Yes,' said Peter, beckoning him to come in. 'I want you to find out what action is being taken to provide support for the dependants of people who drowned when the ice on the Thames broke apart. The families of those printers, for instance.' There had been a whole paragraph about the printing presses, which had been churning out commemorative pamphlets and the like, and how they had plunged beneath the waves. 'They will have lost not only the main breadwinner, but also the equipment by which they earned their living.'

That was how Miss Mitcham had managed to change him. She'd made him think about how a poor person, a person far from home, could survive in severe adversity. Had made him imagine every kind of disaster that could befall a lone female in particular, so that now he only had to read a story about a disaster and his mind was running along similar paths, rather than just taking the bare facts at face value and letting them glance off him like snowballs off an oak door.

'Sir,' said Pettigrew, with a touch of reverence, whipping out a sheaf of paper from the case he carried under his arm, and making a note with the pencil he drew from behind his ear. 'I shall get on to it at once, sir.'

Peter dismissed him with an irritated wave of the hand, then glared at the door through which Pettigrew had just gone. His secretary had never looked at him that way before, as though he was an admirable person. Because the fellow had never witnessed him doing anything admirable. Well, he never had put his mind to doing anything that was not directly related to his own welfare. His own pleasure.

He'd lived selfishly, he supposed. Though he was no more selfish than any other member of his class.

However, he could no longer use the excuse that he was no worse than the next man. Not now that Miss Mitcham had opened his eyes to the fact that other people...*mattered.*

Good lord. She'd made him capable of being a better man.

Or at least of *appearing* to be a better man. This inconvenient compulsion to share the concerns and fears of others would probably wear off before the day was out.

It was to be hoped so, anyway. Because a better

man, a decent man, would not be so consumed with exacting vengeance upon a woman. A woman he'd professed to wish to marry, at that. A better man might even recall that he'd set the whole series of events in train by kissing her. And refusing to listen to her irrelevant and, as he'd thought, half-hearted attempts to refuse his proposal.

Why hadn't she bloody well accepted his proposal gratefully, rather than going running off into the night as though he'd threatened her with…with…medieval thumbscrews?

How had she gained the power to reach deep into what passed for his soul and remake it in the image of…well, some other man? Not him. In fact, how *dare* she change him, in any way, when she didn't give a rap for him? It was not fair. It was not just.

Hah. There went the altruistic mood which had prompted him to send for his secretary and discuss sending aid to the victims of the thaw. Vanished. Now he was…he was…

Hell, he was furious. If he were to run across her today, there was no telling what he'd do. Certainly not let her off the hook. Or curtail the days of her punishment. Not by so much as one single hour.

He strode back to the table, sat down and sawed off a large chunk of his by now congealing sirloin. Just as he'd expected. His better self had rolled over and gone back to sleep. He'd suspected, even while he'd been sending for Pettigrew, that his impulse had no more substance than a phantom. And he'd been right. Because now he felt no reluctance to plan what he'd say to Miss Mitcham during their next encounter. How he would increase her torment. He had a brief and highly satisfying flash of imagination, where he pictured himself as the man with his hand on the lever and Miss Mitcham as the victim bound to the rack.

He sat back, a hard smile on his face. Unlike his sirloin, revenge was a dish best eaten cold. He'd given her fair warning, last night, that he was going to make her pay for her original offence. But now he was also going to have to prove to himself that she had *not* made him become a better man. That on the contrary, she'd made him harder. Less vulnerable.

It was this version of him, this hard, determined man who would not permit anyone, let alone a female, to influence his feelings and decisions, who decided to attend a card party at which he knew she would be present. The man whose pride had been bruised who dressed with the greatest care. It had taken him days to achieve his present state of cool, calm self-control. He'd been determined to wait until his anger no longer blazed out at the slightest provocation, making him fling newspapers across the room, or pursue them so he could ball them up and consign them to the flames. Until his anger cooled to the consistency of ice. He regarded his cool, elegant reflection in the mirror. To his satisfaction, the man who looked steadily back appeared hard enough to withstand any amount of pressure. Even unto, he was convinced, the weight of a veritable elephant.

Eleanor laid one hand upon the Duke's arm as he assisted her from the carriage. He had lovely manners, she had to give him that, though so far she hadn't been able to detect a solitary spark of genuine warmth about him. It was as if he held himself back from other people. And no wonder, when even his own staff treated him like an interloper in his own house!

After only a few days, she'd actually started to feel sorry for him.

And the Duchess had noticed. 'Do you know,' she'd said with an arch laugh, 'I'm starting to think you find my stepson attractive.'

'No! I do not find him *attractive*. I just feel a bit sorry for him, that is all.'

'Sorry for him?' The Duchess looked at her as though she'd grown two heads.

Eleanor had pretended to be busy picking through a tray of bugle beads to avoid looking her benefactress in the eye. She couldn't very well explain that, as far as she'd been able to see, the poor man was guilty of nothing more than being the son of a man the Duchess hated. He probably didn't understand her reluctance to move to the Dower House, because the Duchess would scarcely speak to him, let alone confide the revulsion she felt at being forced to go back and live in the place that held so many awful memories.

If only they'd just sit down and talk to each other...

But, no. The Duchess was frosty with her stepson and he was guarded in his responses. She, as an outsider, didn't feel she had the right to intervene and force them to thrash out their differences. Besides, they both outranked her by so much that, when they were both at their most haughty with each other, all she wanted to do was fade into the wallpaper.

'I suppose,' said the Duchess, 'that is a start. He is definitely showing signs of being interested in you.'

'No. He is not interested in me.' How could he be when he did not know the first thing about her? Besides, she knew what it felt like to have a man interested in her. Lord Lavenham had looked at her with lust, and with loathing, but never with the cool detachment that was all that ever showed in the Duke of Theakstone's eyes. 'He is acting the way any man would towards any guest in his house, I think.' And it was his house, even if the servants treated him like an interloper. 'Perhaps he is even showing you some respect by refraining from asking searching questions, which I think he would dearly love to ask.' Sometimes he actually made her shiver with dread when he turned those keen dark eyes on her, in a manner that seemed to pierce right to the heart of things.

'Respect for me?' The Duchess snorted in derision. 'I think not. Or he would not refer to you as my latest protégée, in that cynical way he does.'

Yes, he did do that. Of course he did. Because he suspected they were up to something. Although for some reason, he had not, as yet, asked either of them outright what it was. But he could do, at any moment. And then what would she say?

As if it wasn't bad enough that she already had Lord Lavenham circling her with malicious intent, she now had the Duke as a potential enemy, too.

It was no longer just sleeping she was finding difficult. Her appetite was almost non-existent and, every so often, a little muscle at the corner of her eye would start jerking so that she had to put up her hand to conceal it.

It twitched now as they entered the house. She turned away from the Duke under the pretext of handing her cloak to a servant, dithering over the business until the spasm passed. Though it was bound to happen again. One day somebody would notice it and comment on it, and wonder why she was in such a state that she'd developed a nervous twitch.

And she was very much afraid that if that person asked her in a genuinely sympathetic manner, or when she was feeling particularly low, she might very well tell them.

Chapter Fifteen

She spotted Lord Lavenham the moment she reached the drawing room in which several card tables had been set out. He spotted her and gave her that look, the one he normally sent winging her way, wherever, of late, she went.

He didn't often speak to her, but he would always watch her in a way that made her pulse race and her stomach churn. Because every time she glanced his way he'd be looking at her, a veritable whirlpool of the darkest emotions blazing from his eyes.

What with him watching her whenever she went out and the Duke observing her every move indoors, it felt like having two great buzzards circling, while she waited for one or the other of them to swoop. She was starting to feel as if she knew what a field mouse felt like just before it got torn to pieces.

Tonight, it appeared, was going to be one of the times Lord Lavenham chose to speak to her. To torment her face to face, rather than from across the room, because he was walking over.

'Your Grace,' he said, bowing to the Duke. 'I do hope you will not mind if I detach your lovely young guest from your side. I would like her to be my partner at the whist table, as it is a game at which I know she excels.'

The Duke, rather than relinquishing her at once, glanced at her and raised one brow slightly, as if to check whether it was what she wanted. For a second, she wasn't sure. If she had any sense, she'd seize this chance to steer clear of Lord Lavenham. On the other hand, at least she knew where she was with him because he knew exactly who she was, whereas she had no idea what the Duke knew, or even suspected.

'Thank you, Lord Lavenham,' she therefore said, since playing cards with him sounded like less of a strain than sticking with the Duke and having to watch every single thing she said in case she roused his suspicions. And landed his stepmother, as well as her, in his black books.

'I should like,' said the Duke as she placed her hand on Lord Lavenham's sleeve, 'to make a contribution to the fund you have set up for the victims of the Frost Fair disaster.'

The what?

'My secretary is dealing with all that,' said Lord Lavenham, confirming that he had, indeed, set up the fund she hadn't heard of until this very moment.

'Then I shall instruct my secretary to contact yours,' said the Duke, before sauntering off without a backward glance.

'You have set up a fund for the victims? What victims?'

'The idiots who went on to the ice when anyone with any sense could see there was a thaw,' he bit out. 'I couldn't see why their families should suffer just because they were so reckless.'

The disparaging way he spoke of those people didn't fool Eleanor. If he thought so ill of them, he would not have done anything about it. It was being found out doing something charitable that was making him uncomfortable.

She felt a wry smile tug at her lips. Because she'd been right about him and the Duchess had been wrong. He *was* capable of achieving anything he wished to do, once he set his mind to it.

'You really ought not to look so pleased to learn that I have set up such a charity,' said Lord Lavenham, shaking his head. 'It does not mean that I am a flat.'

Oh, so *that* was why he was reluctant to let people know he was capable of being charitable. She supposed that made sense, considering how wealthy he was.

'And you need not think that just because I have been charitable in that regard, I meant to extend that softness of heart to you,' he said vehemently.

No, she would not think that. He'd made his position clear. In fact, she wasn't sure, now, that she'd made the right decision in abandoning the Duke. It was just that something drew her to him, like a sort of magnetic pull. Which was a touch ironic, considering he was her avowed enemy.

'And if that enigmatic smile was because you have set your cap at the Duke, be warned, Miss. One word from me and not only will your ambition to become a duchess come to naught, but I can make sure that you are utterly ruined.'

'I'm not setting my cap at the Duke.' Why did everyone keep accusing her of setting caps at people?

'No? Why, then, have you made yourself into exactly the kind of woman he prefers?'

'I have done no such thing.'

'Yet you chose a black wig, rather than a blonde one. Is that not because every mistress he has ever had, as far as anyone knows, has been dark of hair and eyes?'

But she hadn't chosen it. The Duchess had.

'And have put about a rumour that you are a princess. The very kind of high-born woman he would seek out for a wife, if he was looking for one.'

He *was* looking for a wife. And the Duchess had made no secret of the fact that she'd hoped he might find Eleanor attractive.

A cold swirling sensation started up in her stomach. Even though she'd refused to try to make the Duke fall for her, it looked as though the Duchess had gone ahead with her plan, by making her over into the type of woman everyone knew he did find attractive, pushing them together as often as she could.

'Just so,' said Lord Lavenham, with a hard smile.

It took a moment to work out that he must be referring to his threat to expose her and put a halt to a conspiracy she'd only just worked out she was up to her neck in.

'I suppose at least I can acquit you of pursuing young Spenlow.'

Mr Spenlow? Why was he bringing up that young man?

'But then he is only the heir to an earldom. And

since you've already turned down an earl in fact,' he said bitterly, 'it seems unlikely you are prepared to wait an indefinite amount of time to get your hands on a coronet, like the other silly chits who flutter round him wherever he goes.'

They did flutter round Mr Spenlow, now she came to think of it. And she'd never been able to work out why, since he was only of average looks and intelligence. This explained it, but not why Lord Lavenham was speaking to her the way he was.

'I have no wish,' she said indignantly, 'to get my hands on a coronet of any sort. If I ever marry, it will only be because I truly love the man who proposes to me.'

'Hmmph,' he grunted. 'We will be playing General and Lady Cormscroft,' he then said, ignoring her comment and leading her to a table at which an elderly couple were already sitting opposite each other. As he held out the chair for her to take her seat, she noted the empty bottle at the General's elbow. From the way he slouched in the chair, and the rather glazed sheen of his eyes, it looked as though that bottle had not been his first. As she sat down, Lord Lavenham leaned forward and murmured in her ear.

'You may have heard it said that men fall in love with their eyes. I have to tell you that it is only fools who do so. And the Duke is no fool.'

Why wouldn't he listen when she told him she had no interest in the Duke? And how on earth, she wondered, reaching for a wine glass and holding it up for a waiter to come and fill it, had she become caught between two such powerful men? As if she was a person that mattered, when the highest position she'd ever reached on her own account was as companion to an elderly lady? She really was no more than a little mouse, caught in the open by two powerful predators. Hardly worth them bothering over, really. Not more than a mouthful, for either of them.

She downed her wine, when it came, in two very unladylike gulps, hoping it might soothe nerves that were becoming so frayed, it could only be a matter of time before she came unravelled altogether.

'That's what I like to see,' said the elderly General, slapping the tabletop with one rather pudgy hand. 'A woman who knows how to enjoy herself. Eh?' He cast a scornful look at the drooping lady who was sitting opposite his side of the table. A lady who looked as though life, or her boor of a husband, had beaten her down.

'Oh, Miss White knows how to enjoy herself right enough,' said Lord Lavenham, taking the seat opposite her. And giving her a smouldering look that took her right back to the one time she'd been in his arms.

Perhaps that was why she'd come with him so readily. Because, in spite of everything that had happened since, she couldn't totally shake off the feelings that he'd roused that night. Feelings that came over her whenever he looked at her. Actually, worse than that. He didn't even need to look at her. All he had to do was be in the same room and her heart would trip up, and her pulse would become erratic with a combination of nerves and...excitement.

'Best leave the bottle, then,' said the General, totally misunderstanding Lord Lavenham's remark, thank goodness, and grabbing it out of the waiter's hand before he could make off with it.

Eleanor wasn't sure, afterwards, how on earth she and Lord Lavenham managed to win, when she was so distracted by the alternately smouldering, and vengeful looks he kept on shooting at her across the table. It could only have been down to the fact that the General kept on drinking, which addled his own wits, and criticising every discard that his wife made, so that she became increasingly flustered, before eventually giving up even the pretence of trying to focus on the game.

'Another hand?' The General reached for the pack and began to shuffle the deck. 'Give us a chance to recoup our losses?'

They'd only been wagering shillings, since this was a private party, not a gambling den. And Eleanor wouldn't have minded taking more of the General's money, since she'd grown to heartily dislike him for the way he treated his wife. But neither was she all that bothered when Lord Lavenham declined on their behalf, because it was his wife who would pay for any losses they suffered, she could tell. The General would make her the scapegoat for his own incompetence, as he'd been doing all evening.

'Regretfully, I must decline.' Lord Lavenham got to his feet. 'Miss White?' He held out his hand as though offering to escort her somewhere. 'Let us take a stroll about the room.'

The tone in his voice was not an invitation, but an order. And since he held her destiny in his hands, she didn't think it wise to oppose him. Even though the look in his eyes had suddenly turned so implacable she was sure he was going to say something unpleasant. Or several somethings. But in spite of this, she couldn't prevent a little frisson of pleasure at having his arm beneath her hand as he led them across the room to a long side table, which held a selection of light refreshments. She supposed, once a girl had kissed a man, she couldn't help recalling the way she'd felt when he'd held her in his arms. Not when it had been such a wonderful feeling.

A *dangerous* feeling. Or she wouldn't be following him around like a little lost lamb.

Lord Lavenham came to a halt, regarding the plates of cakes and savouries as though making up his mind which to select.

'I have been lenient with you for too long,' he said, leaning across her to pick up a plate. 'It is time I put a stop to your little game,' he said, thrusting the plate into her hands. 'If you value your skin,' he said grimly, picking up a random selection of food from what was on offer, 'as soon as you have eaten this supper, you will go to the library on the second floor of this house where I will be waiting for you. If you don't, then…' he said no more, but the way he slapped a sprig of parsley, which she was certain was only meant to act as a garnish, on top of the heap of food struck her as a threat.

He turned and left her, sauntering across the room as though he hadn't a care in the world. Rather the way the Duke had done. Only something about the set of his shoulders told her that his insouciance was for show, whereas the Duke really hadn't been all that interested in what she was going to do next.

She picked up the parsley sprig and, rather than putting it to one side, deliberately put the whole thing in her mouth and chewed. It was a foolish act of defiance to consume the symbol of threat he'd used. But then it was the only bit of defiance she could allow herself. She had to do as he'd bidden her. She had too much at stake to risk calling his bluff. Had, thanks to the Duchess, behaved with such impropriety by posing as foreign royalty, that she would never live it down if he chose to expose her. It hadn't seemed so very dreadful at first. Well, it had, but after only a token protest she'd given way because the Duchess had made it sound as if it would be great fun and had assured her that nobody would find out because there was hardly anybody in Town. And that anyway, she'd likely be gone before any real harm could be done.

But that had been weeks ago. And people *had* started to return to Town. Not least Lord Lavenham and the Duke. And everywhere she went, people watched her, talked about her, made guesses about her. She was a topic of gossip.

And she hated it.

Whatever punishment Lord Lavenham decreed, at this meeting, she would thoroughly deserve it. Still, she put off the moment as long as she dared, toying with her food and darting nervous glances around the room to see if anybody in particular was watching her at the moment. If anyone would notice her slipping out. But it was one of those evenings where everyone was too intent on their own games, and their own gossip, to pay much attention to one lone female by the buffet table. Even Herr Schnee, who was supposed to be convincing everyone he was her bodyguard, was keeping his attention firmly on the game in play. But then he and the Duchess, who was his partner, were doing extremely well, to judge from the pile of coins in front of him. And from what she'd learned of him so far, earning a few shillings was far more important to him than a mere country miss, which was all she was to him.

And so she turned slowly and put down her plate.

Because there was nothing for it. No excuse to avoid it. She'd have to go in search of the library and bear whatever it was that Lord Lavenham wanted to say to her. It couldn't be anything worse than she'd been saying to herself, of late, she didn't think. Nevertheless, her spirits quailed when she slipped between the double doors to the room on the next floor up, which spanned the entire front of the house. For he was standing with his back to the fireplace, watching the door, his arms folded across his chest, his face set and hard.

'So, you decided to come then?' He marched past her and locked the door, then turned to look at her, giving a bitter laugh. 'I was beginning to wonder if you had the gall to call my bluff. But, no, you are admitting your guilt, by coming here at my command.'

She was. But then she was guilty. And could think of no clever response to make. She just clasped her hands together and braced herself to bear the torrent of scorn she could see he was dying to let loose. Or he wouldn't have demanded she meet him in private, would he?

Chapter Sixteen

'You disgust me,' he said. Although she didn't. It was his own reaction to her that disgusted him. She made him weak. For days he'd been plotting and planning, enjoying dreaming up increasingly inventive ways he could wreak his revenge upon her, but all she had to do was give a little half smile and all his plans melted away under a surge of lust so powerful that it was all he could do to keep his hands off her.

He'd briefly toyed with the idea of wrestling the heat of that lust into a plan for revenge that took a different course. But other things also seemed to have melted some of his ice-cold determination to punish her. The General's behaviour, for instance, had sickened Peter. He'd detested the way the man treated his wife. Had started to feel sorry for her. How could any man treat a woman so badly?

Which led him to question how he could treat *this* woman, who was standing before him with her head bowed, her hands clasped at her waist, in a similarly cold and cruel manner.

He gritted his teeth. It was only justice that he... do something that would change her, since she'd had the audacity to change him from the kind of man who would have sneered at Lady Cormscroft to one who felt pity for her. From the kind of man who could walk away from any unwilling woman, with a shrug of one shoulder, to a man who lay abed at night planning ways to bring this specific one to heel.

Why couldn't he just shrug and let her go?

'You turned down my proposal of marriage,' he said aloud, as the answer hit him, 'as though I was not fit to lick your boots. You preached about wanting something higher, something deeper, and then ran off without a second thought to those you left behind fearing you were lying frozen in a ditch somewhere. You didn't even think to write a note to alleviate our anxiety once you got where you were going. And where did I find you, after scouring the hills and the byways, and thinking I saw you in every random woman who was about your height? Frolicking about at a fair, wearing furs and eating gingerbread!'

'I was going to write a note, once I reached...'

But he wasn't in the mood to listen to excuses. 'You sneered at what I was offering,' he went on, 'saying you were holding out for love, but you behaved more callously than any woman I have ever met. You didn't care how badly worried everyone was about your welfare. And not only that, but, after refusing to enter into a relationship you derided as being dishonest, you are now perpetrating what amounts to a fraud upon society by masquerading as a foreign princess.'

'I know, you are right,' she said, wringing her hands.

'But it wasn't as if I planned any of it!' She looked up at him with pleading eyes. 'I just took the only step I thought I could, to begin with. And then one that seemed frugal. And then one more that I thought wouldn't do anyone any harm. And then before I knew where I was, I was stuck. Trapped. Do you think,' she half-sobbed, 'do you really think I would still be here in London, if I had any other choice? Do you think I want to make people speculate about whether I am a foreign princess or not? Do you think I enjoy wearing this…this stupid wig?'

With that, she reached up, pulled out half-a-dozen pins and wrenched the elaborate wig from her head. She flung it away with such force that it flew across the room, slid across the polished floor and ended up wrapped round the leg of a table, looking for all the world like a cat run over by a brewer's dray.

'There!' She lifted her head, for the first time since she'd come in, and looked him straight in the face. 'I'm sick of all the pretence. I just want to be me again. Here I stand, unmasked. Or unwigged, at any rate. At your mercy. Do your worst. I don't care any more.'

And having said she didn't care, she proved the exact opposite by bursting into tears.

Peter stood still for a moment, reeling from the perverse reaction he was experiencing. Far from feeling triumph at his complete victory, what he wanted to do more than anything was to go over to her and pull her into his arms, and tell her that she needn't cry. That it was all over. That he would never hurt as much as a hair on her head. What hair she had left, that was. It had been cut short, criminally short, so that the wig would fit close to her skull, he supposed, and look as natural as possible.

Though it didn't detract from her beauty. It framed her little face, making her look…no, he wouldn't conjure up similes of elves or fairy creatures! She was a woman. Just a woman. A woman who'd led him a merry dance and…

'What do you mean,' he said, as one of the things she'd said came back to him with some force, 'you have no choice?'

'That I have no choice, you…idiot man,' she retorted. 'What else should I mean?'

Her defiant rejoinder made him want to laugh. Snapped the mood that had held him fast while he fought the urge to go and comfort her, leaving him free to stroll to the nearest sofa and sit down, as though he wasn't so moved that he scarcely knew himself.

'Explain,' he said, leaning back and crossing his legs as though he hadn't a care in the world, but was merely curious about her own state of mind. Although it was as plain as the tear tracks streaking her anguished little face.

She made a frustrated noise and raised her hands to about elbow height. 'Why should I?'

'Because it will affect how I deal with you, from now on.'

She sighed. Bowed her head. Opened her reticule, which hung by its strings from her wrist, took out a handkerchief and blew her nose. 'I… I suppose I do owe you an explanation for the way I ran away, that night,' she said. 'Without leaving a note. I thought that if I stopped long enough to write one, my opportunity to escape would pass. I had to get out before it grew too dark to see where I was going, you know. And also I thought nobody would notice me leaving while you and Lady Bradbury were at dinner.'

'They didn't,' he said as she tucked her handkerchief away and lifted her head to look at him as though awaiting his verdict on her plea for clemency. 'They didn't notice you'd gone until the next morning, when some maid or other went to collect your dinner tray and found it untouched.'

'I didn't intend to worry anyone. Indeed, I didn't think anyone would care all that much.' She tipped her head to one side, a frown pleating her brows as she added, 'I certainly never thought you'd come looking for me.'

'You didn't think the fact that you'd set out on foot, in vile weather, would make any of us wonder if you'd met with some accident?'

'I would wager Lady Bradbury never turned a hair. She probably shrugged and said good riddance, or something of the sort.'

She had said something of the sort. And the fact that Miss Mitcham was correct about that didn't do anything to improve his mood.

'And you thought I would do the same?'

'Well, you'd never given me any indication that you cared tuppence about me.'

What? 'I asked you to marry me.'

'Only to annoy Lady Bradbury,' she reminded him. Funny how he'd forgotten that.

'Besides,' she continued, 'you were planning to treat me like a mistress and abandon me after a month or two. That,' she said with a militant lift to her chin, 'is not, to my mind, an indication that you had any concern for me beyond your own convenience.'

She was correct again, damn her. At that point, he hadn't cared all that much. It had only been when she'd apparently disappeared off the face of the earth that he'd grown a conscience. As well as discovering just how much he really *did* care.

He shifted in his seat. It was time to change the flow of this conversation back to her actions. Make her explain herself, rather than make him rake over his own part in things.

'That was the step you felt you had no choice but to make? To leave while you could? Did you think I would keep you prisoner? Is that what you thought of me?'

'No! It wasn't like that. I have never been any good at…at arguing my case. With anyone. Nobody seems to believe that I mean what I say and I don't have the courage to stand my ground.'

'I am not a bully!' He *wasn't.*

'No,' she said, ignoring the way he'd deliberately hovered wherever she went lately, watching her, letting her know he could step in and expose her at any moment. 'It was more that I was afraid that if you kissed me again, I'd lose all sense of self-preservation and crumble…'

Well, that made him feel a lot better. She wasn't immune to him. The reverse, in fact.

He spread his arms along the back of the sofa, suddenly picturing himself as a pasha in some far eastern country, and her as a girl from the harem, hoping he would make her his favourite.

'And I did mean to write once I'd got to where I was planning to go, truly I did, only I never got there,' she put in, shattering his erotic fantasy of her dropping to her knees and offering to pleasure him.

'Where, as a matter of interest—' and since they were discussing real life, and real choices, not fantasies '—did you plan to go?'

'To my uncle's, in Suffolk.'

About as far away from a harem as a woman could get. 'And why did you not go there?'

'Well, first of all, the Duchess offered me a lift in her carriage as thanks for helping her find the way when her coachman got lost in the fog.'

Ah. So that was the decision she'd made out of frugality.

'She invited me to stay in London for a while, until the weather picked up, because it really was an awful time to be on the roads. Then, well, he just never answered any of my letters.'

A prickle of foreboding ran down his spine. 'Any of your letters? You wrote to him more than once?'

'Yes. And at first I thought I hadn't heard from him because of the weather. Well, the papers were full of accidents to mail coaches and the like. Then I thought that he must be too busy to want to bother with me...'

'Before we continue with your uncle in Suffolk,' he said, his mind racing, 'would you mind explaining why you are posing as a foreign princess if it isn't what you want? No, wait,' he said, holding up one hand to still her. 'It is obvious. The Duchess put you up to it for some twisted reason of her own. And this, I take it, is an example of what happens when you speak your mind, but nobody believes you mean it and they override your better judgement.'

She nodded, dumbly. And something about the way she was standing put him in mind of the way Lady Bradbury had treated her. The way she'd accepted it as a matter of course. Which led him to recall the way he'd sneered at her when she'd told him what she wanted from marriage and why he wasn't it. Which reminded him that his victory was only partial. She'd given him no sign that she'd changed her mind about marrying him. If he asked her now, the answer would still be the same.

But then he no longer wanted to marry her.

He didn't. What kind of man would keep on wanting a woman who'd made her revulsion for him perfectly plain? A man with no pride was who.

Anyway, she had such a knack for falling into scrapes that he'd probably have spent the rest of his life rescuing her from the results of her folly. He'd never have had a minute's peace. She'd have been tiresome. Troublesome.

'What you really want, anyway,' he said, the moment he'd run through the list of all the reasons why he shouldn't want to marry her, 'is to go to your uncle's?'

She nodded again. And sucked her lower lip into her mouth and started chewing on it.

It was funny, how now she was totally at his mercy, he no longer wanted to destroy her. But then he had no need to make her pay for what she'd done. Because she was so miserable that providence, or some form of divine justice, whatever you wanted to call it, had clearly been punishing her already. She'd been looking more and more drawn by the day. And hunted. Which was one of the reasons why he'd decided to bring things to a head tonight. She hadn't looked as if she could take much more.

Also, now that his anger had cooled to the point where he could see why she'd done what she'd done, it was plain that she'd never meant to act so badly. She'd taken one misstep, then another, and ended up very far from where she'd intended to go. Where she would definitely not have gone without the influence of the Duchess. The damned Duchess.

'Has it never occurred to you,' he said with a touch of impatience, 'that the chances of two letters going astray is extremely improbable?'

'Well, the weather, you know,' she said, spreading her hands.

'The weather has improved during the last couple of weeks. Have you written since the roads have cleared?'

She nodded.

'And you handed those letters to the Duchess, no doubt, or her servants?'

She nodded again.

'I doubt,' he said, 'that any of them got further than the kitchen fire.'

She began to shake her head. 'She wouldn't…she has been very kind to me…she…'

He laughed derisively. 'She has practically kidnapped you. Oh, she may have put you in a gilded cage, but it is a cage none the less. She is using you, if I am not very much mistaken, in her ongoing feud with her stepson.'

She shook her head. 'She wouldn't,' she said, but with far less conviction than before.

'Let's put it to the test, shall we? Why don't you write your uncle another letter, and give it to me to frank for you? And give your return address as mine. He's not going to know that the kind friend with whom you are staying in London lives in Grosvenor Square rather than Albemarle Street, is he?'

She lifted her chin. 'Fine. I shall do that.' She looked round the room as though searching for paper and pen, then began pulling at drawers in tables, with increasing desperation.

'There is no need to write it this minute,' he said, going to the remains of her wig, and picking it up.

'Yes, there is,' she said angrily. 'The Duchess would never do anything so…despicable.'

'You always did have a foolish habit of looking for good in everyone, didn't you?' he mused, going to sit on the sofa again so that he could tidy up the mess of hair that had once been a very expensive wig.

'Because there *is* good in everyone,' she insisted, stomping across the room to rummage through the drawers in the last remaining desk.

'Even me?' he couldn't help asking.

She whirled back to him. Planted her fists on her hips. Glared at him. Noted the way he was trying to mend her disguise. And all the anger leached out of her like water from a sieve.

'Yes,' she conceded. 'You worried about me. Came looking for me. And now you are forcing me to face up to the truth about the Duchess. But in such a way that you are also providing me a means of escape. When you could be…' She sucked her lower lip into her mouth again.

Yes, he could be coercing her into the only kind of relationship he ever really had with a female. Something transitory. Something played out entirely on his terms. He could make it a condition of franking the letter. Instead of which, he was going to help her escape. Both the Duchess and himself.

Because she deserved better. She deserved a man who could be all those things she'd said she wanted from a husband. A man who could both feel and inspire love. A man who sounded like the complete opposite of him.

He sighed. Got to his feet. Held out the wig. 'Here. You had better put this back on, I suppose.'

'Thank you,' she breathed and came over to take it from him. She put it on her head. 'Is it straight? Is there a mirror where I can check?'

'This is a library,' he pointed out. 'Why should there be a mirror?'

She patted at the wig with frantic hands, her forehead creased with anxiety.

'Oh, for goodness sake, woman,' he said, taking her hands and pushing them away from her head. 'You are making it worse. Allow me. Although,' he couldn't resist pointing out when she meekly submitted to his ministrations, 'I know far more about disarranging a lady's hair than arranging it.' He couldn't help thinking about bedroom hair when she stood this close to him, allowing him to touch her head, her neck, her ears, when all the while he was breathing in the delicate floral scent that hadn't changed. That reminded him of the way she'd gone up in flames the last time they'd been standing this close.

She gave a disdainful sniff, which shattered the sensual mood.

'My, my, what a little puritan you are.' He tweaked at a curl. Tucked a strand of hair that had come loose into one of the little pearl ornaments that glowed between the artificial curls. 'Just for that, I am going to demand you pay a forfeit.'

She darted an anxious glance up at him. 'What do you mean?'

'You know what I mean,' he said, taking her by the shoulders and turning her to face him. 'You must kiss me.'

Her breath hitched. Her pupils dilated. A blush stole across her cheeks.

'Or…or what?' Her voice was breathy. 'What will you do?'

'I will… I will confiscate this wig and oblige you to face the world as Miss Mitcham. It is what I should have done in the first place, isn't it, rather than allowing you to continue playing the Duchess's game?'

'Perhaps it is what I want you to do,' she said. 'It is what I ought to want you to do, isn't it? To face up to what I've done. And accept the punishment.'

'Yes, but my punishment will hurt you far less, don't you think?' Besides, she wanted an excuse to kiss him. It was written all over her expressive little face.

'Very well,' she said, lifting her chin and gazing straight into his eyes. 'You give me no option.'

Chapter Seventeen

Her heart beating wildly, she reached up, took his face between her hands, pulled him down to her and placed her lips against his. He had given her no choice, she told herself as her fingers slid round to the back of his neck and flirted with the soft curls at his nape.

But thoughts about choice and virtue, and hypocrisy all flew from her mind like so many startled pigeons taking flight when he put one arm round her waist, angled his head to the side and took charge of the kiss. All she could do was hang on. Like a hoyden clinging to a runaway horse. It was exhilarating. Scary. Wonderful! Just like before.

But didn't last anything like long enough.

No. It had lasted quite long enough. In fact, it was a good job he'd had the sense to end it. If they'd carried on devouring each other's mouths like that, who knew where it would have ended? On that sofa over there? On the rug?

She stood for a moment, just staring into his hard, handsome face, wondering how long it would take to get her breath back, wishing she had the courage to leap up at his face and snatch another kiss.

Wondering, if the Duke had a preference for a certain type of woman, if all men did. And if so, what was Lord Lavenham's type?

Variety, she suddenly remembered. He'd warned her, while making his proposal, that he wouldn't be satisfied with one particular woman for very long. And, just as if he was remembering that fact, he began backing away. Not only physically, putting a slight distance between them, but emotionally, too. The fire that had been blazing in his eyes while they kissed was dying. His expression was cooling. Turning cynical.

She could see what he was thinking. That she was a little hypocrite. And she was. That was why she'd run from him in the first place. Because with one kiss, he could overturn all her long-held beliefs about marrying for love. He was just so…so…irresistible! Still. She had learned nothing. After all this time, nothing had changed. She still wanted him. Even though what he could offer her was far from what she'd been brought up to believe was what she ought to want.

No, wait, that wasn't right. He *wasn't* what she actually wanted. She didn't want a husband who would discard her when he grew bored and sought variety with other women. She wanted a solid, dependable…

Oh, why did such a decent, good man sound so boring?

'You had better return to the card room,' he said, putting another step between them when all she was able to do was stand there, gazing up at him like a child with her nose pressed to the sweet shop window. 'Before anyone notices you are missing.'

Yes. She should. Shouldn't she?

When she remained standing exactly where she was, he took her by the shoulders. But instead of resuming the kiss, he disappointed her by turning her round and thrusting her in the direction of the door.

No, she wasn't disappointed. He was doing the right thing. If he'd kissed her again…

With a sigh of resignation, she opened the door herself, stepped through it and back into the world of polite, sensible, behaviour.

She was sure that people would notice that she was still thrumming all over from the power of that kiss. That they'd take one look at her and be able to tell what she'd been doing. She certainly *felt* like a…hussy.

But nobody paid her the slightest bit of attention. The pile of coins in front of Herr Schnee had grown considerably. His face was flushed, as was that of the Duchess. And nobody else in the room did more than give her a cursory glance, and that only if she walked right by their table, before going back to their cards.

Nobody cared tuppence about her, or where she'd been, or what she'd been doing. Because she was of no consequence to anyone. Apart from Lord Lavenham, who was only intent upon…

She rubbed a little tense spot between her brows. It no longer felt as if he was intent upon revenge. Not after the way he'd offered to contact her uncle and set her free from the Duchess. Not after he'd stopped that kiss before it had gone too far, and sent her back to the relative safety of the card room. He was still angry with her, yes, but…

He'd also been worried about her. Had searched for her. She hugged that knowledge to herself the way a lonely child might cling to a rag doll. Because if not for that, she would feel as if nobody cared one way or the other.

Over the next few days, that feeling kept on growing. She'd already begun to suspect that the Duchess was more interested in using her to achieve her own aims than to really do her any good. Herr Schnee had always looked down his nose at her. And the Duke, she suspected, was biding his time before making up his mind about her one way or another. The staff at Theakstone House were all friendly, since she was helping the Duchess. But she was pretty certain that their friendliness would vanish if she fell out of favour with their mistress.

In fact, she didn't know why she kept on delaying writing the letter to her uncle, which Lord Lavenham had promised to frank for her. She was miserable in London, wasn't she? The fun of seeing the sights, and rubbing shoulders with famous people, as though she was their equal, had long since palled. Once the frost and snow melted away, the magic seemed to melt away with it, leaving grey streets and grey skies, and a grey, depressed feeling in her soul.

The only person who noticed that, beneath the calm, social smile she pasted to her face whenever she went out, she was utterly miserable, was Lord Lavenham. His eyebrows would rise. He would approach her. Ask her how she did. When she gave the expected, polite response that she was well, thank you, he would shake his head and frown.

'You are far from well,' he would say. 'This life is not for you.'

No. But even though she knew she wasn't cut out to live the way these titled, wealthy people did, she resented his implication that she'd be better off in an out-of-the-way town in Suffolk, with a country parson. Perhaps that was why she kept on putting off writing to Uncle Norman.

Or perhaps it was because he was forcing her to trust him with her future. Forcing her to face her stupidity in trusting the Duchess.

Or perhaps it was because, once this interlude ended, she would never see him again.

It was that last suspicion that made her sit down, one morning, and write the letter, telling her uncle that she'd left her post in the Cotswolds and that, though she was currently staying with a friend in London, she very much hoped that he would be willing to let her stay with him while she sought her next paid position.

Even when she had written it, it was several more days before she took the opportunity of passing it to him, one evening when they were promenading round the outskirts of a ballroom, after dancing together. And that was only after she'd given an exact copy to the Duchess, hoping that she could prove him wrong about her.

'About time,' he said, tucking his copy into an inner pocket of his jacket. 'I was beginning to think you had set your sights on the Duke, after all. And was wondering to what lengths I'd have to go to put a stop to it.'

'Don't be ridiculous,' she snapped. 'I couldn't marry him without telling him that I'm really only a paid companion. Which is, in effect, the position I'm occupying now, with the Duchess.'

'A position which requires you to wear a disguise?'

'Yes. That is one way of looking at it,' she said, seizing on the excuse to justify her behaviour. 'A companion has little freedom to be herself. She must do as she is bid, or face losing her post. I had to suppress a great deal of my personality when I worked for Lady Bradbury—'

'Is that what you tell yourself so that you can sleep at night? That you are merely doing as your employer bids you?'

'No.' She flinched. How was it that Lord Lavenham had become the voice of her conscience and she was the one justifying the way she was living, when, to start with, she'd been the one to look down her nose at his supposed lack of morals?

'And please believe me, I could never marry a man under false pretences. I'd have to tell him—'

But he snorted, cutting her off. 'Oh, yes. I know all about how blunt you can be when a man proposes to you. I can still recall the sanctimonious little speech you made about how two people ought to live together in companionship and harmony.'

'Well,' she said slowly, marvelling that he'd recalled her exact words. 'You should know then that there can be no harmony between a man who thinks his wife is a foreign princess and a woman who would have to put on her wig before she could risk her husband seeing her in the mornings.'

'What about at night? Good grief, you really have no idea how a married couple would carry on behind closed doors, do you? A wig wouldn't last five minutes in the marriage bed.'

She had a brief, but very vivid vision which comprised Lord Lavenham and a bed, and a lot of very energetic activity which would, without a doubt, cause a wig to tumble from its moorings. 'Well, there you are, then,' she said, wondering how she'd managed to keep track of the conversation, with that sort of thing going on in her head. 'I'd have to remove it. So, I couldn't marry him, could I?'

'And that is that the only reason you won't marry the Duke? Because you daren't take off your wig? You don't have any complaints about his morals? Or his inability to be your *friend*?' He said the word with a sneer.

'I know nothing about *his* morals,' she retorted.

'You knew nothing about mine, apart from what Lady Bradbury told you.'

'I soon learned about them when you spelled out what form you envisioned our marriage taking.'

By this time, they'd stopped walking and were facing each other so that they could argue more conveniently.

'Oh, how I wish I hadn't given you that letter,' Eleanor breathed.

'Why? So that you can prove that you can ensnare a duke?'

'I have no intention of ensnaring anyone,' she said,

barely resisting the urge to stamp her foot. 'I never have done. And I don't know why everyone thinks I'm the kind of woman who could.'

'You have no idea how beautiful you are, do you?' he said, taking the wind out of her sails and replacing the burn of anger with a flush of startled pleasure.

'At least, you were, before you started adopting this air of mystery,' he said, eyeing her elaborately curled and bejewelled wig with distaste. 'And wearing cosmetics. I liked the fresh innocence of Miss Mitcham,' he finished, cuttingly. 'I would have married her and been tolerably happy, I think, for a while. Miss White, on the other hand...' He looked her up and down, his upper lip curling. 'She is a complete fraud. The creation of a scheming, devious woman, with no backbone, no personality and no morals.'

It was true. That was what hurt so much. Not the knowledge that she'd given him a disgust of her. It was that Miss White was like a walking waxwork dummy. She had no conversation, since she daren't say anything that might make her too interesting and would therefore tempt people to become her friends. She could not make friends, since any relationship formed under these circumstances would be based on lies and subterfuge. She was, in any case, not going to be living in London, or in this social milieu, permanently. And now she didn't even have the respect of this man who...who...

Her eyes stinging, she turned and made her way back to the chaperons' bench, where the Duchess should have been sitting waiting for her. Only the Duchess was dancing a waltz with Herr Schnee, to the scandalised amusement of the rest of the matrons.

* * *

The never-ending social whirl kept on spinning Eleanor in its orbit as people began returning to London in greater numbers. The days grew longer and spring flowers began to poke their heads above the sooty soil in the parks and gardens. But no letter came from her uncle.

Not to the house in Grosvenor Square, anyway.

But at length, one night, Lord Lavenham approached her, to ask her to dance, with the light of what looked like triumph in his eyes. And Eleanor knew, even before he told her the news, that he had received a reply.

'I have the proof that the Duchess is using you. And that you owe her no loyalty for what she's done.'

In spite of already knowing it, deep down, Eleanor's heart sank.

'You have received a letter from my uncle.'

He nodded.

'May I see it?'

A feral smile pulled his lips into a tight curve. 'Of course you may see it. Whenever,' he leaned in closer to murmur the rest of his words into her ear, 'you come to my house to collect it.'

She glanced up at him in alarm. 'How could I possibly come to your house? Single women simply do not go to the houses of men to whom they are not related. I would risk being ruined.'

She couldn't even take a maid with her, if she did go, to lend the appearance of respectability, because all the maids were loyal to the Duchess and would be sure to tell her. And since the whole point of going was to collect a letter that would prove the Duchess had lied to her and kept on lying to her, right from the start, she had to keep the errand secret.

But she really wanted to learn what her uncle had to say. She really, really hoped he was going to have written that she could go to him and stay with him. That he'd give her a way to get away from the Duchess and Lord Lavenham, and Herr Schnee, and the whole intolerable mess of lies and deception.

Which meant she'd have to visit him, alone, and risk her reputation.

Or rather, she saw on a sudden wave of relief, the reputation of Miss White, who didn't really exist. Even so…

'It won't be easy to slip away unnoticed…'

'It shouldn't be beyond the means of a woman so steeped in subterfuge,' he said nastily, 'to fabricate some excuse.'

And that was that. Her last hope died. A hope she hadn't even realised, until he snuffed it out, had still been flickering. The hope that even after everything, he still liked her. That he was on her side.

But he didn't. He wasn't. For he would never have spoken to her like that in the old days at Chervil House. He had always treated her with respect back then. Had behaved as though he was an ally against Lady Bradbury.

By falling in with the Duchess, she'd ruined everything. To think she might have been his wife…

But, no. The proposal he'd made had been impossible for her to accept. It was all over between them. Had been over from the moment she'd walked out of Chervil House. Their next meeting would merely be the final scene before the curtain came down on what had been a very sorry, rather silly sort of drama.

'Very well,' she said, lifting her chin, for she refused to let him see how badly he'd hurt her, with a few curt words, spoken in that abrupt way. 'I will call on you tomorrow.'

Chapter Eighteen

Eleanor hadn't been able to think up a good excuse for leaving the house without a maid or footman, so she decided to slip out through the back garden while everyone was at breakfast.

Her heart pounded as she put on the bulky coat she'd worn when she'd escaped from Chervil House. Though she wasn't sure if it was because she was afraid someone might discover her trying to sneak out of the house, or what would happen if she succeeded.

Fortunately it was one of those chilly spring mornings which meant it was perfectly plausible she should wish to wind a thick scarf round the lower part of her face. And it was so early that the only people about on the streets were the more ordinary sort. People who were too busy going about their business to pay attention to one more lone woman in a shabby coat. People who weren't likely to be interested in her, or in a position to report back to the Duchess that they'd seen her, if they did recognise her in spite of her precautions, where she shouldn't be.

* * *

Nobody noticed her leaving and nobody challenged her on the street, which meant that in just under a quarter of an hour she was approaching Lord Lavenham's residence in Albemarle Street. She mounted the steps quickly, rapped on the door and waited, breathing rapidly from the exertion of walking here as fast as she could, with her head down, in order to avoid detection.

And waited. And waited. Outside the house of a known bachelor. A bachelor with a reputation for being a rake, what was more. By the time she heard the steps of a servant approaching the door to let her in, she was hopping from one foot to the other.

Had he made her wait on purpose to humiliate her?

The servant, a perfectly respectable-looking butler, raised his eyebrows when he opened the door and enquired what her business might be. Just as though she had no business visiting his master during the hours of daylight. Just as though Lord Lavenham had never had a visit from a lone female before.

'His lordship commanded my presence here,' she told the servant and felt her cheeks heat as his eyebrows rose even further. But he stepped to one side and indicated she might go in. She was so relieved to be off the street and out of sight she didn't bother to remonstrate with him. Besides, it wasn't his fault his master was…luring women into his house in broad daylight.

The servant led her into a cosy little room at the back of the house, where there was a fire blazing in the grate.

'Please make yourself comfortable, Miss…'

'White,' she replied, after a moment's hesitation. If Lord Lavenham's servants gossiped, and news of this escapade got out, it would be Miss White's reputation that would suffer, not her own. She shook her head as she sank down on to one of the chairs set before the fire. How had she reached the point where she could think of herself as two separate people? Or as Miss White as someone other than herself?

The Duchess, that was how. She wasn't as much a… person as a force of nature, sweeping lesser mortals before her will like so many autumn leaves. Scattering their wits in the process.

Eleanor leaped to her feet, her heart beating wildly, as the door opened again.

Only it was not Lord Lavenham, but a younger male servant, carrying a tray bearing a teapot, a cup, milk jug and so on.

'Thank you,' she said as he set it down on a conveniently positioned table. 'A cup of hot tea is just what I need.' Both to settle her nerves and to warm her. Her hand, she noted as she poured some tea, was trembling. Which was infuriating.

By the time the door opened again, and Lord Lavenham strode in as though he'd hurried to get there from somewhere a touch more important, she'd drunk three cups of tea, eaten a whole plateful of biscuits and plotted all sorts of ways she could humiliate him in return for putting her through this ordeal by tea tray. Including a particularly satisfying vision of training a herd of mice to eat their way through his entire wardrobe of clothing so that he'd have to go about Town in rags.

Unaware of the fate she'd planned for his clothes, he tossed a letter on to the tea tray in front of her as though throwing down a challenge. She stopped thinking about which cheesemongers she could buy the necessary bait to train those mice with the moment she recognised her uncle's distinctive, somewhat impatient handwriting. She pounced on the letter, broke the wafer and read the single, cramped page of writing swiftly. Then went to the head of the page and started again.

'Well?'

She looked up to see Lord Lavenham standing with one shoulder propped against the end of the mantelpiece, his arms folded across his chest, watching her with a grimly mocking expression on his handsome face.

'My uncle writes,' she said, with a sinking feeling, 'that he would be glad of a visit from me, as his wife is expecting again and she is somewhat overwhelmed with parish duties, particularly since Easter is just around the corner. He further says that they would both welcome my help and hope that I may consider waiting until the baby is born before starting to seek another position.'

What he hadn't done was ask why she'd sent him two letters from different addresses. Or explained why he hadn't answered any of her earlier ones. Instead—although she wasn't going to tell Lord Lavenham—he'd said he was glad she'd written as it had been such a long time since they'd heard from her and they were beginning to wonder if she'd been ill.

Which meant that the Duchess hadn't posted a single one of the letters she'd written. Not to her Uncle Norman or any other of her relatives.

Which made her feel a bit...sick. And stupid, for

not seeing what Lord Lavenham had seen from the outset: that the Duchess did not regard her as a friend, but as a tool she could employ to further her feud with her stepson.

She let the letter fall to her lap.

'So, you are going off to become a kind of serf to a parish priest's wife now, are you?'

'What?' She blinked up at him, puzzled by the anger she could hear in his voice. Shouldn't he be…triumphant? After all, he'd just proved he'd been right about the Duchess. That she'd been a gullible fool. But if he wasn't going to crow, she wasn't about to bring it up.

'Why should I not help my aunt by marriage, since she is going to give me house room?'

'Good God! You are still determined to ascribe decent motives to people, when all they wish to do is make use of you. Have you learned nothing?'

Apparently not. She hung her head.

'In fact,' he went on, 'the only person you make an exception for is me, isn't it?'

'Well,' she flashed back at him, since he'd touched a raw nerve, 'that is because your motives are never decent.'

'Typical!' He pushed himself away from the mantelpiece and strode over to stand right in front of her, forcing her to tilt her head back at an extremely awkward angle to look into his face. 'I got the letter for you, didn't I? With no ulterior motive?'

'Oh, no, you didn't! You wanted to prove the Duchess untrustworthy. And find some pretext for getting me to your house alone. So that you could…' She faltered to a halt as a wild look came over him.

'So I could what? Ravish you, is that what you were going to say?'

'No... I...'

'No. Because I have never taken a woman against her will. Believe that of me if you will believe nothing else, because I have never had any need.'

She gasped at the implication that he wouldn't need to use any force to get her to bend to his will. 'You are so...arrogant...'

'Realistic, you mean. I could even have you panting for me, if I wanted.'

If he wanted? Was he implying that he didn't want to...seduce her? But then she'd behaved so stupidly, blindly falling for the Duchess's wiles, and so badly, by leaving her post without an explanation, letting everyone worry about her, and then by getting involved in a scheme to persuade the *ton* that she was a foreign princess, that it wouldn't be surprising if he felt nothing for her now but disgust.

'Think what you like,' she cried, leaping to her feet, since she couldn't bear the way he was, literally, looking down his nose at her. 'Your...your moral code is so twisted that I...' She swallowed. 'You are the kind of man who thinks it is acceptable to behave however you wish, while expecting your wife, or any woman worthy of marrying you, to be a paragon of virtue... well, anyway, I don't care.' She tossed her head. 'I am now impervious to your dubious charms.'

'Haven't you learned yet that I can always tell when you are lying? Your whole body gives it away, even as your mouth breathes out the falsehood.'

'I am not lying...'

'Yes, you are. And I can easily prove it. If I were to take you in my arms, right now, and kiss you, within two seconds you would be on fire for me. Begging me to take you. Right there...' he turned and pointed to the hearthrug '...on that bit of carpet.'

Chapter Nineteen

He'd tried to pay attention to his better self. But his better self was still young and weak, and no match for the adult male who wanted what he wanted.

For weeks he'd been watching her attend events on the arm of the Duke of Theakstone. And go home with the Duke of Theakstone. The Duke was so attentive to her comfort, placing shawls round her shoulders, or handing her into or out of a coach, and the Duchess was looking so increasingly triumphant when she watched the way the pair of them were together that it had started to eat away at him. Some evenings it had been all he could do not to plant the fellow a facer, grab her and pull her away from the pair of them, and declare that she was *his*. That she'd been his before she'd ever met either of them.

And now she was standing there, practically daring him to do his worst, telling him she was impervious to his charms, when he already knew that he had only to kiss her and she'd go up in flames.

So naturally he thrust the better part of himself

aside, hauled her into his arms and proved her a liar. She didn't even pretend to struggle. The moment he set his mouth upon hers, she flung her arms about his neck and kissed him back for all she was worth.

Just what had she been trying to prove, anyway, by saying he couldn't move her? It was the Duke who couldn't move her. She barely glanced at the Duke when they were together, although she couldn't stop darting him greedy little glances. And those shy, guilty little glances acted as powerfully upon him as the most practised caresses of his more experienced lovers.

Just as her moan, and the way she pressed up against him now, was far more exciting than any sound he'd ever heard any other woman make. It made him feel like a conqueror because he knew she'd been trying to fight her attraction for him. Had denied it, run away from it, lied about it. But she wasn't fighting any longer.

She was his.

He could push her down on to that hearthrug he'd just threatened her with and claim her irrevocably.

Only then it would all be over. And he needed to savour this moment of triumph. So he broke off the kiss, to trail open-mouthed kisses along her neck. She moaned again and shivered, her eyes rolling shut.

'I hate you…' she whimpered.

'No, you don't,' he breathed into her ear, nipping at the lobe. 'You only hate the fact that I'm right about you. And yourself, perhaps, for not being able to resist me, in spite of your proud words.'

'And because you are only doing this,' she said as he deftly undid the top few buttons holding the back of her gown together, 'to make a point.'

'Is that so?' He pushed the top of her dress down her arms, so that he could nip at the sensitive point between shoulder and neck. She gasped and shuddered, and plunged her fingers into his hair, holding him to her, not even protesting when he moved from that relatively innocent spot to the valley between her breasts.

'Oh! Oh...'

'Much more of this,' he said, dipping one hand into her bodice and tweaking at a nipple that was already hard, 'and you will be *begging* me to take you to bed.'

'No...no, I wouldn't...' she protested weakly, but she didn't stop twining her fingers in his hair.

'Still lying.' He chuckled. 'To the bitter end.'

He pulled back so that he could look down into her passion-glazed eyes and an outrageous solution occurred to him. 'Do you know, it would solve the dilemma for both of us,' he said, glancing down at the way their bodies were straining together, 'if you were to become my mistress. Then we could slake this madness that is raging between us.' He backed her to the couch since, even though he'd threatened her with the hearthrug, he wasn't so lost to lust that he'd take her for the first time on the floor. 'Get it out of our blood.' Sat down and drew her on to his lap. 'Then, when we tire of each other, which we certainly will since we agree upon practically nothing, we can go our separate ways.'

Yes, yes, that was a far better idea than marriage had been. Neither of them would end up hurt if they both just admitted they wanted each other, in spite of their opposing views on just about everything else.

Everything else? No, part of him began to remind

him of the connection he'd so often felt during all those conversations at Chervil House.

He told that part of himself to hold its tongue. It helped that she shifted on his lap just then, bringing his mind right back to the here and now. Lord, but her bottom felt good upon his thighs. He ran his hand up the curve of her back. She was clinging to his shoulders. 'No legal bonds tying us to each other for life to make us miserable. To make us hate each other…'

She started shaking her head. 'No. I don't want that.'

'You *do* want me, though. Don't keep denying it. You are burning for me. And you would enjoy being my mistress. I guarantee it,' he growled, nipping at the spot just below her earlobe, where he'd already learned she was as vulnerable as just about every other woman he'd ever bedded. 'I shall shower you with jewels and pretty clothes', since she looked so gorgeous in the silks and satins she'd been wearing lately. 'Buy you your own carriage and horses, if you want them', since that was what most men said their mistresses all seemed to want. 'Once you've let go of your foolish, prudish principles…'

'I would hate myself,' she whimpered and somehow managed to wriggle off his lap and land on the sofa next to him, even though he still had his arms round her. 'You are right that I would enjoy…this aspect of things,' she said, running her hand down the front of his chest. Making him harder than ever with her innocent, ignorant little gesture. 'It is so…strong, you are correct about that. I admit it,' she said, as though tossing him a bone. 'But it would be going against everything I believe in. I'd have to abandon every principle by which I live. And what's more, I think you've forgotten that it would go against your own principles, too.'

'What?' She thought he had *principles*? Didn't she know him at all?

'You told me once,' she said, 'that you don't seduce innocents. What would this be but the seduction of an innocent? You would hate yourself after for giving in to what you clearly think is a weakness. And I would hate myself, too.' Her eyes welled up. 'It would make us just as miserable as you predict marriage would.'

He didn't know if it was the tears, or the fact that she was correct, that made him freeze.

'Don't do this, Peter,' she pleaded. 'Even though you could.'

Perhaps he should regard that last statement as the only victory he would ever gain over this woman. It could be the only thing, in years to come, that would give him any satisfaction whatsoever. Because she was right. He would hate himself if he debauched her, even though she'd just admitted that he could. Easily.

'You are the only woman,' he said through gritted teeth, 'who could use such an argument against me, at such a moment.' Before he gave in to the worst part of his nature. That part that he was beginning to despise. 'And be correct.' How had she managed to remember what he'd said, all those weeks ago, and pluck just exactly the words she needed to stop him dead? 'Because you know me better than anyone else has ever done', that was how. 'Better than I knew myself.' He buried his face in her neck, one last time. He wrapped his arms round her, as though he'd never release her, while the better part of himself, the part to which she'd called, urged him to let go.

But this was everything he wanted. Within his grasp. He had only to take what she would not refuse…

But in the taking, he would destroy her innocence. Rob her of her integrity, which would, in turn, mark him. The way his fingers were stained whenever he carelessly plucked a ripe blackberry from the stem, crushing it between his fingers before he could get it to his mouth. And, just as blackberry juice was hard to remove from his fingers, he had a feeling that if he pushed on with her now, if he listened to the clamour of his body rather than the warning voice of his conscience, he would never be able to scour the stain from his soul.

He breathed in deeply, inhaling her essence one last time, before forcing himself to move away.

'Turn round,' he commanded her. 'Quickly.' While he still had the strength to do the right thing.

She presented her back to him and he rapidly did up the buttons with fingers that were shaking. Fingers that wanted to be doing wicked things to her body. Then he got up, strode to the fireplace and stood with his back to her so that she could finish straightening her clothes.

'So,' she ventured in a timid voice, when he continued standing with his back to her, gazing into the flames, clenching and unclenching his fists as he saw how very nearly he'd come to the brink of disaster. 'What happens now?'

'Now?' He turned to look down at her. She was gazing up at him the way a rabbit would look at a fox. All wide-eyed as she waited for him to pounce. Because he'd all but destroyed her trust in him. She'd made a valiant speech and tugged at his newly born conscience, but she wasn't sure how effective her words had been.

'Now,' he said with a good deal of resentment, 'I shall escort you back to Grosvenor Square, like the gentleman you want me to be. Then,' he said, looking at the letter that lay on the tea table, 'we will confront the Duchess about that.'

'Oh, dear.' Her hand flew to her stomach. 'Must we? I mean, yes, of course I must...leave now that I... only...' She drew back her shoulders. 'There is no need for you to come with me. I don't need you to stand up for me. Now that I know the truth, I can face her.'

'I have no doubt that you can,' he said with perfect sincerity, since she'd just stood up to him and prevented them from taking a step they would have regretted. Which was something she'd been too timid to do last time.

She'd grown up, during this time in London. She was no longer a girl with no confidence. She was a woman who knew her own mind. A woman worthy of respect. A woman he would be proud to call his Countess, if she'd have him.

But she wouldn't.

Nevertheless he wasn't going to abandon her at a point where she might need support more than she'd ever needed it before. The Duchess was the kind of woman who'd stop at nothing to get her own way. And he had to make sure Eleanor escaped her influence, once and for all.

'But you don't have to do it alone.'

A frown flitted across her face.

'But you...' She glanced guiltily at the couch. 'I wouldn't let you...'

'You didn't behave like a whore, you mean? You didn't pay me with your body? So now you think I will not do anything for you, is that it?'

'No, I—'

'Spare me from any more lies, Eleanor. You are determined to think the worst of me.'

'No!' She took a pace in his direction. 'I know you are not...that is, I could not have talked you out of... of...' She gestured to the couch, completely unable to use the words for what would have happened on it, if she'd not appealed to his sense of honour. 'If you were truly a rake, nothing would have stopped you. You wouldn't have cared for anything but your own pleasure. Only, you must be so...disappointed in me.' She clasped her hands at her waist and hung her head. 'Disillusioned. So... I don't think it is fair to expect you to do anything more for me, when I've caused you enough...pain as it is.'

'Just let go of your...stubborn independence, for once, and let me...' He turned away from her, his temper fraying. She didn't want him to be her friend. Hell, he didn't want to be her friend. He wanted...

He strode to the bell pull and tugged on it. He wanted his butler to bring her coat and gloves, get her out of his house and out of London, and see her safely into the depths of the countryside. Somewhere so far away, and so inaccessible, that she would never be able to disturb his sleep again.

Chapter Twenty

It was just typical that the first time she'd ever managed to get someone to listen to what she thought, to take her feelings into consideration and alter their own behaviour accordingly, Eleanor wasn't totally sure it was truly a victory.

No, that wasn't right. Of course it was a victory. She didn't want to join the ranks of fallen women, did she? Her parents hadn't brought her up to sacrifice her principles for a moment's pleasure, had they?

But oh, what pleasure it would have been. She glanced up at his rigid profile as he walked alongside her. Then down at where her gloved hand rested upon his sleeve. His arms had felt so…strong, banded round her at the last minute. As if he'd never let her go. But he had. And now all she had of him was this tiny patch. A few square inches of coat sleeve.

When she could have had so much more. Oh, not marriage. Not any longer. He'd downgraded his offer to that of mistress this time because he'd got to know her much better and found that, far from being honest and intelligent she was so silly she'd ended up living a lie. But then hadn't she always known his interest in her, and especially his proposal, was too good to be true?

The grey skies she could see above the sooty roofs perfectly matched her mood. He'd only ever considered her fit to warm his bed for a short while, but at least, to start with, he'd respected her enough to offer to legitimise the relationship with a wedding ring.

Even just now he hadn't pressed his advantage, when he could so easily have done. She sighed. He'd been right about her. She couldn't have resisted him for much longer. And it wasn't just because he was so handsome. She'd always...*liked* him. Shared his sense of humour. Enjoyed playing cards with him, or conversing, in the days before Lady Bradbury had forbidden it. During the time they'd spent in London, she hadn't stopped liking him, even though he'd been trying to make her believe he was going to wreak vengeance on her. Because she'd always known, deep down, that he was a man of honour at heart. Oh, his sense of honour wasn't the same as hers. But he had an ingrained sense of fair play and honesty. The same honesty that had made him speak so bluntly about the way he intended to behave during their marriage, had she accepted. A different sort of man would have had no qualms about deceiving her. Pretending he'd be a conventional husband. But, no. That wasn't his way.

His way was not how she'd thought a husband should behave when he'd proposed, that was true. But he would never have treated her the way General Cormscroft had treated his wife, not in public. She could tell from the way his nostrils had flared with disdain each time the

General had bullied and belittled the poor woman. No, his solution had been to suggest they live separate lives before animosity tempted him to behave so poorly. In his own mind he'd probably thought of that as a kindness. Thought he would hurt her less if he carried on his affaires out of her sight, too.

She shivered.

'Not far now and you will be out of the cold,' said Lord Lavenham, misinterpreting her reason for her shiver. 'You will also be rid of me,' he added bitterly. 'For good.'

She gripped his arm a bit tighter. Now that she'd persuaded him to leave her alone, she was no longer sure she wanted to be rid of him. Her body certainly didn't. On the contrary, it felt cheated. Her knees were still a bit...*distracted*, while other parts of her were positively humming, burning still. How on earth she'd found the strength to stop him from getting his revenge on her by seducing her, she didn't know.

Yes, she did, though. It was because he was only doing it to prove a point. To...humble her. By demonstrating that he had the power to take her, without benefit of clergy. That he didn't think of her as wife material any longer. When she...she...oh, if only he'd proposed to her again! Or if only she had the courage to suggest...to admit that perhaps she'd been too hasty...

But there was no time to marshal her arguments. They were rounding the corner of Grosvenor Square. She'd never be able to persuade him to change his mind about her between this lamp post and the front steps. She'd left it too late.

Perhaps it was for the best. She'd only have made a

fool of herself if she'd admitted that, well, if he weren't so cynical about marriage, or if he would ever allow himself to feel anything so emotional as love for his wife, that she…

If, if, if. What was the point of dwelling on possibilities? What was the point of considering what kind of husband he might have been? He'd made it quite clear he didn't regard her as worthy of marriage any longer. It was over between them. She'd destroyed whatever he'd felt for her. Apart from the physical attraction, that was. And that would fade. On his part, that was. For she didn't think she'd ever meet another man who'd be able to make her heart leap the way it did whenever he walked into the room. Or who could make her so lost to all sense of propriety that she'd let him undo her gown, in broad daylight, and make love to her on a drawing-room floor.

They reached the front steps. She braced herself lest he bid her farewell curtly before turning and walking away. She would not cry. She must not cry. She didn't want his last memory of her to be of snivelling, abject misery.

For it would be the last time they saw each other. He'd made it obvious he couldn't wait to be rid of her. He'd been grim-faced and silent all the way, apart from that one statement about *her* being rid of *him* when he'd really meant the reverse.

She sucked in a ragged breath as the door swung open.

Don't cry. Don't break down. Not until you reach the privacy of your own room...

'Good morning, my lord,' said Dawes, with a smile. 'And Miss White. I was wondering where you were.'

'I... I...' Oh, dear. She had no excuse prepared. And she'd never been any good at telling lies. Well, not ones she'd made up herself. Even though, she reflected unhappily, she'd become adept at playing the role the Duchess had created for her. And if she couldn't control her voice better he'd know she was on the verge of tears...

'When I encountered Miss White on the street, alone,' put in Lord Lavenham, 'I insisted on escorting her home safely.' He put a hand under her elbow, as if in support. Support? No, surely not. She was imagining it because she wanted his support so much.

'Naturally,' said Dawes, with an unctuous nod. 'Her Grace will be so glad you have brought Miss White home safely,' he continued, holding the door open in a manner which indicated that now he'd performed that task, his services were no longer required.

Lord Lavenham responded to the hint by stepping into the hall, removing his hat and handing it to the butler.

'You will find Her Grace in the drawing room, Miss White,' said Dawes, pointedly ignoring Lord Lavenham, 'where she has some news she has been waiting to share with you since breakfast.'

To Eleanor's surprise, Lord Lavenham still didn't pay any attention to the broad hints that he wasn't going to receive much of a welcome if he insisted on staying. He just took off his gloves and coat, took Eleanor's arm and mounted the stairs at her side.

And now, perversely, she just wished he'd go away.

It was taking all her strength to maintain a calm demeanour when all she wanted to do was run upstairs to her room, fling herself across the bed and give way to her emotions in private.

But he was right beside her, his hand at her elbow again when Dawes opened the door to announce them.

She was so full of conflicting feelings that it took her a moment to notice that Herr Schnee, who was sitting on a sofa beside the Duchess, was holding her hand. And that the Duchess looked radiant.

'Darling,' cried the Duchess, bouncing to her feet and across the room to envelop her in a fragrant hug. 'You will never believe it! I am to be married! To His Grace…' She waved her arm in the direction of the sofa. And Herr Schnee got to his feet.

'Oh, good day to you, Lord Lavenham,' said the Duchess, sparing him a fleeting glance. 'You will stay and join us in a glass of champagne, won't you? It is no secret, is it, Wilhelm?' She turned and looked over her shoulder.

At Herr Schnee.

'You are going to marry Herr Schnee?' Eleanor supposed, now she came to think of it, that the older couple had been spending more and more time together and looking extremely happy with each other. But marriage?

Eleanor was relieved that the Duchess was so jubilant on her own account that she hadn't bothered to ask where she'd been, or what she'd been up to, since she was in no fit state to deflect too many awkward questions. On the other hand, the only thing Eleanor knew, for certain, about the man she intended to marry was the fact that he had an over-inflated opinion of himself.

'Well, you know Herr Schnee is not really his name,' said the Duchess.

Exactly! Nobody knew who he really was.

'He has been living in London incognito, lest republican revolutionaries caught wind of his movements and assassinated him.'

'Zat is the slight exaggeration,' said Herr Schnee, or whatever his name was. 'I have always been available to my loyal supporters. And now that the tyrant Napoleon is on the brink of defeat, it is thought good that I return to Wurtem-Fosse-Wald to take my rightful place once more, as soon as his minions are forced to leave. And with a wife at my side...' He came over to the Duchess, and took her hand in his own, giving it a tender squeeze.

'Warty-Fosse-Wold is the kingdom of which Wilhelm is the Grand Duke,' said the Duchess breathily. 'Which means I won't ever have to become a Dowager Duchess, even if Theakstone can persuade some poor girl to marry him, for I shall be a Grand Duchess. Isn't it marvellous? It is practically like being a princess. Of a whole principality.' She clapped her hands together in that little-girl way of hers.

Eleanor couldn't really see that being a Grand Duchess was much of an improvement on becoming a Dowager Duchess. Both titles conjured up images of older, somewhat weighty matrons. Although on second thoughts, in her head, the Dowager she imagined was wearing a turban, whereas the Grand Duchess sported a tiara. But surely that wasn't a good enough reason to marry the man?

At this point, Dawes came in with a tray of glasses, followed by Gordon, the footman, with an ice bucket containing a bottle of champagne. While Dawes deftly opened the bottle and began pouring, Lord Lavenham led her to the sofa on which the happy couple had been sitting, lowered Eleanor to it and took up a position behind it.

The Duchess giggled as she accepted a glass. 'I feel terribly decadent, drinking at this time of the day, but you know, this is really a cause for celebration.'

At this point, Lord Lavenham leaned down and murmured into her ear, 'What is the matter?'

'The matter?'

'Yes, I can see that this business is worrying you.'

She couldn't tell him she felt as if her heart was breaking. That once he left here, her entire future was going to remain as grey as the skies were today. But she *could* share her concerns about the Duchess.

'Well,' she replied softly, so that nobody else in the room could overhear, 'for one thing, although the allies have armies within the borders of France, Napoleon is by no means defeated yet. She could be going into a terribly dangerous situation. Besides which, we have no real proof that, that, well, Herr Schnee is who he says he is. I mean, I always knew his name wasn't really *that,* but…'

'Still thinking of others,' he said savagely. 'Have you learned nothing?'

'What do you mean?'

But before he could enlighten her, the Duchess began to speak directly to Eleanor.

'You see what this means, don't you? It means I won't have to host any balls for that oaf of a stepson of mine, for I will be leaving this house,' said the Duchess, looking round the room as though she despised it, even though ever since Eleanor had known her she'd been fighting tooth and nail to stay in possession of it, 'and going to live in a castle!'

'A *schloss*, *Liebchen*,' said the Grand Duke of Wherever-in-the-Wold.

'And what is more,' the Duchess continued, 'nearly all the staff here have said they will come with me.'

'Well, we could not possibly allow you to travel to foreign parts,' said Dawes, 'without a suitable retinue, could we?'

'You are not,' Lord Lavenham hissed into her ear, 'to go with her.'

'Lord, no!'

'She will try to convince you to do so. She will probably make it sound exciting.'

'I have had quite enough excitement of the sort the Duchess creates to last me a lifetime, thank you very much,' said Eleanor with feeling. 'The tranquillity of a rural vicarage sounds like heaven, in comparison to going overseas in the train of the Duchess.'

'It is a good job I made sure you got that letter from your uncle, then.'

'Yes, indeed,' said Eleanor, wondering why he was still there. 'And I am truly thankful.'

He looked puzzled for a moment, as though surprised that she could express any gratitude towards him, although he wiped the expression from his face before anyone else could notice it. Not that they were likely to. The Duchess and the man she'd formerly known as Herr Schnee had gone back to another sofa and were holding hands again, and gazing into each other's eyes as though each was beholding a miracle.

'How quickly,' said Lord Lavenham, 'can you pack? That is, if you want to make your escape before you somehow get whisked off to the Continent in the train of that pair of…' He took a sip of champagne, as though swallowing back words better left unsaid, and set the glass aside.

'Not long,' she said, thinking regretfully of the wardrobe full of new clothes the Duchess had given her and the prohibitive cost of taking them with her on the stage.

'You are surely not having second thoughts about going with them?' Lord Lavenham frowned at her.

'Absolutely not!' Even though her words were vehemently spoken, she said them as quietly as she could, not wishing the happy couple, or anyone else in the room, to overhear. 'It will be an immense relief to leave London and escape all this…' She waved her hand round the room, but then realised that she'd have to be more specific if she wished him to understand what she meant. How she felt. And she did want him to understand this aspect of things. Because she couldn't bear the thought of them parting with him still having such a poor opinion of her. 'I have no taste for subterfuge. Oh, I know you will find it hard to believe that, but it is the truth. I shall be extremely glad to revert to being plain Miss Mitcham once more.'

'The Duchess, though,' he said, 'will be in her element in any court in Europe, since she adores drama and intrigue. And I have to concede,' he said grudgingly, 'she will be a great asset to a man attempting to take back his throne, since she is one of the most manipulative creatures it has ever been my misfortune to encounter.'

Eleanor was so pleased that he wasn't saying he thought she was lying that she totally forgot to protest about what he'd said about the Duchess. Besides, he was correct. The Duchess could make anyone do whatever she wanted, even if it was far from what they wished to do, with a combination of winsome smiles and tearful vulnerability, both of which were an act. Why, she'd even managed to get her servants to part with a portion of their own money in order to employ the Grand Duke. Which he knew, she reflected, giving his expression a second, more serious examination.

Now that she was trying to look beneath the adoring smile, she could see a hint of tolerant amusement in the Grand Duke's expression and realised that he knew exactly what he was taking on. And what she would bring to the marriage. To start with, he'd arrive back in his home country with a respectable entourage of servants, all of them fiercely loyal to the Duchess. They'd install her in his *schloss* and treat her like royalty. Well, they already did! On her part, the Duchess would either charm his enemies, or destroy them without feeling a shred of remorse. Because she had no scruples. She didn't care how many lies she had to tell, or who she had to use, to get her own way.

Eleanor sighed. She'd tried to keep thinking the best

of the Duchess, but the truth was that the older lady had never been kind without weighing up what she might gain. And none of her gifts had come without strings, from the moment she'd taken Eleanor up in the coach on the pretext of sheltering her from the cold, when really she hadn't wanted to stay in an inn overnight without the services of a maid.

'You are right,' said Eleanor. He'd always been right. Because he was far more discerning about people than she was. He'd grown up seeing people behave at their worst, within his own family, and had put what he'd learned there to use as an adult. He wasn't cynical for no reason. He was cynical because people very often did behave as badly as he suspected they might.

'They will make a good team, won't they?' she mused. 'I almost feel sorry for the people of…that unpronounceable place, especially the courtiers.'

'I thought,' said Lord Lavenham, 'you adored her.'

'Well, I did. I mean, I do, still, in a way. I am just no longer blind to her nature.'

'Oh, darling,' said the Duchess, glancing over at where Eleanor was sitting with Lord Lavenham leaning over the back of the sofa so that they could converse quietly. 'You do understand that you are invited to join me in my new life, don't you? I should so love it if you were to travel with us and help me settle into my new role.'

'That is very generous of you, Your Grace,' said Eleanor, while, at her back, she felt Lord Lavenham stiffen. 'But you know I have always planned to go to stay with my uncle, in Suffolk, until I can find a new post. Something much more humble than you would offer me, I know, but truly, it will suit me far better.'

'Well, if you are sure,' said the Duchess breezily without attempting to win her over. Without referring to all the letters to the uncle in question that she'd surely destroyed. As though the question of Eleanor's future was immaterial.

As the Duchess turned glowing eyes back to her elderly suitor, Lord Lavenham leaned down and murmured into her ear, 'After all you've done for her, she might at the very least have asked how you plan to make your way to Suffolk.'

'I am sure that Dawes will help me to purchase a seat on the stage,' she said, hating his ability to put his finger on exactly what had hurt her the most about the Duchess's careless attitude. 'I still have enough money left, since I haven't had to dip into my purse since the day I left Chervil House. In her own way, the Duchess has been very generous.' And she must remember that in days to come. Remember the good things, rather than pore over the bad, so that she wouldn't become bitter and resentful over this episode in her life. No, what she would take from this would be that for a few weeks, a lady of extremely high rank had treated her, ordinary Miss Mitcham, as if she was a friend and a confidante. Had made her feel like a princess and enabled her to dress like a princess, even if it had been to further her own aims.

Which was something else she would do well to remember. That people who smiled and treated you with affection did not necessarily feel it.

'You still have no need to do so,' said Lord Lavenham.

'To do what?' So deep in contemplation had Eleanor been, of the way she would remember this time in London, that she'd lost the thread of the conversation she'd been having with him.

'To pay for your journey to Suffolk. I will escort you to your uncle myself.'

'You will?' She turned to gape at him in astonishment. 'Really, I don't know why you should… I mean, there is absolutely no need…'

'There is every need,' he snapped. 'Whenever I leave you to your own devices you end up falling into a scrape. I shall not be able to rest easy until I know you have reached your intended destination, this time, in safety.'

'I do not! I am perfectly capable of…that is,' she added, her cheeks heating as she recalled the mess she'd made of her last attempt to escape him. And her vow to be more sensible next time she had to leave one situation and travel to another.

'Don't say another word,' he bit out. 'I am going to see you safely inside that vicarage and nothing you, or anyone else can say, is going to stop me.'

Chapter Twenty-One

It took several days for Peter to put all the arrangements in place. Several days too long for his peace of mind. She'd been a thorn in his side for the last few months and he needed, desperately, to pluck her out. It was no good hoping the attraction would wear off, the way it did with other women. He was never going to be able to restore his equilibrium by applying the method that had worked with every other female he'd known. He could not simply bed her and keep on bedding her until he'd had his fill of her. She'd rebuffed him. Well, he'd always known she was a woman of superior intellect. And that just proved it. She'd seen right through the outer shell of him. Seen that behind the face that everyone else said was handsome, beyond the polished manners and dry wit, there was nothing of worth. Nothing that could tempt a decent woman to take a gamble…

Even though he suspected that if he had her at his side, in his life, all the time, he might prove worthy.

Hadn't he already started to consider the plight of those less fortunate than himself? Hadn't he…?

But what was the point of justifying himself and his motives in his own head? She wasn't prepared to believe in him.

And he wasn't prepared to grovel.

The only solution was to send her away. Once he no longer saw her every day, rediscovering the appeal of her smile…

Or knowing that, since they were living in the same city, he could go and see her, and talk to her, perhaps hold her hand, dance with her…

Yet strangely, even knowing he had to send her away, that it was the right thing, the only thing, to do, he couldn't summon up any enthusiasm about the day when he'd finally have her out of his life.

He couldn't even understand why he'd stepped in to prevent her from going abroad with the Duchess, when that would have solved his problem for him without him having to go to any effort. Yet when the Duchess had suggested she go to the possibly fictional Grand Duchy of somewhere unpronounceable, he'd been livid. He hadn't been able to stand back and let her go and live in some foreign court, where some foreign princeling would woo her and persuade her to marry him, to make her a real princess, by telling her who knew what falsehoods, because of course he'd do anything to get and keep such a pretty, intelligent, English wife.

A blink of an eye after that, he'd imagined her not making it to the Grand Duchy at all, but instead being captured by Napoleon's brutish troops. Or ending up in a city under siege where she'd suffer who knew what sort of hell.

He'd been so alarmed at the thought of her waltzing into such danger, he'd forbidden her to go. Forbidden her! As though he had any right to have a say in what she did with her life once she walked out of his. She was not his concern. He'd startled her by the way he'd snapped at her. Startled himself, to be honest. If this was how she made him behave, not half an hour after refusing to become his mistress, who knew what follies he'd end up committing if he didn't make sure she was safely stowed away somewhere she couldn't… get at him?

Though he didn't know how on earth he was going to endure the forthcoming journey into Suffolk. It was going to be torture. Perhaps it would help if he looked on it as a form of penance. Penance for all the harm that might have befallen her, because of the way he'd made her flee Chervil House.

Once he'd reached that conclusion, things began to make a bit more sense. The sick feeling that came over him, for instance, whenever another piece of the planning fell into place. It had nothing to do with dreading the prospect of never seeing her again, as he'd begun to fear. It was probably what all guilt-ridden people felt when they embarked on a course of penance. Penance wasn't supposed to be easy, or enjoyable, was it?

And who in their right minds would choose to spend three days travelling on horseback to the back end of rural Suffolk?

Having worked out that this was all that was making him so blue-devilled, he managed to adopt a stoic demeanour as he rapped on the front door of Theakstone House, on the morning of their departure.

He found a sizeable crowd of people in the hall, along with a mountain of luggage.

'I am so sorry,' said Eleanor, coming forward, her hands outstretched. 'I meant to leave with only the things I brought with me, but the Duchess insisted I keep the entire wardrobe she made for me.'

'And the wig,' he noted drily. 'Do you intend to wear it all the way to Suffolk?'

'No,' she said, raising her hand self-consciously to her head. 'But she asked me to keep up the…er… disguise as long as I was under her roof and I don't see the harm in it…'

That was the trouble. She never saw the harm in any of the things the Duchess proposed. Which was why she'd ended up in this mess in the first place. Whereas he would have given her the right to move in these circles for the rest of her life, openly. 'If you had any integrity, you'd throw it out of the window the moment we exit Grosvenor Square.'

She flinched. 'I have enough integrity not to break my word,' she snapped back at him. 'Besides, it was probably very expensive. I couldn't possibly just throw it out of the window…'

She stopped, a stricken look on her face. Was she remembering, as he was, the moment when she had flung it across the room? Declared she was sick of the pretence and just wanted to be herself again?

'Make a present of it to your maid, then,' he suggested.

'Maid? What maid?'

'The one I hired to accompany you to Suffolk.'

Her eyes widened.

'You did not imagine,' he said irritably, 'that I would escort you all the way to Suffolk on my own, did you? It would give a very off appearance. Especially as I am delivering you to a man of the cloth.'

'I never gave it a thought,' she said.

Because she trusted him. Even after everything, she trusted him. A sort of warmth began to melt the edges from his sombre mood.

'I've never had a maid,' she continued, oblivious to the effect her casual remark had upon him. 'Not even in the days before I had to more or less become one,' she finished on a wry laugh.

Which shattered the illusion that she trusted him. It was more to do with the fact that she considered herself of no account. 'If you'd married me, you would have had dozens of maidservants,' he said, even more irritably. 'And while you are in my company, it is essential that you have at least one to lend you respectability when we stop in the inns, overnight.'

'Yes,' she said, sobering. 'I should have thought of that. Thank you. And once again, I am so sorry that you've had to go to so much trouble on my account…'

She really didn't have a clue, did she?

'As I told you, I shall not rest easy until I know you have safely reached your destination.'

Her expression altered. To one of chagrin. 'Yes. Because I'm so prone to falling into scrapes. But honestly, you could have just put me on the stage. You still could. I don't need all these trunks and boxes,' she said, sweeping her hand round the cluttered hallway. 'And I cannot think how we are to transport it all...'

'There will be no problem about that,' he assured her. 'What cannot fit in your carriage can go in the second coach with the servants.'

'Second coach? Servants?' Her brow wrinkled in confusion. But then he'd been deliberately avoiding her, these last few days, in case he lost his head and asked her...

Yes, well, he wasn't going to ask her again. She'd made her feelings perfectly clear. So he'd simply sent her a message, informing her of the day he would be arriving to escort her to her uncle's.

The Duchess chose this moment to glide over and put an end to what might have developed into a sharp exchange of words.

'Lord Lavenham,' she trilled, holding out her hand in such a way that he was obliged to take it and raise it to his lips. 'We are so glad to know you are going to take care of our young friend. It is such a relief to know we are going to leave her in safe hands, since we have so much to see to ourselves.'

If Peter was being charitable, he would assume that her frequent use of the word *we* referred to her and the German fellow as a couple. But to him it sounded just as though she was giving herself airs and using the royal *we*. Besides, her total disregard for Eleanor's welfare made his hackles rise. Eleanor had fled a perfectly safe home in the Cotswolds to escape his unwelcome attentions and the woman knew it. Yet here she was, practically throwing her to him, like a bone to a dog.

Perhaps she cherished hopes that by the time they reached Suffolk they would also have reached an understanding.

Hah! They would never be able to reach an understanding. Eleanor would never get down off her high horse. And he had no intention of begging her for scraps of affection, let alone becoming the kind of man who danced to a woman's tune. There were no two people less inclined to either seek, or reach, a compromise. He was too proud and she was too principled, and a journey to Suffolk was not going to be anywhere near long enough to break the deadlock.

'The people of the Grand Duchy of Wurtem-Whatever-the-Fosse it is,' said Peter through gritted teeth as the Duchess sashayed back across the hall to give some final instructions to the butler, 'have my heartfelt sympathy.'

'Please, not now,' said Eleanor, laying one hand on his arm as if to physically restrain him. Something about the pleading look in her eyes, or possibly the slight weight of her hand, made him bite back the cutting words he'd been about to utter.

'She is exactly what the Grand Duke needs, though,' he acknowledged. 'Not only because of her unique blend of ruthlessness and charm, but also because of her connections to so many powerful English families.'

She withdrew her hand, though not with revulsion. Just slowly, as though she'd only just become aware she'd broken a social convention and didn't want to draw anyone's attention to it.

'That…that has occurred to me, as well,' she admitted. 'If he doesn't get the reception he hopes for from his subjects, he will be able to seek sanctuary with any of her daughters, or her son. Which will be a vast improvement on the lodgings he had to take last time he fled his country.'

He looked down at her with renewed respect. He'd been expecting her to spout some nonsense about true love, but instead she'd demonstrated that at last she was capable of working out the shady motives of a particularly ambitious, self-serving individual. 'Are you not concerned about her going away with a man of... dubious heritage? After all, we have only his word for it that he is a grand duke...'

'Only a little, now. Because the Duke, her stepson...' she said, lowering her voice, which obliged her to step a little closer so that he could hear her above the hubbub.

Which meant that with every breath he inhaled her innocent, yet somehow seductive scent...

'...has been making enquiries. And even though the Duchess keeps accusing him of trying to put a spoke in her wheel, he's actually taking steps to ensure she comes to no lasting harm. The trouble is,' she said, glancing warily over her shoulder, as if the danger lay in the people milling about the hall, rather than from his almost overwhelming urge to seize her and kiss her senseless, 'he goes about everything in such a curt, authoritative way that it puts her back up.'

He was sick of the Duchess. She was an idiot. 'He only has to breathe to put her back up, from what I can tell. He has been trying to protect the totty-headed creature ever since his father died. It was he who offered her the use of this house in the first place.'

'But...she says he has been trying to evict her from it.'

'No. He has been trying, unsuccessfully, to stop her from creating scandal ever since he was fool enough to let her off the short leash his father kept her on.'

She recoiled. 'What a horrid thing to say.'

'That is me. Horrid to the core,' he said, wondering why, this morning, he felt the need to be quite so antagonistic.

Because she'd spurned him, twice, was the obvious answer, and was now willingly going to bury herself in the wilds of Suffolk rather than stay with him. And he couldn't bear the way she'd made him feel when she'd placed her hand on his sleeve and confided her thoughts, thoughts she could not share with anyone else present, as if she considered him her closest friend—when friendship was the last thing he wanted from her.

She turned from him with a huff of annoyance, to make her final farewells to all the people milling about the hall. Then they all trooped outside to see her into the coach and wave her off while he mounted his horse. Everyone was smiling, as though they were sending her off on holiday. Everyone but him, because he couldn't stomach the way she was receiving those smiles as tokens of affection and regard from them, and was deceived into thinking they all cared about her to judge from the way she was dabbing at her eyes with her handkerchief and leaning out of the window to wave at them as they swept out of the square.

Why couldn't she see it for what it was? The shallow leavetaking of people who didn't really care what became of her. They couldn't really care if they could smile like that. They couldn't have handed her over to him, either, when they knew his reputation. When they knew she'd only reached London because she'd been fleeing from him.

Lord, did nobody really care what became of her? Why wasn't somebody looking after her? How could her parents have left her so poorly provided for that she had to go out to work, leaving her vulnerable to ruthless, selfish employers…and men like him?

He stopped glaring at the Duchess and her staff and dug his heels into his mount's flanks, before he lost sight of Eleanor's cavalcade altogether. He eyed the threatening sky with a sense of resignation as he trotted after them. It was typical that the weather had turned cold and blustery, on the very day he'd chosen to set off on a journey, on horseback. Before the end of the day, he'd probably be soaking wet, because it was bound to rain. That was what came of deciding that nothing could be worse than spending hours and hours shut up in a cramped carriage with a woman whose clothes he wanted to rip from her body.

And it wouldn't be for just the one day, either. He'd booked rooms in inns for a couple of nights, so that the journey wouldn't be too arduous for her.

He couldn't have chosen a more suitable penance. While he'd done all he could to ensure her comfort, he was clearly doomed to facing several days of torture.

Which would do him good, in the long run. In future, whenever his mind strayed in the general direction of Miss Eleanor Mitcham, and all the mistakes he'd made and all the sins he'd committed, he could remind himself that he'd paid for each and every one of them. He'd have no need to pay any heed to the annoying, niggly voice of the conscience he'd never known he had and could remember, instead, the fate that befell any man who started caring too much about a woman.

Yes, when he'd seen her into the house of her ecclesiastical uncle, he'd be able to turn round, mount his horse and put her well and truly behind him.

Chapter Twenty-Two

Eleanor was so relieved when they finally reached the long, low, thatched cottage where Uncle Norman lived with Aunt Agatha and his children. The journey here had been one of the most awkward and stressful she'd ever taken. And that included the nightmarish walk over the hills in fog so thick she could barely see her hand before her face.

Because he'd been terse to the point of rudeness whenever they had to converse, ordered her meals to be served to her on a tray in her room rather than sitting down to dine with her, and even got soaked to the skin, several times, rather than take shelter in the carriage with her when it came on to rain. He'd made it plain, in so many different ways, that though he was intent on seeing her off to Suffolk, he would much rather be doing something else. *Any*thing else.

The moment the carriage lurched to a halt by Uncle Norman's front gate, he wrenched open the carriage door and leaned in, his face grim.

'Get out of the carriage,' he grated, reaching in to

grab her arm. 'And get inside safely before I change my mind about letting you go, and throw you up on to my horse and carry you off to some low tavern where I can use you as I truly want to.'

He matched his actions to his words, pulling her out of the carriage so abruptly that if she hadn't been nimble she might have ended up flat on her face on the grass verge. But she didn't care, because his words had turned her assumptions about his behaviour, all the way here, upside down. He hadn't been avoiding her because he could no longer stand the sight of her. On the contrary, he still wanted her so much that, given the slightest bit of encouragement, he'd drag her off to somewhere private where they could carry on where they'd left off on his sofa.

He'd avoided being alone with her because he'd been afraid his resolve would weaken and he'd attempt to seduce her again. It made her feel irresistible.

The moment she righted herself, she whirled round to tell him…

What? What could she tell him? Anyway, it was too late. He'd mounted his horse and was kicking the poor exhausted beast in the ribs, as if he couldn't get away from her fast enough.

Her heart sank. Although why it should, she didn't know. It wasn't as if they'd had any future, was it? Only, this was the last she'd see of him. This was the memory she'd carry of him, in her heart, for the rest of her life. Riding angrily away.

Alone.

'Eleanor!' The voice of her uncle boomed from the front door, making her turn away from Lord Lavenham and all the complicated, contrary, confusing feelings he'd provoked. Feelings which she had to stifle. 'It is so good to see you. I trust you had a pleasant journey.' Uncle Norman came striding down the path, his hand outstretched in welcome. So she had to put on a suitable expression and speak the conventional greeting.

After pumping her hand briskly, Uncle Norman peered over her shoulder at the retreating figure of Lord Lavenham. 'Who was that? And who do we have here in the carriage?' He poked his head inside the open door. The maid Lord Lavenham had hired gave a squeak.

'This is Betty,' said Eleanor, who wasn't ready to speak about Lord Lavenham just yet. 'The maid Lord Lavenham hired to accompany me on the journey.' There, she'd said his name. Without bursting into tears.

'You have a maid?' Uncle Norman pulled his head out of the carriage. 'You didn't say anything about a maid. How are we to pay her? We don't have room to put her up.'

'There is no need to do either, Uncle Norman. As I said, Lord Lavenham hired her to accompany me on the journey and that is all. She will be returning to London right away.' A strange feeling came over Eleanor as she said this. Was she *jealous* of the girl who would be going back to London? Surely not. She'd had such a difficult time there that she'd been aching to get away. No, it wasn't her return to London that Eleanor envied. It was the time on the journey she might spend with Lord Lavenham.

'Good,' said Uncle Norman. 'And that was this Lord Lavenham, was it? Galloping away as though he couldn't wait to shake the dust off his feet? Proud sort of fellow, is he? Too proud to darken the doorstep of a mere country parson?'

Yes, he was proud. But not in the way Uncle Norman meant.

'I expect he has gone to whatever inn he has booked for the night, rather than put you to any trouble,' she said, reverting swiftly to her habit of soothing ruffled feathers. 'After all, as you yourself said, you didn't bargain on feeding and housing a maid, did you? And he has a valet as well…'

'Good point. Well, let's get you unpacked and settled in, shall we? This your luggage, is it?' He eyed the growing mound of trunks and boxes the coachman and groom were unloading from the boot of her carriage and the innards of the second coach. 'Good grief,' he said, planting his hands on his hips. 'Never mind the maid, don't know where we're to stow all this. Agatha!' he turned and bellowed in the direction of the house. 'Not that she'll be of any use,' he said irritably, as Eleanor's aunt appeared in the doorway.

'I am so glad you are here,' said Aunt Agatha, simultaneously leaning against the door frame and laying one hand on the mountain of her belly, which contained what was soon to be her fourth child. 'But I didn't know you'd be bringing all this…' She gazed in consternation at the still-increasing pile of luggage that was now completely blocking the gateway.

'My last employer was extremely generous,' Eleanor explained. 'But I won't be needing much of it. If you have an outhouse of some sort, I am sure most of it can be stored there.'

'Well, it could, if we had anyone to carry it there,' said Aunt Agatha plaintively. 'We don't have any male servants, you know. We aren't a wealthy family...' she said, wringing her hands and shooting Uncle Norman a resentful look.

Eleanor perceived that Aunt Agatha was not the sort of woman who tried to make the best of things. Nor did she appear to have any talent at organisation. In some ways, Eleanor was glad of this because it would do her good to feel truly useful. It would also mean that hopefully she'd be too busy over the next few days, at least, to have time to dwell on the wrenching feeling of parting from a certain man whom she had to consign to her past.

That presentiment proved sound. First she discovered that, far from not having any male servants, there were a couple of them hanging about the stables. It was true that they muttered under their breath that they weren't paid to do household duties, when asked to help with the stowing of her luggage, but Eleanor persuaded them to drag or shove all her trunks into one of the few empty stalls. After she'd seen her worldly goods stabled, Eleanor took a moment to thank Betty for her company, before waving her off on her way to whatever inn she was to stay in that night. Then she met the children, and from that point was promptly sucked straight into the chaos of a family with three lively children under the age of seven, which left her no time to droop into the temptation to feel sorry for herself.

Not, that was, until the moment she crawled into the truckle bed, in the room up under the eaves she was to share with the two girls, Mary and Susan. This was the first moment she'd had since setting foot inside the front gate that she'd had leisure to feel sorry for herself. By now she was so tired that she didn't have the energy to indulge in a really good bout of weeping. Besides, she didn't want to disturb the girls, who were already sound asleep. A few tears did run down her cheeks and soak into the pillow before she could stop them. But they, she vowed, would be the last she shed over a man who didn't respect her enough to offer her a proper marriage.

At least, not what she'd thought of as a proper marriage. She had to concede now, though, after seeing how some of the married couples she'd met in London had behaved, that his notion of avoiding either of them getting badly hurt had been…

No, no, she couldn't have gone into marriage *expecting* it to fail. Waiting and watching for him to commit his first act of infidelity.

She'd done the right thing. At least, she might have taken a few wrong turns along the way, but she was here now, where she'd intended to be, with a family who needed her particular talents.

Over the next few days, as Eleanor became more familiar with the family, and the parish, she revised her initial impression of Aunt Agatha. What woman wouldn't appear lethargic and inclined to complain about every little thing, when in an advanced stage of pregnancy and clearly feeling unwell? Especially if she had a child like Horace, the eldest, who was—well, to put it politely, a bit of a handful.

And far from attempting to discipline the lad, Uncle

Norman spent his time either locked up in his study writing sermons, or in his stables, or out riding to hounds with the local squire, who was also master of the hunt. He left all domestic matters to Aunt Agatha, who was too weary to deal with a boy who had boundless energy, like a great puppy. Nearly every day, before long, Aunt Agatha would lay a weary hand across her brow and tell him to go and play outside.

Which just meant that it was the neighbours, or the tradesmen in town, who had to deal with his pranks and who brought him home with a firm grip on one ear, threatening to dust the seat of his breeches if they caught him stealing buns, or apples, or sausages one more time.

In spite of keeping busy, and her vow to never cry over Lord Lavenham again, Eleanor shed many tears in the darkness of her little attic bedroom, once the girls were asleep. She wept with shame when she recalled the way he'd spoken of making her his mistress instead of his wife, after she'd spent so many weeks behaving so disgracefully in London. Sometimes, she wept because, just as she was about to fall asleep, she'd remember how wonderful it had felt when he'd put his arms round her. When he'd kissed her. Then her body would wake up and rob her of sleep no matter how weary she'd been, by reminding her of every caress, every sensation he'd aroused. She would lie there, hot and aching, and not knowing what to do with her limbs, then she'd dream of him touching her, kissing her, holding her and wake up, wondering who he'd been kissing and touching the night before, while she'd been dreaming of him. Then she'd have to drag herself wearily through the next bleak, lonely day, heavy with the knowledge she'd never experience such caresses again.

As the days grew warmer, and blossom began to appear in the hedgerows, she began to really miss aspects of him that she'd forgotten about since the devastating kiss. Because nobody in the family here entered into any of her feelings, or shared her sense of humour. Every day, something would happen that she wished she could tell him about, knowing it would make him laugh. When the news came that Napoleon had abdicated, she wanted to talk to him about what this might mean for the Duchess, who hadn't written to her yet, in spite of her promises to do so. Had she married the Grand Duke? Had they swept into the Grand Duchy at the head of a cavalcade of loyal supporters and ousted whatever government Napoleon had put in place? Was she busily conquering the hearts of her new people, calling them all darling, and smiling at them in such a way that they believed she was really concerned about their welfare?

Oh, but he'd been so right about the Duchess. The woman had deliberately kept Eleanor in London, so that she could try to get her stepson to fall for her.

Only Lord Lavenham had been consistently honest with her. Even when she hadn't like what he'd had to say, he'd never offered her Spanish coin.

Because he valued honesty. Integrity. That was how she'd forfeited his regard. He'd told her so, that night at Mrs Broughty's, that he'd once liked a girl he'd thought honest, enough to offer her marriage.

His proposal, back then, had been meant sincerely. As sincerely as he was capable of being, considering his cynical attitude to marriage. She could even see, now, why he'd assumed she'd have welcomed that half-hearted proposal. She'd seen the way girls fell over themselves to attract even a dull, dim sort of man like Mr Spenlow, merely because he stood to inherit a title one day. And Lord Lavenham was neither dim nor dull. He was the most fascinating, perceptive man she'd ever met. Or was ever likely to meet.

Oh, why hadn't she been honest with him then? At Mrs Broughty's? Why hadn't she explained why she'd recoiled from his proposal? How she couldn't bear the thought of him growing tired of her and taking another lover?

Well, for one thing, at that point she hadn't developed strong enough feelings for him to have thought that, exactly. She'd just hated the thought of being married to a man who hadn't appeared to care enough for her to promise fidelity. Which was surely the cornerstone of any marriage, wasn't it?

But now…oh, now… She buried her face in her pillow to stifle yet another bout of weeping for what might have been.

She welcomed all the bustle of Easter and the added work the extra church services entailed. It meant that she was so tired, most days, that she could fall asleep the moment her head hit the pillow. Then, just as things in the ecclesiastical calendar were quieting down, Aunt Agatha went into labour. A woman from the village acted as midwife and a local girl came in to act as nurse to the newborn, while Eleanor's job was keeping the other children occupied.

It would be too much to say she kept them out of mischief. Because Horace's favourite occupation soon became poking the baby to make it cry the moment anyone wasn't watching. Eleanor could never fathom how he managed to do it so frequently when the village girl was supposed to be in the nursery at all times. Especially when Aunt Agatha was asleep.

She might have known he'd take to doing something of the sort, though, considering how much he'd always enjoyed dismembering his sister's dolls, or pulling their hair. He wasn't a monster, Eleanor told herself ten times a day as she dragged him out of the nursery, and away from the screaming baby that seemed to fascinate him so. It was just that he had too much energy. When he got bored, he invariably found something to do which made him the centre of attention.

She had lost count of the times she said, *'Horace, stop that!'* Or, *'Horace, don't do that!'* Or, *'Horace, don't even think about trying that!'* Until the fateful day dawned when she uttered the words, *'Horace, if you can't behave, why don't you go outside and play?'*

She sat back, hands to her mouth in horror. She was turning into another Aunt Agatha!

Enough was enough. Uncle Norman was the boy's father and he ought to be shouldering some of the responsibility. And if Aunt Agatha was too worn down to say so, Eleanor wasn't.

That very evening, as soon as she'd settled the three oldest children, who'd become her sole responsibility by then, Eleanor went to the study, where Uncle Norman habitually shut himself away after dinner, and knocked on the door.

'Yes?' He looked up from his copy of the *Sporting Magazine*, which he'd been reading while sipping a glass of brandy. 'Something I can do for you? Only I'm rather busy, wrestling with my sermon for next Sunday.'

Yes, she could see that. But it would do no good to antagonise him by pointing out the newspaper, the racing calendar and the collection of whips and broken bits of tack all over his desk, where anyone might have expected to see a bible, a concordance, a sheaf of notes and at least one pen.

'I was just wondering, about Horace,' she said.

Uncle Norman flung his paper aside irritably. 'What has he done now?'

'Oh, nothing in particular. I was just wondering, well…' She summoned all her courage. It wasn't easy, now it came to it, to break the habits of a lifetime and stand up to the head of the household. A man of the cloth, at that. 'Why he isn't at school?' It had been puzzling her for some time. He'd be far happier, not to mention far less trouble, if he only had other boys his own age to play with. He'd be able to use up some of that store of restless energy which sapped the strength of everyone else around him. That was, after all, what schools were designed for, wasn't it?

'In case you haven't noticed, we're not made of money,' snapped Uncle Norman. 'And I see no reason to shell out on school fees when I can educate my own son perfectly well at home.'

Hmm. Well, that was all well and good, but Uncle Norman was not actively educating his son. He'd left him largely to Aunt Agatha, who couldn't cope with him, until Eleanor had arrived, when she'd taken over his day-to-day activities. And as for the argument he couldn't afford school fees, hah! He had a stable full of hunters eating the best oats and two adult grooms and a lad to care for them.

'I suppose Agatha set you on to me about it,' he said with a shake of his head. 'You don't want to be fooled by those die-away airs of hers. She could manage much better if she made a bit more of an effort.'

She'd manage much better if only she had a husband who supported her a bit. Or at all. Good grief, even Lord Lavenham would never treat any wife of his so shabbily. True, he had a deal more money to spare, so that he could afford schooling for any sons he might have...but...no...that wasn't right. Uncle Norman was choosing to spend what he had on himself, and his own pleasures, rather than providing for his family first. A thing Lord Lavenham had criticised her own parents for doing, now she came to think of it.

He'd make a much better father than Uncle Norman, as well as a far superior husband. Even if he did go off and have affaires, he would always notice what his wife felt and do what he could for her. Hadn't he noticed her distress when she'd heard the Duchess was marrying the Grand Duke? Even though he was angry with her and they'd agreed to part, he had still asked her what was the matter, as though he intended to do what he could to help. And when it was time for her to come here, he'd hired a maid and provided a second coach so that she wouldn't have to leave all her pretty clothes behind...

The pretty clothes that, in retrospect, had played such a huge factor in her downfall.

She shook off the spectre of what might have been, something she was having to do with increasing frequency, and dragged her mind back to Uncle Norman and what was to be done about Horace.

'Well, she's only just had the baby...'

Uncle Norman snorted. 'She ain't any different when she ain't breeding. That's why I was so glad to hear you were planning to stay for a while. In fact,' he said, 'I'd be very glad if you were to make your home with us. Permanently. You would be helping us to do God's work in this parish, think of that.'

Permanently? A cold chill ran down her spine. It was all very well helping out while the baby was so little and Aunt Agatha so tired, and while she was in between paid posts. But to live here? For ever?

'I will think about it, Uncle Norman,' she replied, rather than telling him outright that there was nothing to think about. She'd always valued her independence. She could have made her home with any one of half-a-dozen uncles or aunts in the first place had she not been determined to stand on her own two feet. But she'd made the mistake of telling the Duchess the same thing. And the woman had taken steps to prevent her leaving.

She wasn't going to hand Uncle Norman the same opportunity.

She'd have to start searching through the advertisements for paid companions at once. She hadn't had time since she'd been here to do more than glance along the staff wanted columns of newspapers that were already out of date.

Well, that would have to change. She had to stop moping over her failure with Lord Lavenham and the way the Duchess had used her, put it all down to experience and get on with the next stage of her life. Whatever it was to be.

The next morning, when Aunt Agatha sent her out on a visit that as vicar's wife she really should have done herself, Eleanor took a moment to buy herself a newspaper. With it tucked under her arm, she felt as though, finally, she'd stopped drifting along the current of life, that she'd picked up the oars and was about to take charge of her own destiny.

That feeling lasted until she walked into the front parlour and saw Horace, who was sitting on the hearthrug, in front of the fire, gleefully committing his latest atrocity. She stood there for a moment or two, her stomach heaving as she faced the fact that nobody else in the house was going to clear it up.

What was that saying about virtue being its own reward?

Well, she'd been virtuous when she'd spurned Lord Lavenham's last offer, hadn't she? And what good had it done her? She'd condemned herself to this. For the rest of her life, she'd be clearing up after other people in houses that weren't her own.

When, if she'd had less pride, she might be the Countess of Lavenham, right this very minute. Oh, he would probably have tired of her and left her to pursue another woman, but she would still be living in luxury, in a house stuffed with servants, instead of being one. Because that was what she was. Oh, they might call her Aunty Eleanor and say she was one of the family, but in reality she was just a servant. An unpaid one at that. And if she stayed here she would dwindle into a withered, miserable spinster, at everyone's beck and call. Even her plan to go out and obtain a paid position would not improve her lot a great deal, she reflected, taking the newspaper she'd just bought from under her arm and absentmindedly rolling it up into a tube. She could foresee an endless succession of crabby, elderly ladies like Lady Bradbury.

She'd been an idiot.

And she'd be a bigger idiot if she kept on telling herself she was doing a good thing, propping up a family with difficulties. They needed to sort those difficulties out, that was what they needed to do. And they weren't going to do it if they kept on relying on her to fill in for their deficiencies.

Lowering the improvised weapon she'd inadvertently made, and casting one last look of loathing at the mess Horace was making of the hearthrug, Eleanor went up to her room—which wasn't even her own room, but one she had to share with two little girls—to pack a bag.

Chapter Twenty-Three

Eleanor pursed her lips as she tugged her battered portmanteau from the narrow gap between the head of her truckle bed and the eaves, where she'd wedged it.

Had she learned nothing since the last time she'd reached the end of her tether and fled from a situation she should never have been in, in the first place?

Apparently not.

Because she'd ended up serving yet another set of people who didn't value her. At all. Just as Lord Lavenham had warned her she would. And their attitude had driven her to the point where she'd almost abandoned her principles, and set about a helpless boy with a rolled-up newspaper!

Though at least she'd finally come to her senses.

It had come to her, in a flash, when she'd been standing there gazing down at Horace in revulsion, just as though a stiff breeze had blown away the fog that had been obscuring her powers of reasoning. None of the few paid servants in the house would demean themselves by clearing *that* up. Nor would Uncle Norman or Aunt Agatha ask it of them. Because they could threaten to leave. And good staff were so hard to find. Whereas everyone considered spinsters without means to be ten-a-penny.

Wasn't she worth more than this life she was living now? Shouldn't she be doing exactly what she wanted to do, not what everyone else told her to do?

Well, thanks to the generosity of the Duchess, she still had all the money she'd intended to use to flee to London in the first place. So she could walk into any coaching inn and buy a ticket to wherever she wanted. Also, thanks to the Duchess, she would look a great deal smarter than she had done when she'd fled Chervil House, she reflected as she stuffed a random assortment of clothing into the portmanteau along with her brushes and toothpowder.

Never mind looking smarter, Eleanor was smarter on the inside, too. She *was*. She mentally stuck out her tongue at the vision she suddenly had of Lord Lavenham, folding his arms across his chest and shaking his head in reproof. She wouldn't have any trouble dealing with innkeepers and mail-coach guards now she'd learned how to act as though she was a great lady. What was more, she had learned what truly mattered to her. Last time she'd packed this scruffy portmanteau she'd been little more than a schoolgirl. The opinions she'd spouted when Lord Lavenham had asked her to marry him had not truly been her own. They'd been the ones she'd absorbed from her parents, without question, and regurgitated out of habit when put to the test.

Yet where had all her silly, sanctimonious principles got her? Masquerading as a foreign princess. Living a lie.

She sat back on her heels, gazing blindly into the jumbled contents of her bag. As jumbled as her thoughts had been when she'd fled from Chervil House.

At least her mind was less muddled today. She'd spent a lot of time lying in bed at nights, thinking. About Lord Lavenham, mostly. And all the things that had happened since her impetuous flight from him.

This time, before she went flying off into the unknown, just to get away from a situation she knew was wrong for her, she was going to take a moment to decide what she really wanted. And where she really wanted to go.

The answer to both questions was the same. And it wasn't a place, or a job, it was a person.

Lord Lavenham.

But she couldn't…she couldn't…she…

Hang on, though. Why couldn't she? Just a few moments ago, she'd decided that she deserved better from her employment than to be a drudge for people who neither paid nor appreciated her. She'd decided to seek out a job where she would receive both wages and respect. If she could summon up this much resolution about her working life, why should she not apply the same principles to matters of the heart?

Because it wouldn't achieve anything…

Wouldn't it? Wouldn't it really? How would she ever know, if she didn't at least make the attempt to go to him and tell him the truth? *All* the truth.

Which was…

She took a deep breath and began marshalling her

thoughts. For one thing, she'd learned that she'd been wrong about Lord Lavenham's ability to be a good husband. For another, she'd learned what she'd forfeited by turning down his proposal.

A proposal which he'd made, even feeling the way he did about marriage and his own ability to be faithful. She rapidly reviewed the words he'd used. Had he actually said he had no intention of attempting to be faithful? She didn't think so. He'd promised to be faithful for the first few months, then said he hoped that they'd be able to remain friends if he sought amusement elsewhere. Looking back, that was more in the nature of warning her about his character, and propensities, not a declaration that he would deliberately break their marriage vows when it suited him.

And Lady Bradbury had told her that he'd been visiting Chervil House more frequently since she'd begun to work there.

He'd told her, in London, that he'd liked her enough to think he might be able to make a go of a marriage.

Oh. For the first time, kneeling in that attic bedroom with her bag packed, she saw that the proposal had not been an insult at all, but a very great compliment. Even believing what he did about marriage and his own character and capabilities, he'd taken a chance on her—and she'd done nothing but rebuff him and sneer at his morals. She'd never given him any idea how she really felt about him. Why, after that day in his house, on the way back to Grosvenor Square, he'd spoken of *her* wanting to be rid of *him*.

Oh, Eleanor. She wrapped her arms round her waist and shook her head.

He might not have loved her, but he'd wanted to try to see if he could, one day…

And even after she'd hurt him, he'd searched for her to make sure she was safe. Even in Town, when he'd been angry with her and had threatened all sorts of dire retribution, all he'd done was demand a couple of kisses.

Her cheeks flamed as her mind went over those kisses. Kisses which had been full of passion and need, and promise.

Kisses which he could have turned to his own advantage, but never had. In fact, he'd been the only person upon whom she'd been able to rely, in the end. The only person who'd been completely honest with her. The only one who'd put her welfare before their own desires.

So…

She buckled the strap of the portmanteau tightly and got to her feet, her face set. He'd taken a chance on her. So it was about time she returned the favour. She marched to the bedroom door, vowing not to stop until she reached London. To be specific, the front room of a certain house in Albemarle Street where she intended to tell Lord Lavenham all the things she should have told him long ago, plus a few other conclusions she'd reached since the last time she'd seen him.

And if, after pouring her heart out to him, he wasn't willing to renew his offer of marriage?

She paused with her hand on the latch.

Even if he was in no mood to renew his proposal, he'd jump at the chance to make her his mistress. He wanted her. Even when she'd spurned him, he kept right on wanting her. Through all those weeks in London, and all the way to Suffolk. He'd admitted it.

And she wanted him, too. Whether it was with the blessing of the church or not, she'd never stop wanting him till the day she died.

In the end, would being his mistress be so very different from being his wife? After a few months he had warned her the passion would probably burn out. In either case, she was certain that he wouldn't merely cast her aside, to survive as best she could. He would provide a pension for her, of some sort…

Not that it would be a factor. The point was, she decided, lifting the latch and stepping out on to the landing, that no matter whether she wore his ring, or not, he would be the husband of her heart. Because there was no way she would ever contemplate becoming any other man's lover. She would be as true to him as she would have been had he taken her to a church and spoken vows before a minister. At least she would have shown him how much she loved him. She would be sacrificing everything, her principles, her reputation, just for the sake of being his lover, for however long he wanted her.

Didn't he deserve to have someone, for once, show him that he was worth loving? She considered the stories she'd heard about his parents, using him as a pawn in their battles with each other. No wonder he didn't believe in love. He'd never seen it acted out.

Well, that was about to change.

Her heart lifted as she began to descend the stairs. One way or another, for a few weeks, at least, she was going to have the right to hold him and kiss him, and lay in his arms all night long. And after that?

After that, she might well have to deal with her conscience, as well as a broken heart. But then she would have had to deal with the broken heart even if she'd married him, so where was the difference? If the only way to have him was a way everyone said was immoral, well, then, she'd just have to get used to them calling her a wanton. To the fact that Horace and Mary and Susan would remember her as shocking, disgraceful Aunt Eleanor. Though would that be any worse than dwindling into the dull, dependable doormat they'd make of her if she stayed here? No, it wouldn't. She was sick of being plain, practical Eleanor, the girl that everyone took for granted.

What on earth had come over her? Had it been all the attention she'd gained while she'd been pretending to be a princess? Had it gone to her head? Or had she absorbed rather too many of the Duchess's elastic attitudes to morality?

Or perhaps she'd just grown up and learned what was important, in life, and what wasn't.

Well, whatever had come over her, at least she was going to experience joy, true joy, for a few weeks. Because she'd be with the man she loved. The man she couldn't stop thinking about.

And if that made her a wicked sinner, well, then at least she was finally being honest about what she was. She'd wanted him from the moment he'd kissed her. No, in the spirit of honesty, she would admit she'd wanted him almost from the first moment she met him. During his first visit to Chervil House.

'Oi, Aunty Elly,' cried Horace as she passed by the parlour door. 'Where you going?'

Eleanor paused. It might, perhaps, be a good idea to tell him. It would save her having to go and seek out either of his parents and get into a long-winded explanation of how she'd reached her decision to leave. And she didn't really want to worry everyone by simply disappearing the way she'd done last time.

'I'm running away to London,' she therefore told him. And then, in a spirit of mischief that would have made the Duchess double over with laughter, added, 'To tread the primrose path.'

'I'll tell my ma,' he whined.

She gave him a considering look. While she'd been packing, he'd been busy with some dressmaking shears and the second-best tablecloth. He was enjoying himself far too much, wreaking havoc, to cease immediately, even for the pleasure of telling tales. She'd have plenty of time to get well away from the vicarage before Uncle Norman even thought about coming to look for her. Providing, of course, she didn't hang about to bandy words with a seven-year-old.

'Do as you like, Horace,' she said, turning from the scene of carnage. 'Goodbye,' she called over her shoulder as she made for the front door.

It felt as if chains fell from her feet as she stepped outside. Finally, for perhaps the first time in her life, she was doing exactly as she pleased. Something she'd chosen, in spite of what anyone else would think. She felt like skipping down the garden path and might possibly have done so, had not an elegant carriage drawn up by the front gate at that precise moment.

Bother. Visitors for her aunt and uncle, she supposed. Well, if they expected her to show them into the house and order tea and so on while they waited, they were going to be disappointed. She wasn't going to stop for anything or anyone, not now she'd set her heart on returning to Lord Lavenham.

But she did stop, stone dead, when the passenger of the carriage opened the door and got out.

Because it was none other than Lord Lavenham himself.

Chapter Twenty-Four

Peter's heart kicked against his ribcage as he caught sight of the battered little valise Eleanor was carrying and the militant way she'd been marching out of the front door. It looked as though he'd only just got here in time. She was obviously about to do another flit.

Thank God he'd come now, rather than wrestling with his pride for one more day, or she might have plunged him right back to where he'd been in January, searching for her all day and every day, never being able to sleep, wishing he'd done everything differently.

She came to a dead stop the moment she saw him and dropped her bag.

Why? Was she planning to run? Did she think there was anywhere on earth she could go where he wouldn't, eventually, find her?

Anyway, he wasn't going to give her the chance to run. Not again. He placed one hand on the front gate and vaulted over it, rather than wasting time with the latch. Strode up to her with the intention of telling her that she'd won. That he was ready to surrender.

But he'd only gone two steps when she began running towards him, her arms outstretched.

They met by an overhanging lilac tree that was just coming into bloom. She flung herself into his arms and he gathered her in. He wasn't sure whether he kissed her first, or whether she kissed him. But he didn't care, anyway. The point was, they were kissing. After all the long, lonely weeks apart, they were together again and apparently of one mind.

'Eleanor, Eleanor,' he said over and over, between kisses. Until just kissing her wasn't enough. He had to know where she'd been planning to go, so that if she ever took it into her head to run away again he'd know where to look for her.

'Where,' he managed to grate, 'were you going to go?'

'I was coming to find you,' she panted, as out of breath from kissing as he felt.

'I'm here,' he said, taking her beautiful face between his hands.

'Yes. In the front garden,' she said, slackening the hold she had round his waist, so that she could peer up at him as though she still didn't totally believe what she was seeing. 'What are you doing here?'

'I was coming to find you,' he said, echoing her words. And sighed, because he felt as though he could breathe easily again now she was in his arms.

'Why?' She looked up at him challengingly. Was she going to make him say it? Wasn't it obvious why he'd come all the way to the back of beyond when the London Season was in full swing?

He swallowed. This was where it was going to get

tricky. He'd insulted her so much those last few days. Been brutally rude. The chances were he was going to have to grovel to get her to forgive him. The prospect had been causing him discomfort ever since he'd decided to come to Suffolk to find her. His pride had never allowed him to apologise before, no matter what he'd done, or who he'd offended.

But he owed her an apology. And if nothing else was going to work, he was going to have to swallow his pride and make that apology.

Or, at the very least, explain himself.

'London,' he said, deciding to start with the explanation and see what that could achieve, 'was decidedly flat after you left. I…' He gave a half-shrug, hoping it looked nonchalant. 'I missed you.' There. He'd admitted it. And it didn't feel half as bad as he'd thought it might. Because far from gloating, she simply smiled.

'I missed you, too.'

'Truly?'

'Oh, yes,' she said earnestly. 'I have so much to tell you. Things I should have said when I had the chance.'

'You have the chance now,' he said, dropping a kiss on to the tip of her nose to encourage her to carry on talking. Since it meant he didn't have to. 'What were they?'

She blushed. Took a deep breath. 'Well, to begin with, I have decided it is about time I took a leaf out of your book.'

He wasn't sure that sounded like a good thing. 'In what way?'

'Well, you have always been completely frank with me. Whereas I have always hidden behind…well, I told myself they were principles, but in point of fact they were excuses.'

He'd done his fair share of hiding, too, if it came to it. Behind the reputation he'd cultivated, to start with…

'You were right all along,' she said, looking contrite. 'I was nothing but a sanctimonious little hypocrite. Deep down, I've always wanted you. I pretended I didn't because the way you depicted marriage didn't fit my vision of what I thought it ought to be. But now…' She bit down on her lower lip.

'Now?'

'I cannot fight my nature any more. I don't *want* to fight my nature any more. I just want to…' she drew in a rather wobbly sounding breath '…be yours. I mean, I am yours,' she corrected herself. And then went very pink in the face and clung to him a bit tighter, as if to show him she meant it.

'I want you so much,' she said hastily, 'and I've missed you so much that however few weeks we have together will be worth it.'

What?

'What, exactly, are you saying? You are making it sound as if…you are willing to become my mistress.'

He couldn't believe this. He'd come all the way here determined to do the right thing and here she was, apparently offering to do the wrong thing.

'You are telling me, in your own inimitable way, that you love me, aren't you?' Nothing else would make a woman like this sacrifice so many of her rigidly held principles.

She nodded. 'I think I have done from the first moment I met you. But I told myself it was just a silly, schoolgirl infatuation, because you were so handsome. And then when it wouldn't go away, I kept reminding myself that it was foolish because you were so far beyond my reach in every way and that you'd never look at me that way. Then when you seemed to enjoy my company, that you were just being kind to the dowdy, lowly, dab of a creature I was, because you felt sorry for me...'

He could feel a grin plucking at his lips as she enumerated every stage of her thought processes, one at a time, in a typically Eleanorish way.

'So when you proposed,' she continued, 'I couldn't believe you meant it. *That* was why I rejected you so... rudely. But since then...' She could feel her fingers kneading the back of his coat. 'It is no use. I can't stop thinking about you. Dreaming of you. Wishing I could see you again, no matter what the cost. And hoping that you might still want me.'

'Of course I still want you.'

'Yes.' She relaxed a bit in his arms. 'Or you wouldn't be here, would you? And, look, the thing is, even if you don't want to marry me any longer, and why should you when I've been so...oh, foolish and proud, and sanctimonious, and—'

'Now, just stop right there.'

'No, I won't stop. I have to speak. I've come to accept that I'm no better than anyone else. That I'm a sinner, in fact. That I want to sin, with you, so much that nothing else seems to matter...and I know I'm not like all those sophisticated, beautiful women you usually take to your bed...'

'That doesn't matter.'

'Doesn't it?'

'No. You see, I... I have changed my mind about the way I...things I've always believed, too, since knowing you. Let me explain. The way you explained to me. One point at a time, in a logical manner.'

She nodded, solemnly.

'I set out for Suffolk in a foul mood. Because I'd reached the conclusion that sending you away hadn't worked. That out of sight wasn't out of mind. The wanting wouldn't stop. And I believed that the only way I would be able to bed you would be to surrender to your terms.'

'You mean,' she said, wide-eyed, 'that you had steeled yourself to propose again?'

'Just so. But, here's the funny thing. The nearer I drew to this vicarage, to you, the more excited I grew at the prospect of seeing you. Of holding you. Of kissing you. And for the first time in my life, I began to see there were advantages to all that legal stuff, which I'd always looked upon before as a kind of prison sentence.

'Because I'd have rights. The right to bed you for the rest of my life being the first one. To wake up beside you every morning. And instead of recoiling from the prospect of never having any variety in my bedmate, a kind of calm settled over me. The same kind of calm I felt wash over me when you ran into my arms just now.'

'You want to sleep with me, only with me, for the rest of your life?'

He nodded. 'So much that I went and bought a licence.' He patted his pocket where the document nestled. He'd known he'd have to prove he was in earnest and what could be more earnest than a marriage licence?

'You aren't afraid,' she said, looking a bit worried, 'that you will get bored?'

'No. And do you know why?'

She shook her head.

'It is *because* you are nothing like all those sophisticated, shallow women I've taken to bed before. Nor will this be like the marriages men make because they'd been taken in by a pretty face. When they only get to know their bride once it's too late. I know you, Eleanor. I started getting to know you while you were working for Lady Bradbury. Before I considered marriage at all. And I got to know you even better during those awful weeks in London.'

'When you saw me at my worst,' she put in, uncomfortably.

'If the worst you are capable of is wanting to dress up in finery and be treated like a princess, I have nothing to fear, do I? I *want* to see you dressed in pretty clothes. I want to treat you like a princess. You are, to me, unique. You are as far above any of the other women who've briefly held my interest as…as stars are above grains of sand. The only thing I'm afraid of now is that you won't say yes. You didn't last time, and—'

She flung her arms round his neck and burst into tears.

'Don't cry, sweetheart. Don't cry.'

'I'm not crying,' she said untruthfully, as he wiped a tear from her cheek with his thumb.

But he rather thought he was very close to it. His eyes were definitely stinging. Why? Well, nobody had ever cared a rap for him. Yet this lovely woman had been willing to sacrifice all her principles just to be with him, for as long as he wished. She'd been coming to find him. To tell him she loved him. To show him she loved him if he didn't at first believe it possible.

He breathed in deeply, in an attempt to wrestle back the emotion that was at serious risk of flooding from his eyes. A warm breeze stirred the lilac blossom, releasing a sweet scent.

Spring was here. Winter was over. Eleanor had thawed the ice that had encased his heart for so many years. He no longer worried about any hurt coming to him because he'd lowered that shield. Because the person he'd let in was Eleanor. She wasn't going to use him to further her own ends.

She loved him. She'd always sworn she would only ever marry for love. She wasn't interested in his title, or his wealth, or any of the things so many other women believed to be important. She was putting her faith in him, for more than just the few weeks it might take for the passion between them to burn out. She was trusting him with the whole of the rest of her life.

'Mama, mama,' came a voice from the vicinity of the vicarage. 'Aunt Eleanor's kissing a man in the front garden.' There followed the sound of little feet thundering up a staircase.

Eleanor sighed. 'There goes my reputation in Suffolk.'

'We have only to tell them we have just become betrothed...'

'Oh, no, we don't,' she said, letting go of his hand, going back down the path and picking up her case. 'I've been rather looking forward to becoming shocking, disgraceful Aunt Eleanor. She's so much more interesting that dull, dependable Aunt Eleanor, don't you think?'

She grabbed his hand, then, and tugged him down the path to the gate.

'But you are going to be respectably married,' he protested.

'I hope not,' she said, leaving him feeling as if she'd hollowed him out with a spoon.

'What do you mean by that?'

'I mean that I've come to agree with you about marriage. While I was in Town, well, I had the opportunity to observe how most society marriages played out and I didn't like it. Couples were all either terribly polite but distant with each other, in public, or else downright hostile. Which is why I decided that being your mistress might suit me after all. Just as you predicted,' she said firmly, opening the gate and marching through, though she didn't let go of his hand.

'But, then, what was all the kissing and crying about, when I asked you to marry me?'

'Oh, I'll marry you,' she said, completely confusing him.

'Now you really have lost me,' he said, following her into the coach and giving the driver the office to set off, because no matter what nonsense came out of her mouth, she was with him, coming to London with him, and they could thrash out the rest of it en route.

'I'd decided on the terms, you know, that I would demand before becoming your mistress.'

'And what were they?'

'I didn't want the jewels, or the carriage and horses

you offered,' she said with a wrinkle of her nose. 'As if I'd want to flaunt that kind of relationship in public. No. All I wanted was your assurance that when you tired of me, you would provide me with a cottage of my own, somewhere far away from anywhere where anyone might recognise me, and a pension, so that I could live out the rest of my days as a respectable widow. To know that I would have a place that nobody could evict me from, after it was over. Security.'

'Well, you will have far more security as my Countess than you would have had as my mistress.'

She sighed. 'I know. It's just…' She bit on her lower lip again and gave him rather a naughty look. 'I'd been rather looking forward to behaving disgracefully. With you. Couldn't we…?'

Finally, he understood. 'Yes, we could. But might I just point out, before we shock the coachman, that it's unlikely that I will ever let you go off to live in a cottage on your own.'

'When you grow bored—' she said. He stopped her by the simple expedient of laying one finger across her lush little mouth.

'I could never grow bored of you. You have been haunting me for months. I am obsessed with you to the extent that I cannot even look upon another woman with idle curiosity, let alone full-blown lust. Aside from that, I want to protect you. Make sure you never get taken in by some other plausible rogue, pretending to befriend you so that they can use you to further their own ends. Or have to go and work for a family where some man can take advantage of you.'

She raised one eyebrow at him.

'I want the right,' he continued, ignoring the sarcastic tilt of that brow, 'to challenge any man who made you an indecent offer to a duel, so I can put a bullet through him.'

'You think that is what such a man deserves?'

'I know it for a fact,' he said ruefully. 'Also,' he said more gently, 'I want you to be the mother of my children. My companion when I'm too old and gouty to do more than sit by the fireside. In short, I think you are stuck with me. Until death us do part.'

'Oh, Peter…' she sighed '…do you mean it?'

'I came all the way to Suffolk. Doesn't that prove I mean every word?'

'Suffolk isn't that bad,' she said.

'Then why were you leaving?'

'Because, as you well know,' she said with a twinkle in her eye, 'it didn't have you in it.'

'My point exactly. Nowhere is going to be any good if you aren't there.'

'But, with me there?'

'Heaven on earth,' he said and pulled her into his arms to prove it was true.

Even in a coach.

* * * * *

If you enjoyed this book, why not check out these other great reads by Annie Burrows

A Marquess, a Miss and a Mystery
The Scandal of the Season

And be sure to read her Brides for Bachelors miniseries

The Major Meets His Match
The Marquess Tames His Bride
The Captain Claims His Lady